DANIEL

By

Jeff C Clark

Copyright © 2024 Jeff Clark

All rights reserved

The characters and events portrayed in this book are fictitious. Any similarity to real persons, living or dead, is coincidental and not intended by the author. No part of this book may be reproduced, or stored in a retrieval system, or transmitted in any form or by any means, electronic, mechanical, photocopying, recording or otherwise, without express written permission of the publisher.

This book is dedicated to Mary Wilson, the best English teacher ever.

Contents

Chapter 1

Chapter 2

Chapter 3

Chapter 4

Chapter 5

Chapter 6

Chapter 7

Chapter 8

Chapter 9

Chapter 10

Chapter 11

Chapter 12

Chapter 13

Chapter 14

Chapter 15

Chapter 16

Chapter 17

Chapter 18

Chapter 19

Chapter 20

Chapter 21

Chapter 22

Chapter 23

Chapter 24

Chapter 25

Chapter 26

Chapter 27

Chapter 28

Chapter 29

Chapter 30

Chapter 31

Chapter 32

Chapter 33

Chapter 34

Chapter 35

Chapter 36

Chapter 37

Chapter 38

Epilogue

A Dream within a Dream

Edgar Allen Poe

TAKE this kiss upon the brow!
And, in parting from you now,
Thus much let me avow —
You are not wrong, who deem
That my days have been a dream;
Yet if hope has flown away
In a night, or in a day,
In a vision, or in none,
Is it therefore the less *gone?*
All that we see or seem
Is but a dream within a dream.

I stand amid the roar
Of a surf-tormented shore,
And I hold within my hand
Grains of the golden sand—
How few! yet how they creep
Through my fingers to the deep,
While I weep—while I weep!
O God! can I not grasp
Them with a tighter clasp?
O God! can I not save
One from the pitiless wave?
Is *all* that we see or seem
But a dream within a dream?

Chapter 1

Wednesday 17th October 2018, France

My name is Joseph, but most people call me Joe. I'm 63 and a retired firefighter from Liverpool, England. I'm married to Pam, my second wife.

We live in rural France and have done since 2015. Our property is a house with a barn that we run as a gite. We only rent out for the summer months, making enough to keep us going, and the rest of the time we read, stroll through the peaceful countryside and enjoy the easy-going lifestyle that attracted us here in the first place.

We'd been working outside, tidying hedges, deadheading and the like and we came in about 1:30 for a light lunch of tea and a baguette with cheese and figs from our own tree.

I'd just taken a first bite from my sandwich when a WhatsApp alert lit up my phone. It was Lydia, one of my remaining sisters. I say 'remaining' because I used to have three sisters. The eldest of the three, but still younger than me, died in 2017, just a few days after her sixtieth birthday. She had never married, never even had a boyfriend to my knowledge.

Carla and I had not been on speaking terms for a long time. Decades. I wish it could have been different but it wasn't. I always secretly thought that maybe she tended towards misandry. It would be understandable if she did. Or had.

I opened WhatsApp. *'Joe?'* was all that Lydia said. I instinctively knew that something had happened. It wasn't a normal opening from Lyds. She would normally open with something along the lines of *'Hi Joe, how you doing?'* I thought that maybe something had happened to Emily, Lydia's twin sister. Emily hadn't been very communicative since Carla had taken her own life, but then, not being communicative was our default position. It could also have been about Dan, my older brother. He and I had been estranged for a couple of decades or so, in fact, he'd cut himself off from other members of his family from time to time but with me, it was more or less the norm. I don't know why. Of course, there could be something amiss with Lyds, she wasn't the healthiest of people, either physically or mentally. Mind you, none of us were mentally healthy, we all had issues, some probably quite serious. It wouldn't have been possible to grow up in the house we grew up in and not have some issues. Thanks to our parents, mainly our father.

My phone lit up again. Same message from Lydia. *'Joe?'*

'Hiya Lyds.' I typed. *'How're things with you?'* I finished my tea and decided on another.

As I watched the kettle doing its thing, I became slightly agitated. I'm not exactly certain why but suffice to say that when our family had 'dealings' with each other it was always somewhat strained, which was quite understandable, to me at least, when you look at our flawed history. I am a very distrusting person, and my siblings are all the same. I tend to see the bad in someone before I see the good and, if that happens, I often don't bother looking too hard for the good, which probably explains my dearth of friends. Such is life.

Obviously, as a kid, you trust your parents, though you never think of your belief in them as trust, it's just an unsaid, unwritten belief in these adults you know as mum and dad. As things turned out, for me, and probably all my siblings, that belief, that trust, was misplaced. To say the least.

For instance, from a very early age, it hasn't been possible for me to have a normal everyday conversation. I tend to overthink things and look for hidden meanings in words. I subconsciously monitor body language and I never take people at face value. This is very normal and I'm ok with it. I probably wouldn't have it any other way. When I talk with someone, my subconscious notes and pictures get filed away somewhere in my head. The things I can drag from memory, as clear as the day they happened, are amazing. At least they are to me. If only I could've remembered facts and figures from my school lessons in the same way, well, there wouldn't have been an exam that I couldn't have passed with ease. If only. Those little files get revisited at odd times, usually when something said or done by someone jars with me. Often, the thing that jarred will fit, like a jigsaw piece, with the old information. This little 'knack' has stood me in good stead over the years.

My phone lit up. It was Lydia. *'Emily has had a visit from our Daniel's solicitor today to tell us that Daniel passed away 3 days ago. I'm so sorry to give you this news x.'*

My mind emptied. There and then, everything went down the plughole. I stared at the phone, looked out of the kitchen window. Francis and Marie-Therese, our closest neighbours, were digging in their vegetable garden and I could hear them chatting in the sunshine. A bird of prey landed at the top of a pine tree over by the back road to Paizay. Daniel was dead. A thousand memories from our childhood flashed through my mind, none of them staying long enough to mean much.

I suddenly felt tired and I realised that hope had just died in me. I hadn't been ready for my brother to die, had never thought about him dying. In my heart there was always a belief that I could get to live more of my life with him, that somehow, we could sort out whatever it was that had come between us. And now it could never be fixed.

A movement outside caught my eye, and I watched as the bird of prey launched into the air, the tree bending slightly. Its wings flapped majestically, and it seemed to soar straight towards me before veering off and landing on a fence post no more than thirty feet away. It was beautiful. The bright yellow of its legs and feet was so vivid it was hard to imagine how it maintained the colour. Daniel would have loved it. He loved the countryside, especially the wildlife. I remembered him at nine or ten years of age, nursing and nurturing a young sparrow he'd found in grandad's yard. We lived with grandma and grandad when I was younger, as families did back in the fifties. Down by the North Liverpool docks. So close to the river that we could see Goliath or Samson, the gigantic floating cranes, drifting along over the rooftops, dwarfing the three-storey houses on Brassworks Road.

North Liverpool, June 1959

It was sunny. A balmy breeze ruffled the sheets hanging on the washing line that ran the length of the back yard. Me and my big brother, Dan, were playing cowboys and Indians. Dan was always the cowboy, and I was always the Indian. I liked it that way because I preferred the weaponry. Dan had a pair of Wild Bill Hickock silver cap-guns that came with a fancy black twin holster set-up. They made plenty of noise when he pulled the triggers, make no mistake, but I had a bow with six arrows. Mind you, four of those arrows now belonged to various neighbours, once I shot them into their back yards. And one of them belonged to the Rag and Bone man. He took it because I managed to hit his horse on the rump, and it whickered, lifted its tail and cacked all over the road. So, I had one arrow left. It had a red rubber sucker on the end but no feathers on the other end. They'd come off during the battle of the wrecked car at the top of the street. My grandad made my bow and arrow from the finest bamboo and string. All I had to do was wait for my brother to appear from under the sheets and let him have it. Easy.

Dan appeared and I loosed, missing him by barely a foot. The arrow went end over end and clattered the kitchen window. Grandma shouted at me to be careful and then shouted at grandad for being so bloody daft as to make me a bow and arrow in the first place. Grandad said something that I couldn't hear but grandma did and she went into the living room and said that he should have used some common sense and made me a machine gun like anyone else would have done. I would have liked that. Lots of kids had these machine guns made from scrap fence-palings by grandads with nothing better to do. I picked up my arrow and was about to ask grandad if he could maybe find some common sense in the bomb shelter and make me a machine gun when Dan shouted out, 'Grandad! Grandma! Come and see what I've found!'

It was a baby bird. It was lying on the floor, shuffling about in little circles. I retrieved my arrow, loaded it onto the string and started to draw. 'Shall I shoot it?' I shouted. 'Can I shoot it?'

'No y'bloody can't!' shouted Dan, pushing me away.

Grandma came bustling out of the kitchen door, wiping her hands on her pinny. 'You mind your bloody language my lad or I'll wash your mouth out with soap and water!' she said in her broad Yorkshire accent. 'What is it?'

'It's a baby bird grandma.' said Dan.

'Can I shoot it please grandma?' I asked. Politeness personified. Grandad came out, his newspaper rolled up in his hand, like he was ready to whack a spider. Or a cockroach. We had lots of cockroaches everywhere, even under the wallpaper. My mum told me that they ate the wallpaper paste. I always wondered what it tasted like. Semolina probably.

'What is it?' asked grandad.

'It's a baby bird grandad!' I shouted. 'Grandma said I could shoot it; can I shoot it grandad?'

Grandma wagged her finger in my face. 'I never said no such thing you little fibber.' she said, 'Neck it Albert and put the poor bugger in the bin.'

The bird shuffled a bit faster. Circling towards the back gate. I think it knew what grandma meant. I know I did. My arm was shaking from holding my bowstring taut, ready to fire. Melvin, my best mate from next door had heard the commotion and had climbed up onto the wall between the yards. The walls were about six and a half foot high, and most of the kids were like mountain goats. We spent virtually the whole summer on the wall tops, walking around, looking in people's back windows, jumping back and forth across the back entries; the walkway that ran between back-to-back terraced housing, just wide enough for the bin man to get down. 'What are you gonna shoot Joe?' He sounded excited.

'He's not shooting anything,' said grandma, 'and get down from that bloody wall!'

I was intent on blood. 'I'm gonna shoot this bird, me grandad said I could.' I said in the direction of Melvin. Grandad cuffed my head with his newspaper and my already tired thumb somehow let go of the taut string, which then twanged my bow hand. I dropped both bow and arrow with a bambooey clatter and jammed my hand up into my armpit. 'OWWW!' I shouted, hopping about until I realised it wasn't a good look and Melvin was watching. Melvin was younger than me by at least a month or so, which was a lot when you're a five-year-old alpha male. Grandma was still looking in Melvin's direction, so he slid off the wall and out of sight.

Grandad bent to pick the little bird up and groaned because of his back. This proved to be the little bird's lucky break because Dan picked it up instead. He cradled it gently in his hand and the little bird tweeted and opened its mouth wide.

'I'm gonna feed it and help it to grow up.' he said. 'Can we get a box to keep him in grandma?'

'You'll not be able to help it Daniel,' said grandad, 'poor little bugger's best put out of its misery, give it 'ere now.'

'No grandad, no! I need to see if I can do it ... it needs me to try.' Dan said, covering the bird with his free hand. *'Please let me try.'*

My twanged hand had recovered and I picked up my weapon, stringing the arrow expertly. 'Can I shoot it please grandad?' I asked.

*

Over the next few weeks my big brother nurtured the little bird that turned out to be a sparrow. He got a crisp box from May's, the corner shop where the one-armed man worked, smart in his blazer with what I took to be his school badge on the breast pocket, the sleeve neatly pinned up. A little gold aeroplane was pinned to his tie and I always stared at it because I wanted it. He asked me once if I liked it and I was scared because the one-armed man had spoken to me. Of course, now, I know he was a paratrooper who almost certainly lost his arm fighting for his country against the Nazis. Now, I know that if it wasn't for that one-armed man and his many comrades, my brother and me might not exist, the corner shop may have been bombed to bits and May might have ended up in Auschwitz or Belsen. The sparrow would probably have been ok though. Or maybe the sparrow would have been crushed under the jackboots of the Nazis. My grandma was always going on about them doing stuff with their jackboots. Mind you, I did try to obtain permission to shoot it with a bamboo bow and arrow.

The crisp box was kept in the bedroom that me and Dan shared. He put pages of the Echo on the bottom of the box and changed it every day. He made a nest out of newspaper that he shredded into little strips and moulded it with his hands. An eyedropper was used to feed the little bird something that he made. He might have found out what to feed it from the RSPCA. Me and Dan were members of the RSPCA, we had certificates and badges. I can't really remember how we came to be members, but I can remember the man who came to our Sunday school to 'recruit' us. Tall, with grey hair, a limp, and a smart uniform. I thought he was a policeman, so was automatically scared of him, but Dan spoke to him a lot and the result of that seemed to be that we got certificates off the postman in a big envelope. Really nice they were, though I can't really remember what they looked like, but they had the RSPCA emblem in an arc across the top and my name, my full name, Joseph Croft, was under it on mine. I was very proud of being a member of the RSPCA. I think. I'm not sure what they would have thought of me wanting to shoot the baby bird, but it didn't really matter because we rescued it instead of shooting it. Or Dan did. The badges were really nice as well, more like a brooch I think, but the colour was mostly blue and gold and it reminded me of medals, like grandad's.

After a while, the baby bird had feathers and looked quite fat and fluffy. And it became really noisy. Tweeting all the time but much louder than I would ever have imagined. It used to wake us up really early, tweeting like mad and it crossed my mind a few times that maybe I should have 'taken it out' when I had the chance.

Once it had feathers, Dan started saying that he was going to teach it to fly. I was amazed at what my big brother could do … and I couldn't wait to be as old as him so that I could fly too. I told grandma and grandad that Dan could fly, and he was going to teach the bird to do it. They laughed at me. I thought it was good that they laughed. I liked it. One day, while I was sitting on grandad's knee, watching him cut his baccy up with his little penknife, which I wanted, I told him again that I couldn't wait to be as big as Dan so that I could fly and he laughed again and explained that Dan couldn't fly, that no people could fly. Dan had used a 'figure of speech' he said and explained what that meant. I couldn't work out what he was talking about and asked if I could cut his baccy up for him. He let me and showed me how to do it but told me not to tell grandma, which I never did.

Dan did teach the little bird to fly, sort of. He told me that little birds already know how to fly because they are 'programmed' to do it the same as little boys are programmed to run, wrestle and climb walls. He told me that it just needed to be shown when to do it and where from.

I remember thinking, early one morning as the little bird woke us up when it was barely light, tweeting like a madman … that 'the time has arrived Dan! Teach him to fly … now!'

Dan would slide our window open and put the little bird outside on the windowsill. It would get really excited and strut about, ruffling its feathers and flapping its wings. Then Dan would put it back in the box and shut the window. One day, the bird ruffled its feathers, fluttered its wings, took a deep breath and plunged off the windowsill, crash-landing in the yard, bouncing as it hit the stone flags. Grandma's cat, Ginger, was basking in the sun on top of the wall, licking its arse, when the bird fluttered past. Ginger was so startled that he fell backwards and landed on top of next door's bin with a clatter and a screech. Dan sprinted down the stairs and out into the yard. The bird was sat on the floor with the avian equivalent of a surprised look on its face.

After a few days or so of the bird launching itself off the windowsill, it actually flew off. Just like that. Just disappeared from our lives. The crisp box sat there for days. Empty. It had been a nest, a home, shelter for a little creature from all that is bad in the world and now it was just an empty cardboard box, with a strange smell. It was as if the bird had never existed. As if the few weeks of tweeting and crapping had never happened. There was a void and even though I'd wanted to shoot it, I felt a loss. Dan did too. I could tell. He was very quiet. Dan was a quiet boy anyway, much more so than me, I wasn't quiet at all, far from it. But he was just ... different. Introspective. It was almost like he wanted to have flown away with the bird, like he would have given anything to be able to do that.

The crisp box sat there for a few more days. I think Dan thought the bird might come back to see him. To thank him maybe. I thought it would as well, come back that is, but sincerely hoped it wouldn't. I was enjoying sleeping until it was the right time for a human to think about getting out of bed. But then my father, Dan's father, our father, made sure it wouldn't. One Saturday morning, the sun shining through our open bedroom window, dust motes floating in warm air, our grunts and groans punctuating the stillness as we had our habitual Saturday morning wrestling match, the bedroom door burst open, crashing against the wall and our father was suddenly there, filling the hole where the door had been. Before we even had time to disengage our wrestling holds, he'd hit us a number of times with his thick leather belt. Hard. Neither of us cried out from the attack. Both of us already knew better than to make a sound. He stopped after a while and threw his belt out onto the landing. My eyes followed the trajectory. My mum was standing there in the gloom. Our father picked up the crisp box and upended it out of the window, emptying Dan's nest and bird-raising paraphernalia into the yard. I heard the glass eyedropper smash on the flags with a crisp tinkle. He then wrenched our RSPCA certificates off the bedroom wall. Dan's certificate tore as the drawing pin wouldn't let go of it. The drawing pin holding mine, popped out and ricocheted off the other wall, heading for the floor. I saw it, in slow motion almost, strike the lino and scoot under the bed, where it pinged against our tin potty. Funny how you remember the little sounds so well. He ripped our certificates to pieces, threw them out of the window and stormed out, slamming the door. He hadn't said one word.

Me and Dan looked at each other, tears welling in our eyes. I could feel the welts rising on my back and buttocks where I'd been hit with the belt. We must have decided, telepathically, to not cry because our tears dried up. 'Did you hear my drawing pin hit the po?' I whispered.

Chapter 2

Wednesday 17th October 2018, France

We sat in the kitchen with our second cup of tea. I looked at my phone again. It somehow didn't seem right that I was in France. I felt as though I should be at home, in Liverpool. I hadn't said anything to Pam yet and wondered why, at times, I think I should carry on as though nothing out of the ordinary is happening. I messaged Lydia.

'How?' I asked and wondered briefly about my brother having a solicitor who was willing to drive to my sister's to deliver news of Dan's death. I wasn't certain they ever did such things, not for people like us anyway. Rich people maybe but not us.

A message arrived. *'I really don't know Joe x.'*

'Are you back to being friends on Facebook with Em?' I asked.

Just after Carla had died, Em had unfriended just about everyone on Facebook and Lydia had not taken too kindly to it. I'd just put it down to grieving and suggested to Lydia that maybe she should do the same. She hadn't.

'No. x' she typed. Emphatic but softened with a kiss. It intrigued me the way some people use kisses at the end of messages. Was it just a kind of unthinking punctuation? I used to think it was but then, sometimes kisses are missed off and when they are, it's quite often significant in some way. So, if at times there is significance to a missed off kiss, does that mean there is significance to an included kiss or two? Maybe, maybe not.

Moments later Lydia and I both got friend requests from Em and accepted them.

I set up a group chat and typed a question. *'So, exactly how did we come about the information that Dan had died. Who told the solicitors?'* It seemed a little abrupt but, that was us, that was how we were. Not a lot of sentimentality in the Croft family.

Em replied. *'Wasn't solicitors, heir hunters knocked on my door today, said Daniel had died three days ago Joe.'*

'Heir hunters?' I was a bit taken aback and wondered how they got involved. Do the police inform them? But then, how do the police get involved? An incident of some kind? *'How did he die? Do we know?'*

'He didn't know anything, just that Daniel was dead.' said Em. *'He left contact details in case we want them to deal with things for us for ten percent of anything Daniel has left behind. I don't trust them at all.'*

'Neither do I Em, what about you Lydia?' There was no reply from Lyds, though I could see that she'd seen the message.

'How did they even get involved?' I asked.

'I don't know.' said Em and Lydia typed *'I think the coroner gets them involved but I'm not sure. And no, I don't trust them either.'*

These 'heir hunters' had been 'researching' us, finding our addresses, phone numbers and lord knows what else, digging about in our family, all the while knowing that our brother had died whilst we were all oblivious. Daniel was lying, alone in a morgue, and these people could sniff the chance of a payout. I know they serve a purpose and probably perform a good service for those who might need them, but we didn't.

I typed my brother's name into a search engine and to my surprise he came up straight away. Here he was, famous almost. A Police Notice said that a sixty-six-year-old male had been found dead in his home, there were no suspicious circumstances and they wanted relatives to get in touch. It took me no more than forty-five seconds to get this information.

For the last three days, my brother had carried a sliver of importance to some people, whilst his siblings were just going about their business. I was angry. At myself for being oblivious to his death, and at the others who had opened files on my brother. And I was angry at Daniel, my big brother and hero, for setting himself against his world. I was angry at the wasted years and the inescapable fact that there could never be restoration of our brotherhood, something I had yearned after for over half of my life. Whatever had happened in his mind to turn him against me would never be discovered or understood. Yet more damage to add to the long list of irreparable harm caused by Charlie, our father, the father who just keeps on giving.

It transpired that the 'heir hunter' had wanted to access the property before my sister, presumably to discover documents relative to his job and this was something we would need to do for ourselves. I knew that Dan had been a keen photographer and so I expected there to be lots of photos important to us. My brother had been a sensible man, so I expected all his important documents to be safely stored in an obvious place and I did not want some stranger being the first person to lay hands and eyes on Dan's possessions. It was only right that it should be one of us. I asked Emily for the phone number of the company who'd turned up at her house.

I phoned the heir hunter company and had a brief conversation with them, thanked them for their time and made sure they knew we didn't need them.

Back in the WhatsApp group, we chatted on about things for at least another cup of tea and two biscuits, anecdotes, sadness at what had happened, vitriol aimed at our father for our young lives, now distant behind us but still very much relevant. My mind started to wander, and I admonished myself for losing focus. It was strangely important to me to always try to be 'professional'. I still always thought of myself as a firefighter and still always tried to stay focused, especially at stressful times. In that strange way such times work in your mind, my grandma's voice suddenly intruded and told me to put my thinking cap on. That made me smile as I tuned in and out of the group conversation.

I suddenly regressed to the back parlour of my grandma's house, aged about four or five. I'd been asked a question by my mum, to do with her leg. She was sitting on the sofa, having a cup of tea and I'd been playing with my cars on the floor by her feet. Her legs were crossed, and I was intrigued by her calf and the way it wobbled when I poked it. I was a bugger for poking things to see what would happen. I poked grandad's ear once when he was sitting in his chair asleep with his mouth open. He'd growled and puffed his cheeks out, still asleep, and his teeth slid out of his mouth and clacked on the watch chain of his waistcoat then seemed to turn around as if they were looking at me. Which was a massive shock as I didn't know anything about false teeth. I thought me poking his earhole had somehow caused him to jettison his teeth, all in one lump, and I had a quick look about for witnesses, before disappearing to the parlour to play with my soldiers.

So, anyway, mum asked me what I was poking at, and I said that I was wondering what was inside her leg that made it wobble. She asked me what I thought it might be and as I pondered the question, grandma said 'Ey up ... he's got his thinking cap on', which made me feel the top of my head for this cap, making them laugh. I decided that my mum's wobbly calf must be full of blood and said so. They both laughed and then when grandad came in from 'down the yard,' which meant he'd been to the toilet, they told him, and he laughed as well.

I returned to the group chat in time to see that my sisters had just had a little bit of a set-to. Nothing too dramatic but a definite thread of anger had seeped into the chat. Nothing was being said and I assumed that they were re-reading what had gone before. It was a scenario only too common to the

Crofts and their dealings with each other. I didn't really understand why that was the way it was, but it just was.

From nowhere I was suddenly upset, which was out of character for me. I could feel my eyes filling with tears and I glanced up at Pam to make sure she wasn't looking my way. I never wanted anyone to see that I was upset and certainly never wanted anyone to see that I was close to tears. I wasn't supposed to show that I was anything other than in control of myself. I wasn't supposed to show that I was upset or scared or … anything. I was supposed to just be … me.

As a youngster, I couldn't ever show the wrong emotion. To do so would attract the attention of my father, something I never wanted to do. I'm ashamed of the fact that, as a kid, I was happy, if happy is the right word, if one of my siblings broke and showed unwanted emotion, because his attention would be drawn to them and not me.

The emotions I *could* display as a kid, nearly always centred around making my father feel good about himself. So, I could laugh when he said something funny, especially if it was disparaging to my mother or a sibling, even if it was said about me. If I was to laugh, I had to properly laugh, even in the eyes, because he would check your eyes. If you were not showing the correct face, the correct expression, the correct *look*, then his eyes would narrow as they stared at you, his face would … change somehow … like the change you might expect a time-lapse film of drying concrete to show, subtle but there. His face would take on a look that terrified me well into my teens. It wasn't a look that could be seen, as such, more a look that could be felt. It was a set of the face, a deepening of his blue eyes, a set of the mouth that was indefinable, a tenseness about the shoulders, the hands, that just simply told you that you were in danger and that the danger was approaching fast. Sometimes, this *set* of my father, as if for battle, would be held for seconds or even minutes, like there was an argument going on in his head, and then it would disappear, like water down a plug hole. But that didn't mean you were safe because, sometimes, in those first seconds of clemency, he could snap, almost like there was another person whispering in his ear, jeering at him because he'd shown mercy, taunting him because he'd 'gone soft'. And when that happened, it was like he suddenly thought to himself '*Aaah y'know what ... fuck it! Let's just go for it!*' and you could get a beating that, given you were a child, and he was an ex-army boxing champion, could only be described as savage.

My sisters had apparently repaired their spat and were chatting again. I asked them if they knew the whereabouts of the keys to Dan's place. Em said that the heir hunters must have them, as they were going to let themselves in. I wondered where they'd got them from and could only think of the police. I asked my sisters to get in touch with the heir hunters to ask about the keys and I had a look again at the Police Notice on Google. There was an email address, so I quickly wrote to them, telling them who I was and asking where the keys to the flat were.

Half an hour later I returned to the chat room. Emily said that the heir hunters didn't have any keys and that the police had told them they didn't need any. My sisters were discussing what that meant when I returned.

'Just had an email from the police.' I told them, *'Says they had to break the door down and that it was boarded up later by a security company.'*

'So how do we get in?' asked Lydia.

'Jemmy.' I said, 'Then put the boards back when you leave.'

As an ex-firefighter I knew that the police breaking into the flat was a bad sign. A lack of neighbourly sightings of Daniel plus, maybe, a strange smell in the vicinity, meant that the police had to do what they had to do. The thought of what I now expected to have been found at Daniel's place had an unexpected effect on me, given my experiences at such incidents myself.

As a professional dealing with something distasteful, you put your mind in a certain place, you don't concern yourself with the victims, you just get on with your work and move on to the next job. But, as I now discovered, when the victim is part of you, it is very different and I realised that I would have to somehow find a way of dealing with it, find a way of manufacturing another level of me to house and contain the thoughts that would inevitably result. And that was when I realised, I already had that place. I just hadn't been there for a while.

That little-used place, little-used since I was a youngster, was my 'cupboard under the stairs', the place where I could hide inside myself, where I could perform some kind of mind-trick that convinced me that my abnormal life was really normal. If, in a blink, you can make abnormality normal, then you have, not only an antidote to the toxins coursing through you, but also a weapon to fight back. When my instinct told me an attack from my father was imminent, I shifted my mind to this place of safety. My brother used to go there too, but always looked like he struggled to find the door. I could tell.

Once I was in my sanctuary, another person, who I think of as my caretaker, took over and spoke for me, composed me, made me use the right voice, the right body language, made me see the world correctly and without emotion and so gave me a solid platform for good decision-making. I didn't like this other person very much, but I definitely needed him.

It's a strange thing to say, but there is a third person who resides in my place of safety, who is almost like the opposite of my caretaker, much softer of thought and kinder. Without this person, the caretaker, I think, would become too strong and so this third person keeps us in balance.

And so, sat at my home in France, I started to mentally prepare for what lay ahead, to shake off the dustsheets of my sanctuary. But first I had a few things to settle and sort out before I could head over to England. I stared at my laptop screen, lost in thought. Emily's green dot had gone out, so she'd gone to do whatever her day held. Lydia's dot was still there.

'*Are you ok Lyds?*' I typed.

There was no reply and I realised that her green dot still being lit didn't necessarily mean she was still there. Then the three little grey dots started dancing. She was typing something. But then they stopped. Her profile picture stared at me, her dark blue eyes seeming to look into mine. I glanced up at the little camera lens in the rim of my screen and suddenly felt as though I was being watched. Naturally, my mind went into some kind of overdrive and the lens became my father, his eyes narrowing as they weighed me up, his jaw muscles rippling under the skin as he chewed over the pros and cons of attacking me.

I closed my laptop and went out into the sunshine.

Chapter 3

Thursday 18th October 2018

I woke up about seven thirty, which was a little late for me. It was still quite hot where we live and the sun was overcoming the curtains, the warmth beginning to build. October back in Liverpool could easily be sunny but cold. Here, the cold didn't arrive until mid-way through November, though once it did, it was just the same as Liverpool but with much more rain.

As I lay there, I remembered waking from a disturbing dream, one of those dreams that seem so real that when you wake up, it's hard to work out what's what.

In the dream, I'd been outside. It was dark and raining quite hard. The rain was warm and ran in rivers down my face, dripping onto my chest. My brother was standing about thirty feet away from me, in front of a stand of large fir trees, which were silhouetted black on the slightly lighter black of the night sky. I shouted to him, but no words came out. I couldn't see his eyes, but I could feel that he was staring at me. I tried to walk towards him, but my feet wouldn't move. I tried to beckon to him, but my arms wouldn't move. The rain got heavier, the sound of it roaring in my ears and drumming on the top of my head. It was so heavy that my brother became obscured by it, slowly fading and receding and then, I just couldn't see him anymore. He was gone.

When I woke from the dream, I could still hear the rain drumming on my head. I felt hollow, as if something was missing from inside me. I had never stopped loving Daniel, but he had turned his back on me over three decades ago and now, it was as if we had always been close, always been best of friends and his departing had torn a huge hole in my existence. It seemed strange to think, to feel, that for the first time in my life I was living in a world that my brother didn't inhabit. Not for the first time in my life, I realised what a big thing this was, this dying. I got up and got dressed.

We had breakfast outside on the patio, taking advantage of the lovely weather. Coffee and croissants with a good English marmalade, dark and bitter. Francis and Marie-Therese were already busy in their vegetable garden, and we exchanged waves and bonjours and then I went into the gloom of the living room and opened my laptop.

My sisters were in the group chat, talking about going to Dan's flat to see what was what.

I said my 'good mornings' and was about to ask what today's agenda was, when Lydia typed, '*Spoke to the coroners. Daniel might have died five to six weeks ago. They are doing a post-mortem today. The police were called after a neighbour reported not seeing him for a while. They forced entry. Found him under a pile of rubbish. Had to get the fire brigade in to get him out x'*

A six-week-old corpse being dug out from a mound of rubbish by my ex colleagues. I didn't have to imagine what the scene would have been like. The sight, the smell that lingers, the scattering vermin. I could go on.

I'd known for some time that Dan was a bit of a hoarder, but what did they mean by 'rubbish'? His fishing magazines, which he'd had stacks of? I also knew that he tended to collect flattened beer cans until the bin was full before putting them out, so, in the years since I'd last had proper contact with him, had he taken to 'collecting' other stuff?

'My God!' I wrote, *'that's terrible.'*

My sisters chatted about Daniel and what would have to be done, the ins and outs of funerals and sorting belongings out. I zoned in and out of the conversation, pondering my brother being dug out of a mound of rubbish. It was hard enough to think of him as a corpse, let alone a corpse hidden under a pile of rubbish. How had he got there? Did it fall on him? Did he burrow into it? Lie down and scoop it onto himself? What?

I decided that I'd try to speak to some old colleagues, see if I could find anything out about the incident.

My sisters were talking about going to the flat as soon as they were ready and, though it would have its difficulties, I could see no reason why they shouldn't. It was important that someone went there quite soon. I made sure they knew what tools would be required to gain entry and then replace the board and was about to sign off and finish our work in the garden, when, from nowhere, another typical Croft row erupted between my sisters. It went from nought to sixty in two blinks and I think if they'd been in the same room, skin and hair would be flying. I attempted to pour oil on troubled waters, but I was wasting my time. Better to just let them get it out and dealt with, I thought.

On and on they went, neither taking any notice of what the other had to say. In an instant, I was transported back in time, back to my childhood, back to the living room of our house in Halewood, where my father had come in from the pub one Saturday afternoon, full of joy and happiness, a rarity in that house.

Sometime in the late 1960's, Halewood, Liverpool

He'd probably had a good win on the horses, his football team had won, and everything was good in his world. He told my mum that they were going out to eat and to get herself ready. He boiled a kettle of water to take up for a shave and, for some reason known only to her, my mum took against this rushing about to get ready and it showed. I, like all my siblings, was, excited I suppose the word is, because our parents would be out for ages and we could watch telly, eat crisps and drink lemonade all night without a care in the world. It was a taste of freedom, though we never actually thought of it like that. And so, I was put out at my mum being put out. Don't get me wrong, I get where she was coming from. He comes in, full of the joys of spring, looking to get ready and go straight out, whereas she'd been shopping, cleaning, cooking and all the other things she would have done that day, and suddenly here he is, the big man, he comes in, clicks his fingers, and hey presto! we're all supposed to be full of the joys of spring along with him. I get why she would not be jumping through hoops. I get it. But doesn't there come a time when, for the greater good, you just go with what makes life easy for everyone? Shouldn't that be a consideration given that the person 'calling the shots' is, basically, a thug, and can and will cause murder for everyone if a stick is shoved through his spokes, shouldn't that *be a consideration too? Maybe I'm right, maybe I'm wrong, but I know that on that day, in my mind, a voice was shouting out to my mum to just go with the flow. He was not, no matter what you* wanted, *no matter what would be the* right *thing, the kind of person you could reason with, so, why try? Not that trying to reason with him was what she did because she didn't. She went at things as if she was deliberately trying to cause trouble. Which is exactly what happened.*

My mum had recently bought a new kettle. One that you put on the gas ring, not an electric one. Electric ones were only for posh people. Having said that, this new one was a bit special. It was metallic red and instead of having a whistle that came off, it had a hinged whistle, and instead of whistling it hummed, almost like a harmonica. It was my mum's pride and joy. Her red kettle.

On this day, it was used to carry up some boiling water for our father to have a shave. We could hear him singing in the bathroom. He was a good singer. My mum was too, and they would sometimes duet while getting ready to go out. He was singing a Matt Monro song, Born Free. Me and Dan had been to see the film, which was great, we loved it. Suddenly, the bathroom door was wrenched open and then there was an almighty crash and smashing sound, as the kettle came hurtling down the stairs, bouncing on one of them, and smashing through the window at the side of the front door, going down the path like one of the Dam Busters' bouncing bombs and hitting the front gate with a clatter. The funny thing was, the hummer hummed as it went past the living room door. I almost laughed.

There was a stunned silence in the house for a moment, then we heard my mum go up the stairs and a row started that went from a few imperceptible words to anguished muffled screams within seconds. There was the sound of a struggle on the landing and I thought my mum was going to get thrown down the stairs, then footsteps ran into my bedroom above us, the door was slammed shut then it was slammed open, crashing into the bedroom wall, then another scuffling, fast-moving struggle that danced across the floor above us, muffled screams and shouts, noises like something hard hitting something solid but not like, say, a piece of wood hitting a stone, more of a solid meaty sound and then there was just silence.

A few minutes went by and then footsteps, soft and light, moved quietly across my room and along the landing. Soft footsteps, like the kind I'd expect from my mum, not aggressive enough to be my father's. I looked at Dan and it was obvious, to me anyway, that he was thinking the same as me, that the footsteps belonged to our mum, which meant that she was walking away from him, that she was walking along the landing and our father was still in my bedroom, not making a sound. That maybe she'd killed him. Maybe, I thought, maybe she'd gone upstairs with a knife or something and maybe she'd stabbed him, and he was dead. Hope blossomed in my heart as I realised that those retreating footsteps had been my mum's, they must *have been my mum's. I almost wanted to cheer as I realised that it was her who had emerged triumphant from my bedroom.*

All of us were too scared to move. We didn't even speak. We just looked at each other and at the ceiling, like we were trying to see through it. Our eyes were wide. The faces of my siblings were pale, ashen. I assume mine was the same. Carla was trembling. I was desperate to know what had happened but daren't move. All we could do was wait.

A door closed quietly upstairs. It was the door to our parents' room. I knew all the sounds of the house. Or nearly all. Footsteps came softly down the stairs. I was staring at the living room door, waiting for it to open, waiting for my mum to come in to tell us that it was all over, that we could breathe and live, when, instead, the front door opened, then quietly closed. And then I saw my father walking down the path, dressed in his going out stuff, suit, white shirt and tie, shiny shoes. He opened and quietly closed the gate as he went through it, the kettle softly grating on the path. I jumped up and hid behind the curtains to watch where he was going. He went to the bus stop on the main road. Which meant he was going to the pubs in Hunts Cross or Woolton. Maybe even Liverpool city centre. I waited a few minutes until a bus came. It stopped and I could just see the back half of it sticking out beyond the walls of the pub. If he got on it, he'd go upstairs where you could smoke, and he'd go to the back. I saw him walking to the back of the top deck and he was lighting a cigarette as the bus pulled away.

We went upstairs and found our mum lying on the floor of my bedroom. She was conscious but covered in blood from her nose, which was broken and skewed across her face. Her lips were split, and her left eye was already massively swollen, black, purple, and closed. Her face looked strange, and it transpired that her left cheekbone was broken too. A thought was running through my head, over and over. I couldn't stop it. 'You should have just got ready and gone out mum.' *was all I could think.*

Dan was helping mum get herself together and I retrieved the kettle from the path. It had a few dents, and a few scratches but I needed it to make my mum a cup of tea. I filled it and put it on the stove. It still worked. The hummer still hummed but sounded a little bit weird. Funny. As in humorous. But weird.

*

I returned to the here and now, an image of the kettle in my mind's eye. Emily and Lydia were still bickering, still typing furiously into the group chat, both apparently intent on emitting as much bile as they could in as short a time as possible. I just had to sit and wait it out. Eventually the sniping slowed down, then ground to a halt. I gave it a few minutes then asked when they would be going to Dan's flat and they were going to meet there as soon as they were ready, which could mean anything.

Lydia brought up the task of identifying the body, then said that she could only go on this day or that day because she had appointments at the hospital. Then Emily did more or less the same and threw in her own hospital appointments. When this happened, it sometimes felt like a competition to determine who was the sickest and I have to say, I found it a little dismal.

I noticed that the group chat had gone quiet so had a quick read at what had been said. They'd now gone off to get ready to meet at the flat and would be there in about an hour or so.

An interesting little part of their 'friendly' chat centred around the state of Daniel's home. Emily was saying how, if we didn't secure the place as quickly as possible, the local scallywags would be dossing in the living room and Lydia said they would have trouble getting in there because *'there's piles 'n piles 'n PILES of rubbish x'*.

I was amazed but then not amazed at the health issues my younger sisters had between them. Problems with innards, skeletal problems, sleeping problems, dietary problems, problems with breathing. I knew about them all, or most of them, but I was still staggered at the sheer amount of time they both spent at their various clinics and appointments. It was almost like they had part-time jobs as patients.

Not for the first time I pondered the role that my father and cortisol had in their current state of health. Not that I'm an expert on cortisol or anything else health-based. But I do know that when my mum was pregnant with them, her body must have been flooded with the stuff. That, added to the beatings she took from him during her pregnancy, must have had, I thought, an impact on their general wellbeing. As was usual, whenever I thought about this subject, I was briefly transported to a particular Saturday afternoon at our house in Halewood.

Summer 1966

It was a Saturday, sometime after July 30th, the day England won the World Cup, but before September 26th, the day my sisters were born. In fact, I tell a lie. It was sometime between August 6th at the earliest and September 26th, because, the day England won the World Cup, I'd just arrived in Colomendy, North Wales, for a week's holiday with my brother Dan and our old school, from when we used to live at grandma's.

I don't know why we were allowed to travel with our old school, but mum told me it was because Dan was famous on account of having won a scholarship to a Grammar school. Mr Wentworth, the headmaster, liked our Dan because he was dead clever. Our Dan that is, not the headmaster, though I suppose he must also have been dead clever. My mum once told me that he liked me as well, the headmaster, not our Dan, though I suppose our Dan must have liked me too ... back then anyway. I say 'must' have liked me, but you don't have to like someone just because you're related to them, do you? I never liked my father. In fact, I hated him. Still do. A fact that makes me sometimes envious of people who talk in glowing terms about their dads. I say 'sometimes' but I really mean all times. I'm very envious of people, especially men, who quite obviously thought the world of their dads and miss them when they've died. Me? I couldn't wait for mine to die. I wished a sudden, violent death on him a million times. I daydreamed about it. I even had a spell of praying for it. My prayers usually went along the lines of 'Please God, can you make my father have an accident of some kind, doesn't matter what, as long as it kills just him. If you do this for me, I will go to your church every week and light candles and brush the floor and stuff.' I was and still am an agnostic. As a kid, I'd go to Sunday school, and learn all about God, about how he loved little children and looked after them, then my father would beat me with his big leather belt, break my things, beat my mum and my brother Dan, so, it was a bit hard to reconcile the teachings of Sunday school with what happened in real life. Nevertheless, not one to look a gift-horse in the mouth, I had a spell of praying to the big man, woman, whatever God was or is, to grant me a little wish or two. Instead of granting me that little wish, and ridding the world of my father, he apparently chose to ignore me. He saw me and heard me because, as we are taught, he sees and hears everything, so therefore he must have chosen to ignore me. Maybe he didn't like me asking for a fellow human being to be killed. But, as he didn't seem to mind men slaughtering other men in the name of God, I thought that he could do me a turn and get rid of my father. Instead, he or she just carried on letting my father do whatever he wanted to do to my mum and us kids, so I gave up on the praying after a little while.

So, my mum told me that Mr Wentworth liked me too, on account of the gruesome stories I wrote in Comprehension, usually involving fires in houses that killed babies, or battles where lots of Germans were shot and bombed or Normans were slaughtered and thrown from their castles, smearing the walls with their blood as they plummeted into the moat. The stories were all accompanied by pictures crayoned in full colour. Looking back, maybe Mr Wentworth was a little ... intrigued... by the five-year-old with the bloodlust. Strangely, by the time we were invited on this week-long holiday to Colomendy, my brother Dan was fourteen and I was ten, so, truth be told, I have no idea how we got to go on this trip, nor do I really care. Suffice to say, we were there.

Colomendy was, maybe still is, a camp owned by the old Liverpool Education Committee and allowed kids from inner city Liverpool, to get to see the colour green, to see cows, sheep, and trees. I liked it at Colomendy. It was exciting. We got to swim, walk up hills and roll down them, look for wild animals, of which there were none, though one evening after tea, a lad shouted that he could see a lion. Everyone, by which I mean all the kids, believed him, and ran to the tuck shop. I waited to see this lion, which of course, wasn't there, and by the time I got to the tuck shop, all the crisps had gone. Not the first time in my life I'd been duped and not the last.

So anyway, we were in Colomendy for a week. I got to sleep in a bunk bed, swim in an outdoor pool, see England win the World Cup, walk up my first 'mountain', Moel Fammau in Mold, eat Nut Brittle, which I'd never seen before, and see the movie, Gulliver's Travels, which I thought was fantastic and made me want to go to Lilliput where I could be someone. I loved the scenes of Gulliver dragging the navy of the little enders or the big enders, can't remember which, but I think it was the big enders, and I wanted to be a hero just like Gulliver.

We got home from Colomendy on the 6th August, the Saturday after England won the World Cup, and it, the 'event' didn't happen that day, so therefore, it happened on one of the other Saturdays leading up to September 26th, which was a Monday. There were seven Saturdays and I'm guessing it was a good few weeks before the birth because maybe the hospital would have noticed bruising on my mum and done something about it. Or maybe I'm just being naïve, maybe times were very different back in the mid 1960's or maybe God just didn't allow any kind of natural justice to occur, whether to do with mums being beaten by fathers or kids being abused by parents. Either way, it doesn't matter. What happened, happened, and the best way of dealing with it is to file it away as best you can and move on.

It was probably about teatime, which meant five or six o'clock in our house. Us three Croft kids, me, aged ten, Dan, aged fourteen and Carla, aged eight, were watching telly, so I assume we were waiting for our tea. We were watching a typical British Saturday evening variety show. It ... the event ... started with voices in the kitchen. Not a row as such but not a normal discussion. You could tell because there was something about the voices that didn't belong to an everyday mundane conversation. As normal, we strained our ears, trying to catch a word or two, to work out the tone. It was hard to make out words but if you could catch an 'edge' to a voice or an 'abruptness', you could possibly be forewarned of trouble heading your way.

As well as voice sounds, other sounds could be used that might give you an idea of the seriousness of the event. The way something is put down or moved could be discerned and take on meaning, maybe give an indication of whether or not violence was on the horizon. I say 'horizon', which implies distance, but the fact is that my father's 'horizon' was something that could approach very rapidly, sometimes literally in the blink of an eye. He could have genuine humour in his eyes and around his mouth, but by the time his eyes re-opened from a blink, the humour had been replaced with malevolence. The humour was sometimes still evident in the creases around his mouth but the malevolence in his cold eyes injected cruelty into the situation in huge doses, a cruelty that took pleasure from the terror it invoked. Once the violence began, the mouth lost its humour and took on a workmanlike expression, as if getting the job done in a satisfactory way was of paramount importance.

The sounds from the kitchen went quiet and we exchanged glances of relief. There was no row. It had just been a few short words, that was all. But then a low moan was heard, a low moan that rose in pitch, as if someone was in pain. In that moment I knew that my father was twisting my mum's arm up her back. I remembered uttering a similar, involuntary moan when he had taken me by surprise one day, twisting my right arm up behind my back, holding my right wrist in his huge vice of a hand and my left shoulder with his left hand so that I couldn't twist free. One second, I'd been making myself a jam butty and the next second, my right arm was being pushed and twisted up my back, the pain sudden and excruciating, like an electric shock. And just like an electric shock, some mechanism in your brain, decides to let a sound come out of your mouth, forces a sound from your mouth, not a word but simply an expulsion of sound. On that occasion, I'd been guilty of helping myself to food, a crime in my home that I wasn't aware of until the punishment was meted out. I didn't know what my mum had been guilty of on this occasion, but my mind's eye could see her at the sink or the cooker and him holding her still with his left hand while he pushed her arm up between her shoulder blades.

The next second there was a sudden loud scream or shout and a flurry of angry words from my mum that came closer to us in the living room as she made her way from the kitchen. The door burst open, and she rushed in, going straight to the dining table, where her coat rested on the back of a chair. There was no sign of our father. No sound from him. No sound from the kitchen. Not for the first time, I hoped she'd stabbed him. We didn't look at our mum because if he had come in and saw any one of us acknowledging that something was amiss, you became part of what was about to happen. So, we kept our eyes on the telly, though Carla stole a glance at her but quickly looked away.

I could tell from the sounds she was making that my mum was hurt and was crying. I could hear her putting her coat on but struggling. I very briefly thought about helping her when my father silently appeared, moving fast, like a panther.

He didn't glance at us as he moved through the room, his eyes fastened on his quarry. He reached my mum and punched her on the chin, an uppercut, a harsh sound that resulted in my mum dropping instantly to the floor, no screams, no utterances of any kind, just a silent collapse to the floor. I was watching what happened in a silver reflective plate at the side of the radiants of the gas fire. It was slightly distorted but still a good enough view to see what was happening.

He kicked her as she lay on the floor, three or four times, leaning on the back of a chair and the edge of the table for balance. She started to make sounds. Not like any sounds a person would ever make unless you were being kicked whilst semi-conscious. The sounds from my mum started to get louder, more coherent and so he stamped on her back, on her ribcage, again, holding the chair and table for balance. I saw her draw her knees up as high as she could, protecting herself and her unborn children, my twin sisters to be. Carla turned and sneaked a glance. Her eyes were huge, like saucers, and almost bulging from her head. Her little chest was convulsing in dry sobs, like she was choking. I saw my father turn his head and Carla quickly turned back to the telly. Dan was stoically watching the screen, looking like he was completely absorbed in the programme, his eyes unblinking. I could see a slight tremor in his chin. I was terrified. My body was frozen. My mind was frozen. I couldn't think past the moment. I was careful to keep my head very deliberately turned away from what was happening, but my eyes never left the reflective plate on the gas fire. Herman's Hermits were on the TV, singing a song. I don't know what the song was called but it had a lyric that has never left me ... 'I've got a feeling you won't be leaving tonight.'

My father finished what he was doing, finished the job, apparently to a satisfactory level, went upstairs and got in the bath. After five or ten minutes our mum got up and hobbled off into the kitchen. We could hear her carrying on making our tea. We didn't move. Didn't speak. Didn't look at each other. We looked at the telly like nothing untoward had happened. When our father came down, bathed, shaved, and dressed smartly, shirt and tie, trousers, jacket, he threw his shoes at me and told me to go and polish them. I was good at polishing shoes. My grandad had taught me to spit on them to get the shine, a trick he'd probably learned in the army. I liked polishing shoes; it gave me satisfaction. When I came back with the polished shoes, he put them on, and I caught Dan staring at them. Our father tied his laces, got up and walked out of the house, closing the door quietly.

Carla stood up and went to the window to watch where he went. It was important for us to know how far from the house he was going. The further away he went, the harder it was for him to suddenly appear back at the house. He went to the bus stop and when the bus came, he went upstairs to the back and lit a cigarette. Carla went out to the kitchen to see mum, but mum told her to go away.

We ate our tea in silence, not even looking at each other, though I did 'feel' as though I was being watched at one time and when I looked up from my plate, Dan was staring at me while he chewed his food. Flat eyes. I wasn't even certain he was looking at me or was just facing in my direction, lost in his thoughts.

Our mum had a bruised chin and a cut lip from the punch. One of her legs was bruised and that is all we could see. Weeks or maybe days later, our twin sisters were born.

Chapter 4

Two photographs from Lydia arrived on my phone, of the outside of Dan's flat. The boarding over the front door was still in place and looked secure. The garden was covered in a mixture of rubbish and household things. It looked like the aftermath of a gas explosion. Dan's pushbike, minus a front wheel, was lying on the grass.

A message arrived from Lydia. *'OMG it's terrible. It stinks. I'm not doing anything, just having a look.'*

Seconds later, Emily, apparently still en route, joined in. *'What the hell is all that stuff? What's it all doing outside?'*

'What a mess.' I typed. Everything went quiet for a while, and I guessed that Emily had arrived, and they were looking through the stuff.

*

A message arrived from Lydia. *'Shit.'*

'What?' I replied.

'Awful inside.' she said. *'Sounds like the television is on.'*

I was taken aback. *'What?! Can you video it Lyds?'* A minute or two went by and then Lydia said, *'I'm trying, but it's too dark in here x'*.

Another five minutes went by and then a video arrived. It was dark and jerky as Lydia walked. I recognised the staircase in my brother's flat. I'd not been there for thirty years or so, but I still recognised it. It was the same as the day he'd moved in at least forty years before, painted white up the edges with bare wood down the middle. It must have had a carpet on it at one time because I could see gripper rods nailed into the angles. It was covered with years of grime. I could make out the odd muddy boot print here and there … even paw prints from his dog. There was some refuse, as in rubbish, the stuff you'd put in your bin, but not much as the stairs had been cleared by the firefighters. I spotted a muddy footprint on the bottom few steps. A *foot* print, mind, not the print of a shoe or boot, the print of a foot, looked to be about my size, which meant it was probably Dan's.

I could hear voices but not my sisters'. It was the TV, the sound quality a bit tinny, but the volume was quite loud. It sounded like the BBC News. Lydia was sweeping her phone camera, slowly, from side to side. It was very gloomy, but I could make out that the room was full of rubbish, five, maybe even six feet deep, everywhere. The rubbish went halfway up the window, which was covered with something that made the light filtering in, browny-orange.

I heard Lydia say *'Jesus Christ!'* Then Emily said, *'Let me see Lydia, let me get up.'* The phone jiggled about as Emily inched up beside Lydia and then I heard her sob and say, *'Oh my god! what the fuck is this all about?'*

The phone swung round, and I could see a flat-screen TV, probably about a thirty-two inch, perched askew on top of the rubbish. A crisp picture of a BBC News presenter standing on Parliament Green in London was talking about Brexit and in the background someone with a big booming voice was shouting 'Stop Brexit!'

The video picture suddenly disappeared, and about ten minutes later a series of photos started to arrive. They were made stark by the flash. I could see the doorway into Dan's bedroom and the one into the kitchen. Rubbish was piled high everywhere you looked. It was impossible to see how anyone could have lived in there but very easy to see how someone could have died.

I was amazed that the TV was on and had been left on by the police. It had been a police incident, so the fire brigade would have only done exactly what they were asked to do and no more and so too would the coroner's people or undertakers, whoever it was that moved the body.

'I'm shocked that the TV has been left on' I typed.

'I am too,' said Lydia, *'I was scared because I thought someone was in the flat watching it. Emily did too.'*

'I'm disgusted,' I wrote, *'livid.'*

'I am too.' said Lydia, *'Emily said it's disrespectful.'*

I agreed with Emily. I couldn't envisage me, as a police officer, attending that incident and going away, leaving a TV blaring out atop a mound of rubbish. The police would probably claim that it was impossible to find where the TV was plugged in, but the main fuse box was plainly visible right by the front door, so it would have taken two seconds to flip the main switch on the way out. To simply walk away from the incident and leave the TV on beggared belief and I think Emily's words were spot on … it was disrespectful.

A message arrived from Lydia, *'Dan probably set the TV up for it to come on and off. Maybe to wake him up. X'* The thought that someone in the same position as my brother, would set his TV to come on in order to wake him up, seemed, I don't know, wrong somehow. Maybe I was doing my brother a disservice, but I just couldn't see it. *'Yeah possibly.'* I replied.

I was quickly assessing the state of the place, the amount of refuse coupled with a decomposing body. I called Emily. 'Where are you?' I asked.

'At Dan's.' She said.

'No,' I said, '*Exactly* where are you?' Before she could answer the question, I asked another one, 'Are you inside or outside?'

'Outside.' she said.

'Where's Lydia?' I asked.

'Standing next to me.'

'OK good.' I said, 'stay out of the place now, it's very likely a biohazard and you need protective equipment to go in there, so *do not go back in*. OK?'

I could hear her telling Lydia. I butted in, 'Em, you need to flip the main switch in the fuse box by the front door to turn the TV off, then put the boards back on. Can you do that?'

'Yes', she said, and the phone went dead.

Twenty minutes went by and then a message arrived from Em. *'Joe, we're going back to mine for something to drink, it's shocking, can't believe what I've just seen y'know. I'm shaking all over, just can't believe it. What the hell was he doing? I'm struggling with this Joe, we'll speak to you from mine later, OK?'*

We goodbyed each other and I went into the house. Pam was hoovering the living room. I showed her the video. She was stunned and sat down on the settee. I went to make a cuppa then thought better of it and got a couple of Leffe's instead.

We sat in the living room drinking the beers. A huge purple bee buzzed past the open French windows, and then turned back to investigate the dark opening. It came in, heavy and ponderous, did a sweep of the room then hovered for a few seconds at the mouth of my beer bottle. It seemed to give me a glance, saw me giving it the one-eyebrow look, and buzzed off down the garden.

'So, what now?' asked Pam.

'We're going to have to square everything up here and get over there as soon as we can I think, what do you reckon?'

'Agree' she said, holding up her bottle, 'but let's have another one of these first.'

Chapter 5

The next morning, as we ate breakfast, I joined my sisters in the group chat. *'Morning Joe.'* typed Emily, *'Yesterday, we had a scoot through all the stuff outside the flat. It was all over the garden. It was mostly clothes and rubbish, but we found some documents, y'know, letters, mostly bills and some old bank statements. There was a couple of photos of him fishing with a mate, one or two of Midge and that was it.'* Midge was his pet Staffordshire Bull Terrier. Lovely dog. She used to love playing with Sheba, my German Shepherd. Back in another life.

For the next hour we spoke about the complexities of sorting Dan's home out. We talked at length about the importance of protective clothing. The major problem was that a body had been dead in the place for a number of weeks. That would inevitably involve vermin and various moulds that we didn't know the names of but certainly didn't want to inhale or ingest. As stuff was moved, these moulds would become airborne, and we needed to ensure that they didn't become part of us.

My sisters mentioned that they had masks and overalls that they'd used for decorating and decided that these would suffice. It took some diplomacy and guile to explain, without offending, that these items, notably the masks, wouldn't be good enough.

The twins were out of their depth here and it became obvious that they would be putting themselves at risk by working in the flat. I know they were keen to muck in, but it just wasn't worth the risk. I told them that I was happy to work alone, sorting and sifting, if they were willing to organise the removal of the sorted stuff.

'*Listen,*' I typed, '*I don't think it's safe for either of you to work in there, you're not geared-up for this, whereas I am. I'm driving over there tomorrow; Pam has just booked our channel crossing and I'll stay until everything is sorted. If you two sort out all the equipment I'll need and the removal of all the stuff, I think that's the best way of utilising our team. How does that sound?*'

The response I got, from Lydia, was not what I expected. It was instantaneous and seemed hostile. '*And in what way are you geared-up for it?*' she asked. No kiss I noted.

I have to admit I was taken aback at the perceived hostility. I know I was in my sixties but I was quite fit and strong still. I generally looked after myself well and, just a little thing but I thought it was valid, I'd worked at one of the busiest fire stations in the UK for over thirty years, so I had to at least have an inkling of working in challenging environments, I thought.

I knew that Lydia must surely know all these things and that she must be able to appreciate that neither her nor Em were in a fit enough state to contribute in the way I could, so in true Croft fashion, my mind looked for something sinister in her words. The word 'plot' flitted into my mind, though I couldn't think what any plot concerning a hoarder's home could involve. I know that any plot or dastardly plan began with a few words here and a few words there, but then an inner voice told me I was being a bit daft and overthinking things ... as usual ... but it wouldn't hurt to put these thoughts on a back-burner to be revisited, if needed, on another day.

'I used to do this kind of stuff, remember?' I typed, followed by a laughing emoji. I wondered how many million false emojis were sent around the world each day.

Emily emoji-laughed but Lydia made no reply.

For me, after Dan's personal documents, the most important things to recover would be family photographs, probably many hundreds of them. I know that he took lots of the house we started our lives in, our grandparents' house. To me, they would be priceless and I, for one, would dearly love to set eyes on my lovely grandma and grandad again.

There was a lull in the conversation. Pam was busy upstairs packing for our trip. I sat thinking about Dan. I hadn't spoken to him in decades but thought about him most weeks. I often wondered what he was doing and thought about how he would love it where I lived, the peace and quiet, the weather, the wildlife. I always wanted him to come over for a few weeks, or for as long as he wanted. We could have gone walking or cycling together, something we both loved. We could have even had a beer together, something we'd never done, but of course now, none of it could ever come to pass. I would never speak to him again and never get to know what drove him to his final destination.

I was just about to close my laptop when a message arrived from Emily, *'Broke my heart this.'* Both of their little green lights disappeared. They'd gone.

Chapter 6

Early next morning Pam and I were just finishing our breakfast when my phone rang. It was Andy, an old friend of mine. I'd left a message on his phone last night, asking him to give me a call. Andy was a joiner by trade and a good firefighter. We'd served together a number of times on different stations.

After we exchanged greetings and a few pleasantries we got down to business. I told him that I needed a new front door fitting to a property, but it was urgent, as in *now*. We discussed the work. He knew about the job the brigade had attended and was shocked to discover the victim had been my brother. He agreed to go to the property as soon as someone could meet him there and we left it at that.

I arranged with my sisters for one or both of them to go and meet Andy, then Pam and I packed the car and we set off for England. The journey to Calais and the tunnel crossing would take about seven hours and we would stay that night in Folkestone, before making our way up to Liverpool early the next day. We could have done the journey in one go but, these days, driving for too long, especially in stressful circumstances, wasn't something we wanted.

The journey up through France was uneventful. The weather was fine until we got near to Calais when it started to rain and boy, did it rain. I parked up in the car park at the Channel Tunnel crossing and Pam went to get a couple of Costas and a chocolate bar. My phone rang. It was Andy.

'Alright mate, listen, I've finished that job. You were right, the frame needed replacing as well as the door, but it's all good now. The keys are with your sisters, and they've got the bill too, but look, don't even think about paying it until you've got everything sorted.'

I thanked him, we had a little chat about stuff and then Andy got off, 'Good luck with that place mate,' he said, 'you're gonna need it. If you need a touch, give me a call.'

We checked into our hotel at Folkestone, showered, and went down to the restaurant.

Halfway through the meal a video from Lydia arrived but I decided to wait until we were back in the room before looking at it. Which turned out to be a good decision.

The message attached with the video was to the point. *'The new door etc is fine, we've got a key for you. The flat is really small.'* she said, like I didn't know. *'It's covered in piles n piles of rubbish. Really bad in every room. Can't get rid of the smell, all our clothes are in the washer. We've showered but can't get rid of the smell. It's terrible.'*

Two things struck me. One, I hoped they'd worn at least an effective mask but wouldn't be surprised if they hadn't. And two, the smell. I knew the score with this. There were just some smells that somehow clung on inside your nose or your brain, just lingered and there was nothing you were going to do to get rid of it. For me, the smell that lingered forever was that of a burned body. It was a sickly, sweet, meaty kind of smell that you could somehow recall at any time. Some firefighters used to say it smelled like pork cooking, but I couldn't say that it smelled like anything I'd eat. Interestingly though, I remember reading an article somewhere or other that those tribes in Africa who used to eat their enemies after a battle, as a mark of respect, referred to their cooked victims as 'long pig'.

The message from Lydia went on. *'We had to put a new bulb in the living room, so we've got lights. Edward…'* who was Lydia's husband, *'had to use pliers to unscrew a broken bulb before he could put the new one in.'* I wondered how he'd managed to climb onto the rubbish to get to the bulb. Edward needed walking sticks to get about. *'We can see where Daniel died,'* she said, *'I've ringed round it x'*

A photograph arrived of a doorway, through which I could see Dan's bedroom, which meant it had been taken from his living room. The light was on in the bedroom, showing filthy pink curtains drawn closed. Rubbish was piled high across the room, and I could see that, for the most part, if I'd been standing there, at my regal height of five foot eight, I would have been looking across the top of the pile. The door was fully open, and I knew from memory that, hidden from view around the corner, assuming he still had it, was a lovely leather-topped desk, the green leather with gold tooling around the edge beautifully inlaid into the top. I remembered him buying it from an antique shop. He really loved it, and I did too. I thought about the day I went around to see it and recalled our excited and animated conversation about the chair that had to be bought to complement it. His ideal chair, a Chesterfield green leather Captain's chair, absolutely matched mine and we chuckled about that synchronicity. I said that a brass desk lamp with a green glass shade was the only lamp that belonged on it, and he agreed. We'd had a coffee and sat, side by side on the desk, talking about studying, him chemistry and microbiology, me, the science of firefighting and what we wanted to do with our lives. I'd ended up getting too enamoured with actual firefighting and rescue rather than studying it, and he, apparently, had become too enamoured with booze and collecting rubbish to store in his home. I hoped the desk was still there. If it was, I'd rescue it, restore it if needed and use it. Assuming my sisters agreed. I'd sit on it, have a coffee, and ponder what might have been.

In the doorway, in the space between the door, which was flat against the wall, and the assumed desk around the corner, was, I don't quite know how to describe it but here goes. On the Bay of Skaill in the Orkney Islands is a place called Skara Brae, a Neolithic village. People were living there before the Pyramids or Stonehenge were built and it's really well preserved.

Within the houses of Skara Brae, there are beds built from the local stone. The thin slabs of stone were 'slotted' into the ground to form a sort of shallow box that would be filled with moss and grasses as a mattress. The 'beds' were placed around the central fire-pit and must have been very cosy.

The photograph of Dan's place showed something strikingly similar in the space between the open door and the desk around the corner. It looked like he'd used folded cardboard instead of slabs of rock to form the edges, making a sort of box, and then filled the box with rubbish as a mattress. The box was coffin-shaped, the narrow end in the bedroom, and the wider end, the shoulder end, in the living room, close to the photographer.

Lydia had drawn a rough circle on the photograph, around the narrow end of the 'bed'. That area looked very black. Black with a dirty green tinge to it. It looked like something had rotted there, had become slimy, runny paste.

I moved the photograph into Photoshop, zoomed in on it and sharpened it up as much as I dared then re-examined it. I decided that the black and green mess at the narrow end of the bed, was probably where his head rested. I imagined that when a human head rots, the brain turns to some kind of porridge and oozes out. I just couldn't envisage the feet, which, I thought, were mostly bone, sinew, and stringy muscle, causing that much discolouration. I'm no scientist but I had my brother as lying in his coffin-shaped bed, with his head in the narrow end. The wrong way round as far as I was concerned.

I thought that if I had made myself a box-bed from stiff cardboard and rubbish, and shaped it like a coffin, that I would lie in it the right way round, head and shoulders in the wide end, feet in the narrow end. It just made sense. The existence of the bed in the first place made no sense but nevertheless smacked of a certain kind of logic. For whatever reason, the place you would normally rest your head at the end of the day is, shall we say, barred from you, so, you need a place to lie down, to sleep. So, you make one and do so from the materials you have available. Refuse. Simple. In this particular case, strangely complex, but, simple at the same time.

If, as I assumed, the black-green staining, was the remains of his head, I pondered why he would be lying in his Skara Brae bed the wrong way round.

So, scenario one, you lay down to sleep at the end of your normal day … and die as you dream. If it were me, I'd lie down with my head at the wide end and my feet in the narrow end.

Scenario two, you feel ill and need to lie down. You go to your bed and lie down, as the manufacturer intended, with your head at the wide end and your feet in the narrow end. I think I would.

Scenario three, you're having a heart attack or something equally dramatic and you simply collapse. But do you collapse straight into your Skara Brae bed, perfectly aligned with your head at the sharp end? If so, you'd have to have been standing in the bed with your feet perfectly placed at the head end. It was possible but just didn't seem feasible to me.

And finally, there's scenario four, almost the same as scenario two … you're not well. You need a duvet day, to coin a phrase. You lie down in your Skara Brae bed in such a way that you can see your TV, which is atop the mound of rubbish in your living room and in order to do so, you lie down the wrong way round, with your head in the sharp end. And then, for whatever reason, you die whilst watching the TV. Probably of boredom as there is so much crap on TV these days.

I wondered if he'd been lying on his back or his front, and how his arms and legs had been positioned. I needed to know the answers to these questions because it was the only way my mind could manage the grieving of Dan's death. I needed a Q&A session with the people involved with the extraction of him from his cardboard Neolithic bed.

I didn't expect the police to help me in this respect and figured that they would have some sort of party line they'd trot out so as to *spare me*. I needed full, no-frills disclosure, and for me, the only place I knew I was likely to get that was from the firefighters involved. I needed to speak with the fire crew who'd dug him out or uncovered him. I thought that the police would just want the firefighters to properly ascertain his whereabouts and make the area safe for them to deliberate and detect whether or not they were dealing with a crime scene before the body was actually moved.

I decided to get in touch with an old brigade mate, Dennis, and ask him if he could set up a meeting between me and the officer in charge of the appliance. In the meantime, I messaged into our group chat.

'That all looks pretty bad.' I typed. Even on a photo it was quite shocking and once I was there and the other senses kicked in, I knew that it would become a different scene altogether. I studied the photograph of the *bed* again and saw something I didn't like the look of. Not that I liked the look of anything whatsoever but this was a particularly disturbing addition. *'I can see what looks like a 7Up bottle with brown stuff in it. Is that what I think it is?'* I asked.

'Yes I think so.' She said. *'We think it's piss.'*

I asked Lydia about the state of his bathroom.

'The bathroom is full of rubbish' she replied, *'It's about our height. X'*

'Full of rubbish? So, not usable?' I asked.

'No it's not usable.' said Lydia, *'The door is open about six inches and the rubbish is up to my neck. You can't see the bathroom at all.'*

Strangely, it took half a minute for the real significance of this information to bloom in my head. Dan had done away with his toilet. The conversation petered out and I briefly wondered where Emily was and what she was thinking. She hadn't said anything for ages.

Later that evening, before I went to sleep, I came back to the conversation, to see if anything else had been said. There was nothing.

When I woke up, about 7 a.m. I checked my phone and at 03:50, Emily had added, *'Yesterday proper traumatised me. It's horrendous. It's like a movie set, I can't believe it.'*

I had a little think about what she'd said. I understood that, to me, as horrible as some things are, I at least have a part of my mind prepared for it. *I was lucky*, I thought, *I have this facility whereas my sisters don't.* My mind flitted to the things witnessed and dealt with by murder detectives and I mentally winced at the pictures and smells they'd have filed away in their heads. I took my hat off to them.

We went down for breakfast. While I was eating my muesli, my phone lit up. It was Emily.

'I know you've probably seen it worse Joe, but I never have.' she typed, *'I can't sleep, keep seeing the spot where he died. He was our brother, and that stain was his body. It's messed my head up. I've Googled a body*

decomposing and what that black stain is. I know now. It's from him poor man. I feel so bad so sad. I'm broken at the moment, destroyed, no words can describe what is going on, it's mind blowing to me. I know where he died God love him. Poor man.'

I was in two minds. Literally. I had one mind, which found everything upsetting and my other mind, which … just didn't. And that mind was currently in control of me. I decided that I had to try to be less of a firefighter and more of a brother but, I wasn't sure I could pull it off.

'I understand Em.' I typed. *'It must have been hard for both of you. It's not an easy thing to deal with, especially when it's someone you know and love. Doing what you've just done, talking about how you feel, is the way to tackle it … it's how firefighters deal with things. Talking about it, over and over again. Even making jokes out of some things, which sounds terrible but, sometimes you have to break the circle of horror otherwise you'd become ill.'* I stopped and had a little think about what to say next. Just be you, I thought, just say what you need to say. *'Over the years I've become too used to these things, so I'm probably a little bit emotionally cold at times. I use a different mind for dealing with things so when stuff like this occurs y'know, Dan and Carla, I'm lucky, or unlucky, depending on your viewpoint, to be able to put my firefighter's head on and deal with things dispassionately.'* I wanted my sisters to understand how I worked and maybe trust that I was a little bit different to them when dealing with trauma. Things like this family tragedy, made me properly realise how useful it was to have a fireground head.

Chapter 7

Our journey up to Liverpool from Folkestone was, as usual, littered with the stops and starts of phantom traffic jams. Too many cars, not enough space between them. How does it take almost as long, to drive half the distance that we drove to Calais from our house? We stopped for a coffee and a bite to eat somewhere in the Midlands.

As we walked into the services my phone trumpeted the arrival of an email. It was from Emily and attached to it was the post-mortem report.

I knew that the post-mortem was going to be a bit 'tasty' for want of a better word. Once it was known that he'd lain dead in his flat for so long, it was a given that he'd be in a sorry state. It had been about five to six weeks since he'd last been seen when he was discovered on Sunday 14th October. Go back six weeks and we're at about 2nd September, so let's just say he died during the first week of September.

The TV news has been banging on about this year being the hottest on record in the UK, so, a dead body lying in a house, insulated by a layer of rubbish and open to attack from insects and vermin, must have become pretty unsavoury pretty quickly.

We got coffees and some stodgy, sticky, quite wonderful Danish pastries and made our way to a table. I opened the post-mortem and started to read.

It began with some details of the deceased and gave his date and time of death as the date and time he was found. No one would ever know when he died. Except God, and he wasn't giving anything away.

The first section stated that he'd not been seen alive for five to six weeks, that the police had forced entry to the property and he'd been found, '*in an advanced state of decomposition*' on his bedroom floor. It said that the property had rubbish piled high and, made a point of the fact that there were bottles of urine present. I found that comment intriguing. I understood the mention of the rubbish, as it might well have some kind of scientific importance on account of the heat it naturally generates, but did the presence of bottles of urine have any scientific significance? I couldn't think of one. A bottle of liquid is a bottle of liquid. The relevance to a scientific report was lost on me, but apparently meant something to the Doctor of forensic pathology who'd written it. Which is why I was intrigued.

A full body CT scan was performed to rule out stabbing, shooting and strangulation. There were no fractures to the long bones, skull, vertebra, or hyoid, which, bizarrely, I remembered from reading a book by a Home Office pathologist, is a little bone in the neck that snaps very easily when someone is strangled. Funny the things that stick in your mind. The scan also showed that no organs were present.

The *'General Observations'* section told us that Dan was of slim build, 160 centimetres in height and weighed twenty-eight kilogrammes, or sixty-two pounds, which was a bit shocking. Those pesky varmints had certainly feasted on my brother. His height seemed small, and I know that me and Dan were the same height, same measurements exactly, leg, inside leg, chest, neck, everything. We could interchange clothes flawlessly if we'd wanted to, which we never did. I liked the way my brother dressed, he was always very smart, but I didn't like to dress smartly, still don't. I preferred to look a bit, *worn*. He'd always tried to get me to buy similar clothing to him, to use the same shops but, we were different in that way. Though we *were* the same size.

I converted my height of five foot eight to centimetres. I was about 173 centimetres tall. Thirteen centimetres taller than my brother. That equated to over five inches in real money. That was a big difference. Had he shrunk? *Do* you shrink? In life? In death? I looked it up and yes you do shrink as you get older, but without going right into it, it seemed that to shrink more than an inch, you probably had something other than age affecting your height, an illness or something. So, it appeared that Dan had shrunk quite a bit for some reason that we will never know.

The body was completely discoloured a brown/black combination and was covered with pupae cases, maggots, coffin flies and a number of beetles. There were multiple defects, or holes, in the body and some areas of the body were completely skeletonised. There were *'a few teeth'* present in the upper and lower jaws and I thought about the Dan I knew with his perfect teeth and his handsome Hollywood smile. That is, until our father punched him square in the face. A lifetime of boozing obviously hadn't helped either. *Bloody hell Dan,* I thought, *I hope you enjoyed your life but, somehow mate, I don't think you did.*

The *'Regional Examination',* section started with the *'Head and Neck'* and made for stark reading. Complete tissue loss of the right side of the upper face and scalp. Skull and facial bones were exposed, eyes, ears, lips and nose severely decomposed and the trachea was exposed.

The *'Chest and Abdomen'* paragraph was the same, stark and brutal … two full-thickness defects in both left and right sides of the chest, which extended over the shoulders. The right side of the lower abdomen had two full-thickness defects, there was a large defect over the right side of the upper back and also around the anus and perineum. I didn't know what the perineum was. I do now.

Both hands had extensive tissue loss, exposing the bones, to the extent that it was possible to ascertain that no fractures were present. Both upper arms had full-thickness defects exposing both humeruses. Humeruses? Or Humori? Neither sounds right. Let's do it like this. The right arm was eaten away such that the head of the humerus was exposed. And the left arm was the same. Both wrists were eaten through, exposing the bones.

Both feet were skeletonised with no obvious fractures. The right femoral shaft and the tibia were exposed. On the left, the femoral head and left side of the pelvis were exposed.

In the specific *'Head and Neck'* section, the scalp was completely missing on the right and heavily decomposed on the left, the skull being intact but the brain and upper spinal cord were completely missing.

The cervical spine, the neck part of your spine, was exposed and dislocated with the dislocation being put down to loss of tissue. The mouth, tongue, pharynx, and the oesophagus were *not assessable*.

The soft tissue and strap muscles of the neck were missing, and the trachea was *not assessable*.

In the chest area, the chest wall was partially exposed and all the bones, ribs, collar bones and thoracic spine were intact.

The air passages were *not assessable,* and the pleural cavities contained brown powder-like material. I wondered what that was. I quickly checked the rest of the report to see if there was an explanation of this powdery stuff, found that there wasn't, but it was mentioned again as being present in the abdominal cavity, so I fired a short and sweet email off to the coroner's office asking the question.

There were some scraps of lung still in his chest, the right one weighing eighty-eight grammes and the left one weighing fifty-seven grammes. Eighty-eight grammes seemed incredibly small and light to me. The internet told me that the normal weight for a man's lungs is about 1300 grammes, and Dan had just 145 grammes remaining.

Dan's heart and aorta were completely gone, and the coronary and pulmonary arteries were *not assessable*.

The abdomen contained the same powder-like brown material as the pleural cavity and nothing else. Everything that should've been in the abdominal area, was gone. No wonder he didn't weigh much.

The Cause of Death was, as expected, 'UNASCERTAINED'.

We'd asked for the full report and, I've got to say, we got it. Stark, we expected, stark we got. It made for shocking reading, especially when it concerned the body of a person you shared a bedroom with for the first twenty years of your life. The thought that Dan had become a feast for insects and vermin, was not easy to deal with. It was expected, given the circumstances, but the thought of your brother being slowly consumed was … not nice. Yet again, I got angry at Dan for choosing to go down the road he went down. He had a family who wanted him in their lives. He had options available to him that were very different to the ones he'd taken. His life could have been very different, but his mind wouldn't let him out.

As we got back into the car another email arrived. It was from Richard, the coroner's police liaison officer. He said that the brown powder-like material was *'most likely'* the dried remnants of the lungs after complete tissue breakdown and that the majority of his decomposition was mummification.

So, my brother had become mummified. I reckon he'd have liked that. Like Tutankhamun. He always had a fascination with rotting meat *and* Egyptian mummies, so, ending up, sort of like King Tut, would have pleased him, I think.

Daniel studied rotting meat, *really* studied it. He was fascinated by it. He knew all about the different insects that came to feed and how the whole thing worked. He was an angler and we used to have to get two buses to the bait shop near Sefton Park to buy maggots. I say 'we' because Dan was determined to make me into an angler as well, a task he failed at. I liked roaming the lakes in the city parks and the various bomb-crater ponds dotted about the outskirts of Liverpool from the blitz, but I never took to fishing. Dan was always moaning about the cost of bait plus the bus fare plus the Caramac or Aztec bar we had to buy from the shop by the bus stop. So, he decided to grow his own maggots.

He started with some chicken offal he kept from cleaning the chicken out one Sunday. He actually liked cleaning the chicken out and sometimes I'd stand and watch. I hated it, hated the smell and the overall messiness of it but he loved it.

He put the offal on a plate in the little greenhouse in the garden and waited. Sure enough, he was able to harvest maggots from it in no time. I can't remember the details but I think he used to harvest different maggots at different times. To me, a maggot is a maggot but he reckoned anglers liked different maggots for different fishes, or something like that. I found it all a bit boring to be honest. One time, he actually caught a rabbit in Sefton Park, using our box, stick and string trick and brought it home as a pet, but it died soon after and he used that little corpse as a maggot factory. He'd be called an entrepreneur these days.

The box, stick and string trick worked like this. We'd put bread out on the cobbles of our dockland street for the pigeons, but leading to an upside-down box that was held up by a stick that had string tied to it, which led across the pavement and into our letterbox. We'd watch through the letterbox and when a pigeon went under the box we'd pull the string, causing the box to fall and trap the pigeon. Usually, a few seconds later the box would start moving down the street in the same way a pigeon moves. It was dead funny. After a few minutes we'd let the pigeon out and it would walk off, and then, if it could be bothered, fly away. Our grandad taught us that little hunter-gatherer trick. He taught us lots of good stuff.

As we continued the drive up the M6 to Liverpool, I thought about the email from the police liaison officer. I couldn't quite put my finger on it, but it seemed to raise more questions than it answered. I just couldn't think what those questions were.

Chapter 8

We were staying in a holiday cottage up near Southport and we eventually arrived there mid-afternoon. We unpacked, made a cup of tea and watched the BBC News on TV.

When we'd finished our tea, I went to have a shower and while I stood there with the hottest water I could stand running in rivers down my body, the post-mortem penny dropped.

My brother died under a pile of rubbish. He lay there and became a feast for insects and their maggots, rats and mice. The creatures eating him would, to my mind, just keep eating until there was nothing left. From what I can make out, different creatures eat, apart from each other, different parts of the body at different stages of decomposition. All of his internal organs were gone, apart from, approximately, ten percent of his lungs.

While the diners were eating his heart and liver for instance, did they eat his lungs as well, or not? I mean, why wouldn't they? They ate everything else, so surely, they wouldn't have turned their noses up at his lungs.

If they ate his lungs, and, at the same time, his lungs were drying out, and, apparently, turning into powder, then it would seem that the human tissue-to-powder process was faster than the devourers' dining process. I'm obviously no authority on any of this, but I found it to be interesting.

So, his lungs dry out and, to the astonishment of the diners, starts to shower them with brown snow — *I* can't think of many things *worse* than brown snow — so … wouldn't that brown snow simply drop? Straight down? And all end up at the bottom of the pleural cavity? How does it also end up in the abdominal cavity? Blown by the wind that is keening across his body, five feet under the rubbish? Or was it carried there by the diners leaving in their droves because they were being showered by brown snow? If it was carried to the abdominal cavity by the diners leaving, then, wouldn't the brown powder also be in and on other parts of the corpse? Apparently not, because, to my way of thinking, if it was notable enough to mention as being in the pleural and abdominal cavities, then it would surely be notable enough to mention as being in other places too and the fact that it wasn't mentioned in that way, suggests that it wasn't in any other locations.

I know I don't know what I'm talking about, and I know I'm out of my depth but, if something is noteworthy, then it's noteworthy for a reason. Maybe this kind of wording showed up in every case of a corpse like my brother. I don't know, but, bottom line, for me, with regards to the PM report, was this; it was full of the kind of jargon I'd expect but with two noteworthy items that just seemed at odds, the mention of the bottles of urine and the brown powder-like substance.

It occurred to me that maybe the two noteworthy items were connected in some way. Was the doctor making note of something that he expected to be questioned about? Did he have an idea as to what the brown powder was and why it was in two places? And if he was expecting to be questioned about it, where was he expecting those questions to come from? The family? Or the police? I'd already asked the question and been told it was *'most likely'* from the mummified lungs.

To me, the report was as dry and scientific as it could get, so, if you're going to go to the trouble of reporting something a little bit, *out of kilter* with that dryness, then why treat an enquiry of it as a 'bit of a nuisance'? While dealing with the corpse of my brother, there must have been many pieces of information not really relevant to the essence of the report, so why, if there is an apparently normal explanation for the powder, mention it at all? Was the pathologist expecting the police to ask the questions and been informed that those questions weren't going to be asked? Did he *know*, had he been *told* that the police were *not* going to invest time and money into looking further into the death of a man who lived in a rat-infested tip of his own making? Was my imagination running riot here? Probably. Because, surely, in this great country of ours, the police looked into *everything* questionable about the death of *anyone*, regardless of their personal opinions of that person. Surely.

As I got dressed after my shower, my phone lit up. Emily. *'Funeral tmrw, 11 am Anfield Crem. Sorry for the short notice but this slot came up and we took it. See you there xx'*

A slot came up, I thought. Must have been a cancellation. I wondered how that came about.

Chapter 9

We stood in a small huddle outside the crematorium, the rain creating a gentle, almost soothing susurration and watched as the hearse came up the short drive and stopped outside the large double doors.

As the four bearers readied the coffin, we positioned ourselves behind them and the small procession headed for the chapel. I was bringing up the rear and as we were about to go through the double doors, Lydia half-turned and looked towards the big wrought-iron gates at the roadside. Her brow slightly furrowed and she quickly glanced at me before turning back to the bearers. I looked towards the gates and a frail-looking old man in an anorak, hood up against the rain, was just about to move past the imposing sandstone gatepost. He stopped momentarily and looked towards us, probably getting a glimpse of his own future.

Once inside the chapel, I looked around. There was just us, the coffin and the celebrant, a short, plump, jolly-looking woman in a purple suit and white blouse.

The celebrant spoke very briefly about Daniel and then asked if any of us would like to say anything. We didn't. She surreptitiously pressed the button, the coffin slid backwards on a bed of rollers and disappeared from view as a pair of red velvet curtains closed on Daniel's life.

We went to a nearby café for drinks and food. I had a chicken sandwich with a fancy name, and coffee, Pam had the same but with tea. My sisters had toasted cheese sandwiches and when I saw theirs, I wished I'd had the same.

'No Edward today?' I asked Lydia. 'No.' she said, 'He's not been feeling too good. His legs.'

We chatted about what needed to be done at the flat. Our overall aim was to clear the place, find everything we wanted, then do what was needed to get the place sellable. I was given a key to the new door at Dan's place and that was the funeral, done and dusted.

Our meal over, we left the café and parted outside on the pavement after agreeing that I should pick up the box of PPE at Emily's the following morning.

I was tempted to go past the flat, which was no more than ten minutes away, but Pam and I had some grocery shopping to do, and we both really needed to have a bit of a rest. It had been a hectic few days.

Chapter 10

'Cup of tea?' Emily asked, filling the kettle, and switching it on. 'Or coffee?'

'I'll have a coffee please Em,' I said.

I'd just arrived to pick up the box of protective equipment. As Em made the drinks I sifted through the box. Everything was perfect. Exactly the items I'd asked for.

I asked Em about the arrangements made for the removal of the rubbish. A company was going to deliver an eight-tonne skip early in the morning and I intended to use tomorrow just for assessment and planning.

We spoke briefly about how the skips were being paid for. It transpired that Edward had set up an account with the skip company and would pay for them as we went. Em also told me that my plan to bag things up for the skip was a no-no. The skip company needed things to be easy to get at, so, no bags, which meant I had to slightly change how I would do the work but didn't present much of a problem.

There was a scratching at the door and Emily let the cat in. It immediately came and rubbed itself up against my leg. I eased it away as I don't like cats and Em shooed it into the hall, closing the door behind it. She knew I didn't like cats and wasn't bothered, whereas Carla, my dead sister, *hated* me for not liking cats, which I couldn't understand. I don't quite get why some cat owners, and some dog owners too, can't accept that others don't share their love. I mean, I wasn't particularly keen on tapirs either, but people were probably more than ready to accept that. With some people and their pets, you need to love what they love and if you don't, then there is a definite one-sided hostility that exists between you.

The entrance of the cat was my cue for exiting and I got up to leave. We very briefly hugged at the front door, she bade me good luck, then I got in the car and drove away.

Chapter 11

I left the cottage just before eight, leaving Pam gently snoring. She was going to have a lovely lazy day reading and just catching up on rest. She'd worked hard all year and deserved it.

As I neared Dan's place, I recalled the day he came to see me at my first house, a little old mid-terrace built in the early 1900's. It was a cold, draughty place with rising damp, ice on the inside of the bedroom windows in winter, but solid. And solid, apparently, was what mattered according to my mother. 'Solid house that.' she'd said, moving onto the price of a sliced loaf in Asda. I'd asked her what she meant by *solid house*, expecting some olde-worlde wisdom on the way they used to build '*back in the day*' and she said that it '*wasn't gonna fall down in a hurry*'. Which was reassuring, though many of them fell down in an *Olympic* hurry when the Luftwaffe dropped in.

About 1977, Liverpool

There had been a knock on my door and as I approached it, I could see a man with a pushbike through the frosted glass. I knew it was Dan and opened the door. 'Alright Dan.' I said, always glad to see him.

'Hello Joe.' he said, in his quiet monotone, his eyes not looking into mine. He took the bike clips off his jeans, hung them on the handlebars and parked his bike against the wall in the hall.

I made a drinking motion with my hand. 'Coffee?'

'Yes please.' he said.

'Go in and sit down mate.' I said, pointing with my head to the living room. Sheba, my gorgeous German Shepherd had come out to greet him and they both went into the living room. I made coffees, carried them through and sat down in the armchair opposite Dan. Sheba stayed sitting next to my brother while he rubbed his hand in the thick ruff of her neck. Sheba loved that and seemed to smile. She had a beautiful lustrous coat, black as black could be and a deep orangey tan. Her eyes were full of expression and, best of all, she had a lovely personality.

We drank our coffee and spoke about stuff; the way brothers do. Dan was a lab assistant at a large pharmaceutical company. He wanted to be a biochemist and certainly had the wherewithal, but our father wouldn't let him go to university. He had to be bringing money into the house and that was it. The law as laid down.

One day, I said to Dan, 'You should just go to uni and bollocks to what he says Dan, it's your life you can do what you want.' He'd replied that he wouldn't be allowed to live at mum's and not bring money in and so he was stuffed.

I'd told him that he could live in my house while he studied, and it wouldn't cost him anything. But then he said that food costs money and he wouldn't be able to contribute and that he would feel terrible putting lights on and using hot water. I used to tell him not to worry about that, we'd sort something out and to just worry about getting his degree. But I knew that Dan was never going to university. He had the brains in abundance, but Dan was missing something when it came to being decisive. There were times when he seemed to like the idea of living with me while he studied but then a frown settled on him, and he'd switch off from it. He'd see a way forward and you could see it in his face, in his body language. And then a cloud would descend. His eyes would become sort of, smoky. Distant. Like he was trying to eavesdrop on someone else's conversation. A faint, almost imperceptible vertical line would appear between his eyebrows. It was like another person was talking to him and telling him that he couldn't do it, that he wouldn't be able to do it. It was like he was arguing with himself, and his alter ego was so much stronger than him, it always won. Always. It was like he was bullying himself.

'I've bought a flat.' he said, lighting a cigarette. I was taken aback. In a good way. A little concerned that with a mortgage his dreams of a degree had just disappeared but, it was his life as I was forever telling him. Maybe he'd reconciled himself to being someone who would carry out experiments rather than think them up.

'Fantastic Dan! Where is it?' I asked.

'It's a new-build.' he said and mentioned a large national building company. 'Where is it?' I asked.

'A one-bedroomed first floor flat on a brand-new estate.' he explained.

'Nice.' I said. 'So where is it mate?' I asked.

'It's got its own designated car space.' he said, 'For when I get my own car.'

'Where is it, Dan?' I asked. Again.

'West Derby.' he said.

I was relieved. West Derby was a nice area. A very nice area. 'Nice Dan. Whereabouts in West Derby?' I asked.

He described an area that I knew wasn't West Derby. It was off a road called West Derby Road, that led to West Derby from the city centre, but in no way was it West Derby. We talked more and I narrowed down the area of the flat he'd bought. I knew it quite well. It was the next fire station along from where I worked and, like my area, was full of drugs and crime that blighted the lives of the many good people who lived there.

'You do know that's not West Derby, don't you? It's off West Derby Road, but it's not West Derby.' I said.

'Well yeah, but … it's almost.' For the first time since he'd arrived, he looked directly into my eyes, making it feel like a challenge.

Dan was my big brother, I loved him and for all my life he'd been my hero. He gave me my music, my love of photography, my love of mountains and walking in them. I'd looked up to him for ever and that wasn't going to change. But the fact was, the area he'd bought his flat in was not West Derby and was nowhere near being almost West Derby either. 'The main thing Dan, is that you're happy.' I said. 'So, when are you moving in and what can I do to help?'

*

The approach to Dan's place seemed like it was 'around the back', but, strangely, the layout gave two fronts and, effectively, two backs. You went from the front of the terrace and walked around the back, where the front doors to the upper flats were.

I hadn't been to the flat since about 1988. Thirty years ago. That is a long time, a life sentence for murder or a whole career in the police or fire service. That had been after he'd had the fire in his flat and been rescued by my colleagues from an adjoining station. I remember the occasion like it was yesterday.

1988, Liverpool

I was on nights. We'd just returned from a fatality. It had been a protracted job, a 'smell of smoke', always tricky. We'd eventually found the source of the smell, a long way from the origin of the call-out. When we broke into the house we'd found the sad tableau of an old lady dead in her bed with her two pet poodles, one black, one white, lying dead next to her, all victims of a smouldering fire that had filled the house with deadly fumes then, having consumed all the air, had effectively put itself out leaving the smoke to slowly percolate from the house and spread its tendrils to others.

We'd got back to the station and a well-earned mug of tea. It was while I was drinking that mug of tea that the phone in the mess rang. A few minutes later our station PA system clicked on, and I was summoned to the boss's office.

It transpired that my brother, Dan, had just been rescued from a fire in his flat, he had declined to go to hospital and had asked for me to be contacted.

My boss told me to go and help him sort things out and to come back on duty, if possible.

I drove the five miles or so to my brother's flat. The information I had was that a neighbour had smelled smoke and called the fire brigade. That station had turned out to a smell of smoke at more or less the same time as I had. They investigated, just as we had done and, as a consequence, had broken into his flat. Two of my mates had gone in wearing breathing apparatus, had done the same checks and search that I'd done and had found Dan lying on the settee. A smouldering fire in a pile of fishing magazines had done precisely the same in Dan's flat as it had done in the old lady's house. My two mates had found him very quickly and dragged him off the settee, down the stairs and out into the fresh air. He'd been very lucky. Just another five or ten minutes and he would have become a fatality. He was also considered to be drunk. Dan had sat in the back of an ambulance, taking in some oxygen for a while but had refused to go to hospital. The fire, I was told, had been caused by a cigarette falling off an ashtray onto a pile of magazines.

As I drove through the dark streets, Queen's 'Works' album on the CD player, I thought about the strangenesses that occur in life. There I was, crawling into a smoke-filled house, hoping to find either no-one or someone to rescue but instead, finding a strangely familiar scene, whilst just five or six miles away, at more or less the same time, my brother is heading towards the same fate as the old lady but is rescued by my colleagues. Spooky or what? As I pulled up in the little car park by Dan's place, 'Is This the World We Created' *with the haunting lyrics sung by Freddie Mercury had just started.*

The front door to the flat was open. I shouted a greeting up the stairs and his voice, sounding understandably subdued, not to mention slightly hoarse, told me to come up. As I walked up the bare wooden stairs, I noticed that the smoke-line, an almost straight-line discolouration of the walls, was down to about the fifth stair from the top, meaning he'd been lying asleep on his settee and the smoke had overtaken him substantially. He'd been breathing that stuff in for a while. Dan had indeed been extremely lucky.

The stairs took you straight up and into the living room. As I walked in, he was sitting on his settee smoking a cigarette. I sat down in the one armchair after moving a stack of fishing magazines onto the floor.

'How are you, Dan?' I asked and he took a deep breath before replying.

'OK' he said.

I studied the room. The ceiling and walls were coffee-coloured from the smoke. The old dresser in the corner was scorched up one edge, where the smouldering magazines had been stacked, and the floor adjacent to it was burned. The windowsill had burned through in one spot about the size of a saucer. There was a ring of darker brown on the ceiling above the dresser, giving me a clear picture of the size of the fire. The fire had been far enough away from the dresser to just scorch it. Apparently, it hadn't got properly going but had, like the old lady's, smouldered, giving off toxic fumes. The place stunk of the smoke. Heavy and acrid. It was going to take some getting rid of.

'You've been very lucky Dan.' I said.

He stubbed his cigarette out in an already full ashtray. 'I know. I feel stupid.' he said, speaking the smoke out.

'The good thing is mate,' I said, 'you have to be alive to feel that.' I got up to look around the flat. You didn't have to move from the living room to survey the whole place. Apart from the entrance, two other doors led out of the living room. One led to a tiny space that contained another three doors, the left one led to the kitchen, the right one to the bathroom and the third one was an airing cupboard. The other door in the living room led to the bedroom. All the doors, apart from the airing cupboard had apparently been open, and every room was badly smoke damaged.

'I know.' he said. 'I'm glad someone called the fire brigade. I'll have to find out who it was and thank them. Your mates must think I'm a dope. I'll bet they're laughing at me, aren't they? I wouldn't blame them.'

He was sitting there, looking down at the floor, his cigarette held in the fingers of his left hand. He was rubbing the thumb and forefinger of his right hand together, as if he was feeling the quality of a cloth at his tailor's. 'Do you want a coffee?' he asked, without looking up.

'I'll make it Dan.' I said, 'And no one is laughing at you. That just doesn't happen mate.'

I went into the kitchen and put the kettle on. I had to wash a few mugs and a spoon. I looked in the fridge for the milk. There was none. There wasn't much of anything. A tub of butter, some plain yoghurts and what looked like some tomatoes, but they were covered in a silver fur. 'You carrying out an experiment in your fridge here Dan?' I shouted through to him. He laughed, which was good to hear. I carried the coffees through and sat down.

'So, Dan, you've got insurance, right?'

'I don't think I have.' he said, 'I think it lapsed a few months ago'.

'Are you certain about that?' I asked.

He looked directly at me and there was a flash of something in his eyes I couldn't quite put my finger on. 'I just said I think it lapsed, didn't I?' he said. There was an edge to his voice. Belligerent. The thing in his eyes that I couldn't quite work out became more pronounced and I could now see what it was. It was the narrowing of the eyes and the overall set of the face. It was that part of him that was our father coming through. Elbowing its way to the front. Readying itself for ... what?

I took a sip of coffee and held a hand up to him, palm out. 'Just asking a question Dan, that's all.'

The belligerence went out of him, his narrowed eyes relaxed, looked away and his shoulders seemed to sag.

'Is everything OK with you Dan? Work OK?' He looked at me, but his eyes didn't stay on mine for more than a second or two, then they flitted around the room, avoiding me. Fidgety eyes. That was a sign of something. I don't know precisely what, but, to me, it was a sign that something wasn't right. 'Yeah.' he said, 'everything's fine, apart from' he looked around, 'this.'

'Well listen,' I said, 'If you haven't got insurance, don't worry, I'll sort this out for you if you want.'

'That'd be good yeah.' he said. 'Thanks.'

'I can get some chemicals from the Salvage Corp,' I said, 'get rid of the smell of smoke and clean the brown off everything.'

Dan nodded. Looked at the floor. And that was it. I expected him to say something, but he didn't. I felt that something had changed in the few minutes I'd been in the flat. I could feel a barrier, I could feel … I'm not quite sure of the word but, hostility came to mind. A part of me said that I was being too sensitive, but I couldn't shake that feeling of suddenly not being welcome. I was intruding even though I'd been invited. He said nothing more and took to looking anywhere but at me.

Tomorrow was another day I thought. A new day. A sober day, though, to be fair, Dan didn't appear to be drunk to me. I couldn't see any signs, there was no smell on him, though the smell of smoke swamped everything. But then, the lads who'd fished him out of his flat said he was drunk, so, as far as I was concerned, he was drunk. I realised, at that second, that the bond I had with firefighters was a very strong one. Probably stronger than the one I currently had with my brother. It made me sad, and I felt that part of me was becoming lost for ever, was sliding over the horizon, never to be seen again.

We planned for me to return in the morning and we'd work out how we were going to fix things. I left and drove back to work.

The next morning, when I went back to Dan's, he met me at the front door. He'd been watching for my arrival. 'It's ok,' he said, 'I went through my papers last night after you left. I have got insurance and they're going to sort it all out.'

'Well, that's good news Dan. Nice one. You getting the kettle on or what?' I said and went to step in.

'I can't.' he said, looking at the sycamore tree in the small garden. 'I've, er, got to go out.'

I knew I was getting fobbed. 'Not even time for a coffee?'

'Sorry, no.' he said and looked straight into my eyes. His blue eyes looking into my blue eyes, not blinking, not flinching.

'Ok.' I said. 'I'll get off then.' He was already moving back, getting ready to close the door. 'Let me know if you need anything.' I said as the door closed. As the gap narrowed, his eyes were still looking into mine. The latch clicked and I stood there for a few seconds and watched his figure through the frosted glass. He also stood there for a few seconds then he turned and climbed the stairs. I counted his steps on the bare wood and then I heard his living room door close.

*

And now, as I approached Dan's front door, the smell hit me. The little patch of garden was covered in rubbish and a sour, mouldy, sweaty, rotting, rank smell lay like a heavy blanket over the area.

Casting an eye over the mess, it was easy to just see an area littered with refuse and look beyond it, but all this stuff was here because my ex-colleagues had put it here, moved it all out of the building to make a 'clear way' for the safe retrieval of a body. Working like a chain gang, the crew would have cleared the staircase and thrown the rubbish as far away from the entrance as possible.

The rubbish in the garden wasn't 'tidy', which sounds strange, but you could tell that this rubbish had been searched. There was a sheltered corner made by two walls, opposite the front door. Had I been the officer in charge of the incident, I would have had the rubbish piled as neatly as possible in that corner.

Once that neat pile was in my mind's eye, the scattered rubbish took on a pattern and I could see that pattern had been made by someone searching through the mound and throwing each item backwards, using both hands.

Once you accepted that theory, you could see two fan-like patterns of spread. Two people had methodically searched through the pile.

The most startling item of the stuff in the garden, and flung the furthest distance away from the front door, was Dan's green five-speed racing bike, minus a wheel.

He'd had that bike since he was fourteen. He'd got it for his birthday and was the only one of us five kids that ever had a bike, or even a trike, bought for them. I always wanted a bike but never got one. One year, there was a bike wrapped up in Christmas paper, stored in the coal hole, and as far as I was concerned, it must have been mine, me being the next in line age-wise, but it just disappeared. My mum always said that I must have imagined it. Like you do. But I knew that the thing that looked like a bike wrapped in paper, at the back of our coal hole, discovered by me on one of my many Christmas present hunts, had been a bike wrapped in paper, no imagination involved. It had been there and probably had been mine, but my father had discovered that it had been discovered and consequently disposed of it. That happened a lot. A lot of secret discussions between us kids, especially the original three, me, Dan and Carla, took place on the subject of toys and games being found hidden in drawers and wardrobes and quite often those items never found their way into our pillowslips on Christmas morning. The looks of puzzlement and disappointment on our faces must have been a joy to our father. He must have had something against Christmas because he ruined every one that I can ever remember from my first twenty years on this planet. I hate Christmas to this day, and I always will. I've tried to like it, really tried. I've always made it just how it should be for my own kids but, I'm not able to change it for me. Or maybe I don't want to, I don't know. I don't know why I wouldn't want to but, the thought of Christmas approaching fills me with a feeling close to dread, and I always want it to just go away.

I unlocked and opened the front door and was hit hard by the smell. It was abominable. This was not something I had ever experienced in my life and I have experienced some god-awful smells as a firefighter. This smell was very different from the abattoir fires I'd been to, very different from any body job I'd attended. The smell was heavy, and settled on you like a sodden blanket, moulding itself to you, too heavy to shrug off. It made you want to stop breathing but when you did breathe, it made you gag. It made your eyes sting, probably caused by the overpowering stench of ammonia. I stepped back outside and donned a suit, hat, mask and gloves from my box of PPE.

I re-entered the flat. The tiny hallway was filthy. A single light bulb on a short strand of cable hung down, the bulb dark brown, as though it had been dipped in molten toffee. I flipped the mains switch to on. The light from the bulb was next to useless. The walls had never been painted since the property had been built and they were covered in gouges and scrapes. Handprints, like someone who'd been handling coal, were everywhere, like cave paintings. There was a ledge to the left of the front door, about my chest height. It had a small window that had been boarded up. The ledge was a foot high in stuff that had been posted through the door, letters, bills, free newspapers and the like. The ceiling of the hallway had gone, just the joists visible, with the redundant plasterboard nails protruding. The corners of the hallway were festooned in the thickest heaviest cobwebs I'd ever seen, coated in dust that made them dark grey. The staircase was uncarpeted, like it had been 30 years ago. It looked as though a regiment of troops fresh from the mud of Flanders had tramped up them. There were dog prints, prints from work boots or, most probably, fire boots, plus the dark, muddy footprints that I'd seen in Lydia's video. They were underneath most of the other prints, but they were there, as plain as day. My mind flitted to the TV programme me and Dan used to love as kids, Robinson Crusoe. We used to sit on the settee, happy because our father wasn't due in from work for a few hours yet and we were eating jam butties with our school uniforms still on and watching the telly. Our lives just didn't get much better than that. And the footprints in the sand that Crusoe found one day were introduced in such a way as to add suspense and make the next episode a bit scary, even though we knew, from having read the book, that the footprints belonged to Man Friday.

The stairwell walls were dark and grimy, cobwebs hanging in sheets from the ceiling and stacked down the corners. At the top of the stairs, on the one-square-yard landing, a dark toffee-covered light bulb sat in a fixture on the ceiling that looked as though it had been involved in fire. Surely, I thought, that can't be smoke damage from thirty years ago? Could it? Looking down from the top of the stairs I could easily see that the smoke-line caused by the fire of thirty years previous was still very much in evidence.

I stood at the doorway from the stairs into the living room and looked in. The smell was overpowering. My brother's living room was … dramatic, though no theatre-set designer could dream this up. It could only ever exist in your mind because you've seen it.

The room was full of rubbish. The floor wasn't visible anywhere except right at the entrance and a narrow path, obviously cleared by the firefighters, had been cut through it in the direction of the bedroom.

The window, diagonally opposite the door I was standing at, was almost obscured, with only the top twenty-four inches visible above the refuse. There was a filthy net curtain at the window, grey, brown and hung with cobwebs, that disappeared into the midden.

Everything seemed to be dark and looked damp, sodden even. What little light entered by the window was absorbed by the mass of detritus in the room, and it was difficult to determine what the mass actually was. I examined it.

There were what looked like islands rearing up out of it. In the corner furthest away from us, was a fish tank, probably four feet wide, upside down. It seemed to be full of boxes and had what looked like food tins on top of it, some of them obviously empty, their lids peeled back. The twisted legs of an upside-down ironing board stuck up and looked as though they were waving for help. There were the top half a dozen inches of what looked like a large hamster cage, with a newspaper stack forming a roof. Another island, I could see, was a microwave oven, lying on its back, just two inches of its dirty cream carcass above the surface. The last island, the one I'd reach first, was a cardboard box, white with what looked like black lettering on it. You could make out four black lines reaching up out of the refuse, two diagonals angling away from a point beneath the surface and two lines coming straight up. I reckoned the word would be Vodka.

Scattered about the place, on top of and sticking up out of the refuse, like shell-cases surrounding an artillery position, were bottles, the two-litre ones that you'd buy soft drinks in. They were full of something brown, but I didn't for one second think they'd be filled with fizzy cola. The bottles of urine mentioned by the coroner. I reached over to one of the bottles and pulled it to me. The liquid inside was dark brown and viscous, almost like syrup.

The bottle was full almost to the top and around the shoulder of the bottle, was a sticker with writing in black marker pen. Dan's distinctive left-handed writing. He was the only one of our family who was left-handed. Grandma always used to say that left-handers were really clever, but I reckon she might have changed her mind if she'd been standing next to me. There's no doubt that Dan *was* a clever man, no doubt at all, but, looking about the place, there was nothing at all clever about what he'd done here. There was a date on the label and underneath the date was a series of numbers, letters and strange symbols, none of which meant anything to me. Except maybe madness.

The bottles were everywhere, some stacked neatly, some just piled, and others randomly scattered about. Most of them that I could see appeared to have the same stickers on their shoulders, all with their notations in black marker.

Having advanced slightly into the living room, I could see into the bedroom, which was the same, filled to a depth of well over five feet with general refuse. The whole raft of stuff looked solid, settled and permanent. This had taken a long time to collect. *Nothing* had been thrown away in this home for years. Nothing. Apparently not even his waste. Before I took any more steps into the place, I needed to know what he'd done with his number twos. Peeing in bottles was one thing, but solid waste is a different thing altogether. What do you do with that? You can't get that into a bottle. Not that I've tried.

The more I looked at the midden, the more I realised that there was something odd about it all, which sounds like a ridiculous thing to say.

The 'oddness' was the snow. Or what looked like snow. There were large patches of it everywhere, more prevalent in some places than others. I bent down to look at the closest patch and realised that it was chewings, gnawings, whatever you want to call them. Mice, rats or both together had been chewing everything chewable. An army of rodents had been at work here and I wondered how Dan had managed to sleep with all the noise they must have generated. The whole place was one big filthy, smelly rodent nest. A picture of my brother standing by the kitchen door the last time I'd been here pounced into my mind's eye, and I was almost overcome with the horror of his life. I fought it down, pushed it to the back of my mind and pressed on.

Lying on top of the living room refuse was a wooden step ladder that had been my mum's … rickety, bearing paintbrush marks from the time me and Dan had been forced to paint our bedroom because our father didn't like decorating. We were given wallpaper and paste and a couple of one-inch paintbrushes. We painted the ceiling and all the woodwork with those one-inch brushes. We pasted the paper on the kitchen table downstairs and carried each strip up the stairs and stuck it to the walls, not even once managing to match the pattern. Dan was fourteen years old, and I was ten and so we made a mess, as you would expect. It took us weeks, doing what we could after school and at weekends. Not once did our parents come to see how we were getting on. Only when we had finished did he come to see. He laughed at us. Sneeringly, his eyes filled with contempt. He said we were useless and would never be as good as him at decorating. Like I cared one jot about that when I was ten. Or at any age come to think of it. I noticed one of Dan's hands trembling. I think our father did too. He finished sneering at us, sighed, casually took his big leather belt off and beat us with it across our arses but the good thing was, we got to keep our kecks on.

I got to like our patchy ceiling. I could see my grandparent's faces in it, like seeing faces in clouds. And I liked our mismatched wallpaper. It was unique I thought. It was also a good game of mine, discovering the best way to travel diagonally up the paper from one corner to the other, using as much of the pattern as possible. Weird I know but simple things amuse simple minds as grandma used to say. Dan always said to me that he would never decorate anywhere again, and he'd definitely kept to his word on that.

I went to the doorway leading to the kitchen and bathroom. The door immediately in front of me was the airing cupboard. It was closed and was prevented from opening by the refuse. The door to the right, to the bathroom, was ajar, enough for a man to, say, put his arm through. I used the torch on my phone to look inside. It was over five feet deep in rubbish. It was hard to comprehend. This was his bathroom, and it was unusable.

What did my brother do when he wanted to use the toilet. The bathroom had been out of bounds for a long time. So, what did he do? And more to the point, why would you bar yourself from using your bathroom? What is your thought process? Surely at some point during your hoarding you think to yourself, *hang on a sec ... if I carry on chucking stuff in there, pretty soon I won't be able to use the toilet.* Don't you? In my world that question would be asked. What happened in my brother's world for that question to not get asked? Or, scary thought, maybe it *did* get asked ... and answered.

So, what would the answer be? Off the top of my head, I couldn't think of one.

A thought occurred. Dan didn't keep this stuff because he wanted to store refuse. He was keeping it because, somehow, it represented value to him. Did he have so little real value in his life that he thought of his rubbish as valuable? Was he making some kind of statement to us, his family, standing in his home after his death? Was he saying to his family, the family he had shunned for decades, that he treasured his rubbish more than he did us?

I turned my attention to the kitchen door, which was ajar in the same fashion as the bathroom one. The kitchen, I knew, was twice the size of the bathroom and you could see that the cans and refuse were up to within, maybe, fifteen inches of the ceiling.

In the bedroom doorway, his Skara Brae bed was still visible. It was overwhelming to picture him lying down there to die. The black staining that I'd seen in Lydia's photograph was actually more green than black and the whole area looked sodden.

The house, the home of my brother, who had shunned me for three decades, was heartbreaking. He was the boy I'd grown up with, the boy I'd had such fun with and shared tragic and traumatic moments with, he was the boy that I idolised and admired. He was my big brother, and it broke my heart to think of him not so much dying in this place but living in it. In this shitty cardboard facsimile of a Skara Brae bed, Dan lay down and died, listening to the vermin chewing his treasures into shreds.

I spotted an old suitcase on top of the rubbish in the bedroom and managed to snare it with a rolled-up umbrella that stuck up from the midden.

I opened it. It contained old clothes. They were my mother's. I was a bit taken aback. Our mum had been dead for nearly twenty years. What on earth did my brother keep her clothes for? I was taken back to the night she died and the strange way that my brother had approached her as she lay in her hospital bed, hair nicely brushed back, and her body composed and relaxed.

January 30th, 2001, Liverpool

My sister Carla had called me about half one in the morning and I'd driven straight to the hospital, picking up Emily on the way. Carla had also called Lydia, who lived on the Wirral.

We got to the hospital in central Liverpool and gathered at the ward. The nurses took us into a small room and gave us chairs to sit on. I refused a seat and, instead, stood behind and slightly to the side of my sisters who all took a seat in front of the ward sister, who told us that our mum had died of a heart attack and that it wasn't painful. A painless heart attack … I wondered if there was such a thing.

I don't know what reaction, if any, the hospital staff expected but what happened was this. My three sisters didn't flinch. There wasn't a flicker of hurt, not one tear, not even a word. All of us were completely impassive. I saw the two nurses exchange a quick glance before they realised I was observing them and then they composed themselves.

Of course, I was upset. She was my mother. But I was not about to show myself to these people in front of us. And that is all I can put it down to. We were not going to show ourselves to anyone, not even to each other.

We all went in to see our mum. She just lay there. Obviously. I took her hand, and it was still warmish. The nurses had lied because my mum's face showed pain. And something else. Resignation. Acceptance. You can brush hair as neatly as you like, pose the body in a relaxed way as much as possible. But you can't take the pain from the face of someone who died in pain.

We were given a room to sit in where we wouldn't be disturbed. A nurse brought a tray of tea in for us, but I didn't want any. Carla had been ringing Dan's landline, but he wasn't answering. Dan didn't have a mobile back then. Eventually, he did pick up and I asked Carla to tell him that I would come and get him. He lived a stone's throw from the hospital, but he refused and said he'd come up on his pushbike … the one that now lay rusting in his garden minus a wheel.

Dan arrived and I hugged him. He was stiff and unresponsive. There was a smell on him. Blackcurrant. He was cold to touch. The cold, for some reason, seemed to make the smell of alcohol seeping from skin, more discernible.

I led him into the place where mum lay and went to the far side of the bed to stand by her side. I looked up to where I expected Dan to be standing, opposite me, but he wasn't there. He was stood at the foot of the bed, with his back to her, and he was looking at her over his right shoulder.

'Are you ok Dan?' I asked. He ignored me. I don't think he heard me. *'Dan?'* I said. *'Are you alright mate?'* I asked again.

He looked terrified. He started to approach the head of the bed but did so in that same posture, backwards and very slowly, all the time looking at her over his shoulder. He seemed to be entranced, completely in a world of his own.

I stayed quiet and still. I didn't want to break whatever spell he'd cast over himself. He stopped at the head of the bed but didn't once turn to face her. He stared at her face over his right shoulder for a few minutes, then left.

*

And now here I was standing in my brother's flat at the place of *his* death, looking at a suitcase full of my mother's clothing. I had no idea why he would keep these clothes, but then, I had no idea why he would keep all this refuse. I didn't think I would ever get my head around it.

Just inside the bedroom on the right, was his lovely desk, but not quite as I remembered it. It had been a beautiful piece of furniture. It had drawers down each side and a shallow drawer that slid out from the middle front, all lockable. When I'd first seen the desk, all those years ago, I loved it and knew that it exactly summed up who my brother was; educated, refined, handsome. Maybe the brass desk lamp with the green shade that we'd talked about was here somewhere, buried in the rubbish.

The desk was laden with stacks of books and magazines. The stacks reached almost to the ceiling. They were filthy, cobwebbed, damp and looked like they were covered in the snow of rodent gnawings. Every single book and magazine that could be seen was chewed. Along the front edge of the desk were two-litre bottles full of the brown liquid, complete with their labels, all pointing the same way, all immediately readable, like they were standing on a library shelf.

In amongst the books and magazines were thousands of coupons, the little blue ones that came with Embassy cigarettes. You collected them and traded them in for items from a catalogue. How cynical tobacco companies were and probably still are. Why my brother kept all these coupons, I could only guess at because you hadn't been able to trade them in for decades. I wondered what he'd been smoking towards.

The skip arrived and I supervised the siting of it, took all my gear off, locked the flat and drove away. The real job would begin in the morning.

Chapter 12

I parked the car and donned all my gear, standing by the open boot. Walking around the back, I almost bumped into a bent old man walking the opposite way, who didn't even look up or acknowledge me. *Ignorant sod* I thought. 'Sorry mate', I called to his back as he walked away. After a few more steps he gave a hurried glance over his shoulder, turned the corner and was gone. I unlocked the front door and opened it. The smell came rushing out at me, like a guard dog.

As I entered the living room, right in front of me, was a stack of papers and magazines atop a large cardboard box. A tatty threadbare blanket, filthy and brown, topped the stack. On top of the blanket was a plastic sleeve with white A4 paper inside. I was amazed I'd missed seeing it yesterday. It was square-on to the top of the staircase and really quite prominent, like it had been put there specifically for me to find as I entered. I picked it up.

It was a letter from mum to Dan. Handwritten. There were three copies of the same letter. There was something odd about them but I couldn't quite put my finger on it. I read the letter. It startled me at the first reading, so I read it again. It wasn't dated and mum's address was at the top right-hand corner, like my brother wouldn't have known the address he grew up at.

Dear Daniel,

How are you? Why don't you give me a ring sometimes? Or better still call & see me? What's wrong with you? Why do you treat everyone like rubbish? No one has done anything to you Daniel, everyone is concerned & keeps asking about you, but if anyone comes to see you, you won't open the door. If we ring you up, you've never got time to talk & when you do its only to hurt. Why don't you get that chip off your shoulder & start being a human being again & leave the booze alone before it destroys you. You were the only one who was worried about being like your dad & you are the only one who's taken after him except he was at least sociable & had a bit more feeling than you. I'm still your mother Daniel and you have got a family who do care. I do think that if you could make the effort, you might feel better.

Love Mam x

The letter made me angry. *She couldn't possibly be that crass, could she?* I thought and a voice in my head laughed and said, *Yeah! Of course she could be that crass.* Her cold-heartedness was disturbing.

I stood in the living room, surrounded by refuse, just a few feet away from the spot where Dan had died and been eaten by animals, in the place that was sanctuary from his world, the place that my brother called home, the place that his own parents had condemned him to, and she, his *mam*, had sent him this letter that told him he was not as good as his father.

Not as good as his father. It was an abomination. My mother had thought this letter through, written it, put it in an envelope, bought and put a stamp on it, walked to the post box, slid the envelope through the opening and let go of it. This letter was *meant*. It had intent.

There were so many points in time at which she could have stepped back and reconsidered. She could have written no more than love and concern for her eldest. But she didn't. Instead, she attacked him. I understood her anger. I'd been there myself with Dan, used angry words in my own letters, but always mixed with expressions of love and admiration. For a parent to say such a damaging thing to one of her children, without any conscience of the part she played in the reasons for his behaviour; for my mum to make that statement, she had to believe it. Didn't she?

My mother believed that our father was better than my brother.

That phrase looped around in my mind. I was taken back to just a few years before my mum died, sitting in her living room, telling her how all five of us Croft kids were damaged mentally and that at least two of them were alcoholics and were approaching their brink. Those two people, Dan and Carla, were now dead.

I told her about the physical and mental abuse throughout all of our formative years and that such abuse takes a toll that many people find impossible to recover from. I told her that our wounds were the type that do not heal, that are open and raw and the pain of them comes to spend time with you every day of your life.

I explained to her that being beaten with a leather belt, often for no reason and always for just about any misdemeanour, has a lasting effect. That such beatings, when coupled with other stuff, don't just go away. I told her that being made to cut the grass with a pair of scissors, not as a punishment, which would have been bad enough, but as a weekly chore, was not the way you teach your sons how to look after a garden. That being beaten with the leather belt for not cutting the grass short enough or not cutting the grass quickly enough or not picking up ALL the grass cuttings, is just not the way you bring a child up. That punching a young boy, with enough force to knock you over, for no other reason than you weren't fast enough to appreciate a 'joke', is not exactly best practice. That kicking a young boy with a steel-toed work boot, causing the most impressively colourful bruising, is just not bloody cricket. Broken toys, ripped up clothing, beatings for listening to music, punishments for winning a game, having the exuberance and spirit of youth constantly attacked, crushed and ground into dust … do not constitute proper child rearing.

I could have mentioned the brutal beatings given to her, that we were forced to witness whilst pretending that nothing untoward was happening, beatings that resulted in teeth smashed so badly that the dentist had to take all of them out in her thirties, regular black eyes, broken cheek bones, broken noses, a broken jaw, stamping, kicking, strangling, all done in front of the children … but I didn't.

I could have gone on about the sexual abuse. But I didn't.

The very act of voicing the things I'd voiced … to my mother about my father … had set me on a downward spiral to despair and my protector, Big Joe, who'd been monitoring things, stopped me saying all of the things I should or could have done.

And after all that I *did* say, during which she looked at the floor in front of her and smoked a cigarette, she looked up, stared me right in the eye and said, in the most dismissive way imaginable, she said, 'Ohhh it wasn't *that* bad Joseph!' I even got the full name, the full name that she only ever used when she was angry with me.

Without being summoned, not that he ever *was* summoned, Big Joe was in the room, looking out of my eyes. I was banished to the back somewhere and now, suddenly, he was fully in charge, and he was calmly looking at her.

Another cigarette was lit, and she blew the smoke in my direction, but slightly up towards the ceiling. The intent to blow smoke right at me was there but she stopped herself. Big Joe looked at her, keeping my face calm and expressionless, using my eyes to scrutinise her. She watched him, stared at him. Seemed to challenge him. He got my racing heartbeat under control. Then he told me to stand up and walk out. He told me to not say anything, told me to not slam any doors. He told me to get in the car, drive properly, safely, and go home. He told me to put what happened in a box and slide it to the back of my mind for later analysis. And that is exactly what I did.

Now, standing in my brother's flat, the same thing happened. Big Joe took over and told me to physically put the letter in a safe place, to mentally put it in the same box that everything to do with my mother was stored, and slide it to the back of my mind, to be pored over at a later date.

After I packed the letter away, I realised what the oddness had been, the thing I couldn't put my finger on earlier. Why would my brother, who didn't appear to have a computer or printer, why would he take the letter and get photocopies made? Why were the photocopies placed prominently facing the top of the stairs. Who put them there and why? The plastic sleeve and contents were clean and fresh looking. The letter in the sleeve hadn't been there very long, which meant that someone other than Dan had put it there. Recently. Very recently. That person must have been Lydia or Emily. I didn't think it was Emily because I think she was so traumatised by the place that she wouldn't come near it again, not until it was cleaned and the evidence of what had happened been removed. So, Lydia must have put it there. Which meant that it was her who had made a copy of it. Which meant that she must have the original. So, I texted her and asked her about it and she denied all knowledge. I texted Emily but she claimed ignorance as well and said that she hadn't been near the place since that first time and wouldn't be coming near the place any time soon.

Someone was lying. But who? And why?

Chapter 13

When I got back from day one of the clear up, I stunk. In spite of overalls the odour permeated everything, clothing, hair, not that I've got much, and skin. I took my clothes off and put them straight into the washing machine, which, luckily, was in an outhouse. I crossed the little courtyard with a bin bag around my middle and got straight into the shower.

Once in the shower I performed a little trick I picked up as a firefighter, to help rid your nose of smells. You breathe a small amount of soapy water up your nose and then blow it out. If you do this three or four times, it tends to get rid of a lot of smells and crap. Sounds terrible but it works.

I got dried and into a fresh T-shirt and shorts. My phone lit up as I opened a bottle of Evian. It was my mate, Dennis. He'd set up a Messenger conversation later that evening with the OIC or officer in charge of the Dan incident, a fella called Frank Stevens. I didn't recognise the name.

Pam was preparing a bought lasagne which smelled fantastic. I spotted a garlic bread wrapper as well and realised I was ravenous.

As we ate our meal, I was mulling over what I needed to know from Frank.

As the allotted time for the Messenger meeting drew closer, I became a bit edgy and part of me didn't want the chat. I knew why and as the edginess increased, I thought back to something I'd once said, strangely enough, to Dan.

We were having a coffee in Dan's living room, and he'd asked me what it was like in the fire brigade. I'd said it was the best job in the world and that I loved it.

'What about dealing with bodies and all that,' he'd asked, 'do you get lots of jobs involving that kind of stuff? What do you deal with mostly?'

I remember feeling that the question, if answered honestly, would open a window into my mind and part of me hadn't wanted to answer.

I always thought that the death of someone was a very private thing. It was the one thing that was yours, truly yours. The one thing that belonged to you that no thief would ever want to steal. When I became involved in the death of another person I felt like an intruder. My job, as I saw it, was to disrupt their path to this death, violently if necessary, to extract them from their burning home or wrecked car. When I was involved in their rescue, I namelessly became part of their triumph of survival. But as a firefighter involved in their demise I became part of their failure to survive, and their failure sometimes became my failure. Don't get me wrong, I didn't obsess about them, they didn't dominate my thoughts, but they were, nonetheless, woven into the fabric of my life.

I'd explained all this to my brother, but probably made a bit of a mess of it. There had been a few moments of silence, when he'd looked into my eyes and then he raised his eyebrows, lowered the corners of his mouth, glanced slightly to one side as though he was looking at someone behind me, lit a cigarette and asked me if I wanted another cup of coffee. Which I did.

And now, as the time for my 'meeting' with the officer in charge of the incident of Dan loomed, I knew that my brother had become woven into the fabric of Frank's life and, rightly or wrongly, I resented him. I resented that he and his crew had become involved in the history of Dan. The fact that the meeting would take place on a screen made the task of holding my resentment at bay an easier one. His thumbnail photo popped up on my screen.

'*Hiya Frank,*' I typed, '*thanks for agreeing to speak to me mate. I don't think we know each other, do we?*'

'*Hi Joe,*' he said, '*No I don't think we do. To be honest*' ... a phrase that often set my teeth on edge, '*I'm not sure what I can tell you about the incident, confidentiality-wise. Why don't you tell me what you'd like to know and if I can help I will.*'

'*Confidentiality-wise?*' I thought. A very brief battle exploded inside my head and Big Joe wanted to let rip on Frank, wanted to climb into the screen, wriggle through the ether and emerge from Frank's screen to grab him round the throat and shake him. The other person who lived in my head, the reasonable one, said to me, '*I'll handle this mate, you just keep that other fella under control, OK?*'

'Fully understand Frank, I know the score.' I typed, *'So, were you active at the job?'* I asked, just to make sure he was in charge of the appliance and crew and not a more senior officer dispatched to oversee the incident.

He answered straight away, *'Yes Joe I was the appliance OIC'.* I had a quick squint at his thumbnail. He looked too young. A very quick calculation told me that, as I retired from firefighting, he was still at school, probably studying for his A levels. *Christ!* I thought, *Joe mate, you're older than you think you are* and then I thought, *why, how old do you think you are?* and this other voice said *he thinks he's young enough to do the stuff he retired from doing because he was too old to do it, that's how old he thinks he is. He's an idiot.* Enough! I said out loud and typed *'Nasty job to get Frank. I hope you and your crew are all OK and fully recovered from it. I just need to know a few things with regard to the fatality, who, as you probably know, was my brother.'*

'Yes,' he replied, *'I'm sorry for your loss Joe. We're all OK thanks, you know how it goes.'*

I realised that this couldn't be an easy task for him and that this was something he didn't have to do. *'Thanks mate,'* I said, *'I appreciate that. Is it possible for you to tell me which way round his body was, i.e., head towards the bedroom?'*

'Yes,' he said, *'his head was towards the bedroom, his feet in the room entered via the stairs.'* That agreed with my assessment of the photo Lydia had sent me. So, Dan *had* been lying the wrong way round, as far as I was concerned. He wasn't using the 'bed' as the *manufacturer* intended.

'What about the alignment of his limbs Frank, did you see him fully?' There was a tiny pause as Frank gathered his thoughts, maybe assessing whether or not this 'confidential' information could be imparted to me.

'Yes, Joe, I did see him fully, he was lying on his back with his legs straight out and his arms by his side.' In other words, like he was lying in a coffin. I found this a bit strange. Who goes to sleep like that? I understood that you can lie down in that position and suddenly die but, my head kept coming back to the fact that, as far as I was concerned anyway, he was lying in his bed the wrong way around. His head should have been at the wide end. That's not just me being pernickety. After all, it was Dan who'd made the bed, he made it that shape and he did that for a reason, and as far as I was concerned that reason was that it was just a logical thing to do even though the circumstances were completely illogical.

'What was your actual brief for the job Frank?' I asked. *'I know you were just assisting police so what did they ask you to do?'*

'We had to clear the staircase, which was full of refuse, and clear a path from the top of the stairs to the place where the body lay, to make access for them easy and safe, you know the score, Joe.'

'Yeah, I do mate,' I typed, *'and so, was he under the rubbish or on top of it?'*

'He was under the refuse, had about five feet of it on top of him, consisting of household items, papers, food wrappers etc. The police had identified where the body lay, more or less, and wanted as much stuff removing from on top of him without disturbing the body itself. Once we

cleared a path to the site, the removal of the rubbish from on top of him was a bit of a painstaking task.'

I took a few moments to let this sink in, then typed *'Was the rubbish a uniform depth Frank? Do you think he'd burrowed under the rubbish, or what? What's your gut feeling?'*

He was quick to answer this question, *'I couldn't in all honesty say I'm afraid,'* he said, *'he could have burrowed but it could also have fallen onto him some time later. And yes, it was a uniform depth covering him.'*

Good answer mate, I thought, thinking back to my time in the job and the neutral stance that should be taken at times. *Good answer.*

'Ok Frank. Mate, did he have hold of anything?'

Again, he was quick to answer. He probably had a good mental image of what he'd seen, an image that would live with him forever. *'No.'* he typed, *'He was not holding anything.'*

'Ok Frank,' I typed, *'I think I'm just about done.'*

'I hope that I've been of some help Joe and, once again, I'm sorry for your loss.'

'Yeah, you have Frank, a great help and thanks,' I replied, *'just one more thing though,'* I felt like Columbo, *'the rubbish you removed, where did you put it all?'*

'We put everything from the stairs and the pathway to your brother in the garden and the stuff that was on top of him we put to one side because that's what the police told us to do.' he answered.

'Ok Frank, well that really is me done now.' I said. *'Thanks for all your help mate and if you would pass on my thanks to your crew, I'd appreciate it.'*

We said our goodbyes and Frank disappeared. I put the laptop down and watched some TV. A documentary about whales. As David Attenborough waxed on about the blue whale, I was thinking about the conversation I'd just had and the position of Dan's body. What was it Frank had said? *'He was under the refuse, had about five feet of it on top of him.'*

So, the rubbish in the flat was in the region of five to six feet deep everywhere. It wasn't beautifully stacked, it was just, *there*. The beer-can mountains in the kitchen and bathroom appeared random but they weren't, they were thought through, there was a sad logic to them. My brother had *constructed* a bed with cardboard as its bedstead and squashed rubbish as its mattress. He would need to cover himself for warmth at night and so used rubbish as a duvet. So, what were the mechanics of getting into bed. How did he do it? How would *I* do it?

Firstly, even though I am, to the casual observer, chucking my rubbish haphazardly about the place, I wouldn't do that. I would spread it about, but I wouldn't let it get too high in the vicinity of my bed because I wouldn't want the task of clearing the bed of avalanches on a daily basis. So, first things first, I would construct my bed in a place where it's easy to ensure its safety, which sounds ridiculous but, this is what he'd done too. His bed was in a doorway and was enclosed on one side by a wall and on the other side by his desk, which was the only place where the rubbish was piled in a structurally sound way, stacks of books and magazines being relatively stable, even to the height he'd stacked them. The books and the desk, right next to him were possibly the one remaining link to who he used to be, who he *was*, albeit locked away deep in his mind.

I would ensure, as much as possible, that rubbish was not going to cascade down onto me from the two remaining quarters, the head end, and the feet end, by evening it out, never allowing the rubbish to teeter over me. It's a rubbish tip but it doesn't have to be a *precarious* one. You have to *live* there, after all. If you think about those 'bag people', the ones who walk the streets with a mountain of rubbish in plastic bags, often piled into a shopping trolley or strapped to a bike or a pram, they never seem to lose control of their stuff, even though it often looks quite precarious. There is a strange logic and ingenuity in what they do, and I thought Dan had applied himself in the same way.

I reckoned that, if I was of the same mindset as my brother, I would have a bed area that was 'safe' and a ready supply of empty plastic bottles to pull over me at night for warmth. And those bottles I would keep in the vicinity of the foot of my bed, so I could just drag them up at night. Maybe even contained in large bags, like a duvet.

So, I'm lying in my Skara Brae bed, how do I collect a uniform layer of rubbish on top of me to a depth of five feet? With my arms? How? I'm not Mr Tickle, so how did I do this?

Did it fall on me? If it did, and it's fine if it did, where did it fall *from*? And how did it fall in such a way as to even itself out? Strange things happen in life, I know, but that just didn't seem feasible to me.

In my mind, for Dan to have been lying in his bed, covered, uniformly, to a depth of five feet with rubbish, he must have burrowed in, or another person must have placed the rubbish on top of him, spreading it uniformly so that it looked the same as the rest of the room. If he burrowed in and died, that's fine. Sort of. But if someone covered him up in such a way as to make him look like a room full of rubbish, then that smacks of something else entirely.

As I was digesting that thought, the blue whale making its majestic way through the ocean, another question popped into my mind, the brown powder question. The brown powder that was 'most likely' the dried remnants of his lungs.

That brown powder had been present in both the pleural and abdominal cavities and I'd wondered how the dried-out lung powder had somehow migrated to another part of the body. Wind passing over the body had been discounted, which left gravity as the cause. And now, with the 'testimony' of Frank Stevens, I knew that gravity had played no part. Dan had been lying flat, his uneaten lung remnants had dried out, turned to a brown powder-like substance, and dropped into his chest cavity but also his abdomen. It didn't make sense to me.

I went to bed and, as was the norm for me, I got my thoughts into some sort of order, did a bit of pondering and fell asleep.

The next morning, the first thought that came into my mind was a yellow spot that I'd seen when I got up during the night to pee. A small bright yellow spot on the white rim of the toilet bowl. I went to the bathroom and investigated.

Sure enough, the bright yellow spot was there, and it was obviously pee. I hadn't spotted it until I was stood there in the early hours of the morning and, being virtually asleep standing, had just gone back to bed. But it had stayed in my mind and now that I was inspecting it, it looked as though it had tiny little diamonds glittering in it. *Salt crystals* I thought. I rubbed my forefinger over the spot and, in the light from the window, examined my fingertip. The glittery stuff was almost certainly salt crystals. I rubbed the stain between finger and thumb. It felt like fine salt, gritty, dusty, powdery. Pee, I thought, dries into powder.

The bright, almost fluorescent yellow of my pee spot, came from some tablets I took for my restless leg thing and an hour or two after taking one, my pee, no matter how much water I drink, looks like it's *radioactive* or something.

I wondered if pee drying into a powder would be on the internet and looked as I ate my breakfast. I typed the words *dried piss* into the search engine and to my complete surprise, opened a door to a world I didn't know existed. I discovered that I could buy dried urine on the internet and wondered why I would want to do that … and the answer would never, in a million years, have occurred to me. The bags of dried pee are guaranteed *Drug Free!* You simply re-hydrate it.

So, if fluorescent yellow pee dries into fluorescent yellow powder, brown pee must become brown powder. It seemed a reasonable assumption, though it still didn't answer the question of how it came to be in two different body cavities.

I finished my breakfast, brushed my teeth, checked to make sure I'd left no more little spots on the toilet rim and went to the flat.

Chapter 14

The work was drudgery. Pick up, examine if you need to, put it in the document box if wanted or the bucket if not. Fill the bucket, take it down the stairs, put it in the wheelbarrow, do it again until three buckets are full, take wheelbarrow to skip, empty it, start again. And repeat. Hour after hour.

The beer cans had presented a problem. I estimated that there were 20,000 beer cans in the flat, maybe ten years' worth at about five or six a day. I didn't know what his consumption was, but I reckoned five or six a day of strong lager wasn't overcooking it for someone like Dan.

The kitchen, which measured about ten feet by six, was full almost to the ceiling. The door was open a crack, just enough to put your arm in and flick a can up onto the pile. It's hard to envisage and just as hard to take in.

Filling that room the way he'd done hadn't been easy. He must have started furthest from the door. How it got to the state it ended up, is beyond me, I couldn't understand it. What I did understand is that it had taken effort and a certain amount of ingenuity.

Getting it all out again required nothing more than persistence and a little brute force. It was impossible to open the door more than a few inches and so I used my sledgehammer to obliterate the door into component parts. As soon as there was room, the cans avalanched out into the square metre of floor between the kitchen and bathroom. The noise was deafening, and I wished I'd thought of bringing ear defenders.

Every shovelful of cans created space for more cans to cascade into and this terrible noise persisted until the mountain of cans reached some kind of equilibrium.

At the far end of the kitchen I found the skeleton of a dog, lying in its bed and covered by a sack. Judging by the size of the skeleton, the colouring of what hair remained and the underbite, I took it to be Bertie, the Shih Tzu that my brother had bought for my mum and had reclaimed when she died. I wondered if, given the site of the 'burial', the death of Bertie had maybe been the catalyst for the hoarding to begin in earnest. We'd never know and, in the strangest of ways I took it all in my stride, like it was normal. My fire brigade head was in charge, and it was only every now and then that I opened my mind to allow stuff in. When that happened, I'd take a little break outside by the car, sipping at a bottle of water or having a coffee, listening to the real world sliding by.

Every time I looked up at the windows of his flat, I thought about the world he'd created inside, and how those windows were like the bedroom windows of our childhood home, seemingly like every other window on every other house, but, in reality not the same at all. Panes of glass, separating worlds, normality from abnormality, horror from happiness. Each time I thought about windows, the comparison with eyes came to mind. Windows to the soul some say. Through the eyes of every person is a world different to the one you see, every world viewed from inside a world made in the human mind.

The world inside the mind of my brother had created the world inside his flat. I wondered if the world outside his windows looked the same to him as the world inside. When he was a child and spent time looking out through our bedroom window, he saw a world that was at odds with the world inside *that* house. But *that* world had been created by his parents, mainly his father. Did Dan look out of his own windows and see a world he preferred? Apparently not.

There were three wall cupboards above the kitchen worktop, which the mountain of beer cans had completely covered, all perfectly normal in that they were full of the things you'd expect to find in kitchen wall cupboards, sauce bottles, salt, pepper, herbs, dried goods and lots of mismatched crockery. Everything was filthy and well out of date but all the kind of stuff you'd expect. Except for, strangely, a black A4 sized page-a-day diary.

I opened it. It was packed with writing, every square inch of every page. Different coloured inks but mostly black, the writing obviously Dan's but different at different times. Some of the writing was aggressive looking, some of it looked almost unintelligible. And, riffling through the pages, not reading anything but just taking first sight of it, some of the writing was very neat, not at all like his writing but at the same time still obviously his. It was intriguing, not least because it had been 'secreted' for want of a better word in a wall cupboard with the condiments and crockery of a normal kitchen. It was intriguing but it was something that would have to wait for later.

Emptying the bathroom was the same tedious work, the same problems of avalanching cans. The room contained another dog bed, bigger than the Bertie bed, probably Midge's, Dan's Staffy. Dog leads, choker chains and collars, food bowls and dog toys were scattered through the refuse. A selection of Midge's bed blankets, tatty and filthy, hung on a nail hammered into the wall. There was also a full box of boxes of Jaffa Cakes. Apparently, Dan loved the cake sold from the biscuit aisle, the same as me. Or maybe more than me. How, I wondered, did he manage to obtain a full box of boxes of them then seemingly forget what he had and cover them up with refuse.

When the bathroom was emptied, I discovered the toilet was also empty. The water in the U bend had evaporated, opening a conduit for rats to enter from the sewers. I pressed the flusher handle but the cistern was empty as well. I couldn't see a stopcock anywhere but needed to fill the U bend with liquid. I picked up one of Dan's special two-litre bottles, examined the label like a wine connoisseur, opened it and poured it into the toilet bowl. The smell was utterly dreadful and when I'd fought down the instinct to gag, promised myself that I'd bring some big bottles of water and bleach the following day and repeat the procedure.

A shelving unit in the corner of the bathroom contained long-abandoned aftershaves, shaving foams and deodorants. I took the top off a can of Brut deodorant and sprayed it into the air. It smelled just like it did decades before when I'd last smelled it. I wondered when Dan had last had a bath, washed his hair, his clothes or brushed his teeth.

Once the bathroom was empty I moved into the living room. As I picked up a string-tied stack of *Coarse Fishing* magazines a family of mice nesting underneath, squeaked in unison, and scattered, making me jump about three feet in the air. When I recovered my composure, I sat on the stack of magazines and laughed so much that tears streamed down my face and into my mask.

As I worked through the square-yard of rubbish where I stood, I uncovered what looked like the corner of a TV. Ten minutes later, the TV was fully uncovered, and I lifted it up and onto the top of the pile next to me. It was a flat-screen, maybe about twenty-eight inches, with a big hole right in the middle of the screen and a corresponding bulge and crack in the back. It had been hit fairly hard with something, maybe a hammer. Or a foot. Maybe it had been kicked. Maybe there was something on it, a programme or news item that angered Dan and he'd kicked the TV. The instant that thought bloomed in my mind I was transported back in time.

About 1961, North Liverpool

I was sat on the settee. Dan was in an armchair, but not our father's armchair. We were both watching the TV. We'd not long been in from school, and we were watching Torchy the Battery Boy or something like that. Whatever we were watching must have been good because neither of us even knew that our father was in the house. He didn't normally come in from work until teatime and it was probably about four o'clock or thereabouts.

He suddenly appeared, striding quickly into the room, went straight to the TV in the corner, kicked the screen in, turned and walked out. No words, no shouts, no acknowledgement of us whatsoever. When he kicked the screen, it imploded, made an incredible bang, then exploded, showering the whole room with glass. We weren't hurt but we were shocked, such that we didn't move. We didn't even look at each other. I just looked at the wooden box in the corner that used to be the TV. I was too shocked to even be scared.

After a few minutes, our mother came in, looked at the wooden box for what seemed an age, then walked out. And when I say out, I mean out. Of the house. She got the pram with my sister Carla in, walked out, slamming the front door, and I heard her shoes clicking off down the street.

Me and Dan still hadn't moved.

Our father came back into the room with a sandwich on a plate, a cup of tea and the newspaper under his arm. He sat down in his armchair, the one with the best view of the telly, and, putting his cup of tea on the arm, opened the paper onto the back page, the sports page, rested it on his knee and took a bite out of his sandwich. He didn't even look at us. He did, however, quite bizarrely, look at the TV every now and then. As he moved in the chair, the little pieces of glass under him crunched and squeaked. I liked the noise. I don't know why. I still like the noise made by grinding glass.

It was when our father started reading the paper that my brother first glanced at me. A tiny sidelong glance made without moving his head. I copied him. Glancing without moving my head. I didn't know what to do so I just sat and waited to see what Dan did, to take my cue from him.

My father ate his sandwich, drank his tea, and read his paper. He kept looking at the TV and the clock on the mantelpiece, the same clock that years later, in a moment of school holiday boredom, I decided to take apart to see how it worked, which was a big mistake but another story. I knew that he was checking the clock because he was going to go out. Probably to the pub. He finished his drink and sandwich, put the paper on the floor, got up and walked out. A couple of minutes later, the front door opened and closed. We still hadn't moved but were glancing at each other like mad.

A few minutes went by and then our grandparents came into the room. My grandma stood the two of us up and started to brush at the glass fragments with her tea towel. My grandma always had a tea towel. Grandad just looked at the TV and the mess and shook his head slowly. 'By 'eck' he kept saying, over and over.

'Grandma ...' I said, 'can I have a sandwich please?'

They took us out of the room, and we were both given a sandwich. Big thick slices of white bread cut off the loaf the way she used to do it, by turning the loaf around as she cut. I've tried to do it the grandma way and just ended up with a slice of bread that has a crust two inches thick at one end and half an inch thick at the other, with a kind of step in the middle. The sandwich had a thick spread of best butter, a generous slice of the ham she'd cooked the day before and a serious dollop of English mustard, the proper stuff, made by grandma from the powder. The mustard made my nose and eyes water, but I loved it. It's still one of my favourite sandwiches and I still put too much mustard on, like she did.

*

Nothing was ever said about the TV. To my knowledge the same thing happened at least twice more, and nothing was ever said about those occasions either. No-one in the family ever mentioned it to anyone else. Or should I say no-one in the family ever mentioned it to me, nor I to them.

Now here we were, sixty or so years later, in Dan's flat, with a kicked-in TV. I couldn't understand why he'd kept it. Again, I wondered if it was another of the catalysts that had provoked the hoarding of rubbish. Did he keep the TV to remind him of what he'd done? Or did he keep it, knowing that sooner or later, when he'd gone, someone, meaning us, would clear his mess up and find it and know what he'd done. Was it all part of some after-death message he wanted to send to us? I don't know. I couldn't start to think too deeply about it whilst doing the work because, to do so would be a recipe for mistakes at best and disaster at worst. There would be time for analysis later.

Chapter 15

I started to browse the diary I'd found earlier and did so outside the cottage. Even then, I had to give up after just ten minutes, because the smell coming from it was so foul it was making me heave.

I 'spoke' to my sisters in the group chat and suggested that I photograph every page and send them copies. They agreed, though Lydia was hesitant, asking if it was right and proper that we read his diary. I thought that he owed me answers. And I said so. He'd not spoken to me for more than half of my life with no explanation, left a terrible mess behind him that I was in the process of cleaning up and if a diary could shed *some* light into the darkness then I was going to take that opportunity. Emily agreed with me. '*Lyds*,' I said, '*I'll send you the pages then you decide whether you'll read them or not.*'

It took an hour to photograph the diary, Pam holding the pages still in the breeze, and move those photos to my laptop. Once that was done I bagged the diary and put it in the bin.

The diary was an A4 page-a-day diary but Dan had used it to record two years of his life, 2003 and 2004, possibly with the start of 2005, from what I could make out at first glance.

To begin with it seemed as though this had been successful, but the more I looked, the more I realised it hadn't. I picked a random date, 28th May. On that page were the entries for the 28th May 2003, with the entry for the 28th May 2004 written underneath but, at the bottom of the page, because he ran out of room for what he wanted to write, he started again at the top of the page, and overwrote part of the 2003 entry. It looked, at first glance, like a lot of scribble and it was only when magnifying the photo that I was able to see the two entries written, one on top of the other. It was difficult but with careful scrutiny, coupled with the context of what had been written before, it was possible to decipher it.

Although mostly black ink, he'd used different coloured pens throughout, and it was easier to read overlaps when the ink colour changed. *Maybe that's why he did it,* I thought, a certain logical craziness involved.

I started to decipher and transcribe the diary. It wasn't going to be a fast job. Luckily I liked puzzles

Chapter 16

The format he'd used was consistent throughout the diary. Underneath every line showing the date was a line of figures. It was almost like a mantra. For instance, '*2nyt start 7pm 45 x 6 + 112.50.*'

It seemed obvious that it was related to drinking but exactly what it meant was lost on me. I gave the problem to Pam. She's good at research, good at ferreting stuff out on the internet and putting it all together.

It looked like the diary had started as a means of monitoring his habit, both by stating how much he was drinking and giving a brief description of his day. I was saddened by this attempt to help himself. Saddened because he'd failed and that I wasn't able to help him. I feel sure that I could have helped him, but a voice inside my head said that I was not the first person to think that about an alcoholic, and I wouldn't be the last.

His writing showed him to be a different person to the one I knew. It was very matter of fact. At times he seems proud of what he writes and at other times he seems ashamed but soon bolsters himself. Like it's two people writing the same entry at the same time. It's strange to read and hard to reconcile with the boy I knew.

It seemed as if he was writing his diary for an audience, that he expected someone to read it one day, which, I suppose, is exactly what is happening. It struck me that this particular diary was written years ago, and I wondered if there had been others or whether he just did it for the span of this book, then gave up.

His drinking appeared to be quite horrendous during the course of the journal and I couldn't imagine what state his body was in during the run-up to his death. It was such a terrible waste of a life.

Pam, as I expected, didn't take long to produce the info on Dan's mantras. It was all new to me and I found it oddly compelling.

All of the thousands of empty beer cans in his flat were strong beers, the Supers and the Special Brews, all 9 percent abv beers. ABV is an abbreviation for *alcohol by volume* and the number relates to the amount, in millilitres, of pure alcohol in a given volume, meaning that, in Dan's preferred beers, 9 percent of every mouthful is pure alcohol.

Dan's '45', which crops up a lot, relates to the millilitres of pure alcohol in a given drink. All of his 9 percent abv beer cans had contained 500 ml of beer. To arrive at the '45' you multiply the contents, 500, by the abv, 9 percent and you get 45. So, each of his cans contained 45 ml of pure alcohol.

Similarly, the same formula applied to a 750 ml sized bottle of 15 percent abv wine, gives you 112.50.

In the UK, the NHS recommended number of 'units' for an adult, is not more than 14 units per week. One of Dan's 45's equals 4.5 units, meaning that he could safely drink about three cans of his preferred beers, *per week*. In an average week, he was drinking at least 30 of these beers. Dan was consuming about 30 x 4.5 units which equals a staggering 135 or, about 120 units more than the recommended 'safe' amount. Every week. For decades. And that figure didn't include strong wine and whatever spirits he drank.

Looking at the stark figures, it was hard for me to comprehend that my *brother*, the boy and man I had grown up with, had somehow been driven down this path. I felt desolate. *I* felt desolate. *Me*. What did Dan feel? Anything? Or nothing? Did he simply become robotic ... anaesthetised to everything except his base thoughts and desires and the need to fuel his addiction?

It was disturbing.

Sunday 26th January 2003
2nyt start 5:35pm 45 x 7
2nyt gave Bertie firmish slap on side 2 stop him from looking for piece of dog biscuit on floor, because he was in danger of causing landslide of cans, and he wouldn't stop looking when I told him to stop (several times). He walked away and looked at me. I told him to come here and jump up on chair. He did so, and I felt him and he wasn't shaking, i.e., not frightened. But he had been given a mild shock, i.e., he licked his lips and looked at me when I talked to him and stroked him. I went and got him another piece of biscuit and pretended to find it by the landslide. He was ok about it all.

Wednesday 05th February 2003
2nyt start 7:24pm 45 x 5 + 112.50
This morning, b4 7am, started my car (started 1st time) and reversed to other car park, then decided 2 go for a spin. Had at least 45 x 4 inside me, will never do that again, even though my driving was fine. Had Bertie with me, untethered in the front seat. Blue Seat car was parked next to me B4 I went out,

B4 7am. Who's car is it? Where do they go? Came in after engine had warmed up and had another 45 x 3. Didn't put alarm on, and car has had no alarm on overnight into Thursday daytime.

Friday 07th March 2003
2nyt start 7.43 pm 45 x 6? + 112.50

Finished Disneys Atlantis this afternoon PS1.

This morning (late) Bertie on the bed me in the toilet, Bertie screaming with pain, I shouted a lot. Bertie scratching his ear and screaming I assume. This afternoon Bertie same scenario but this time in lounge on chair. I was in kitchen. I lost it and battered him for a few seconds only. I don't know if I was controlling the fast slaps 2 his body (may have been 1 or 2 initial ones to his head, I can't remember, but I hope not), but I appeared to be fast and hard. I don't know if he jumped off chair or was "slapped off" chair, but he didn't cry once, in fact, the screaming from him scratching his ear instantly stopped when I started hitting him. He was very soon back on the chair, he didn't try to run away from me. I was shocked at myself, and soon went from kitchen back into lounge and apologised 2 him. I felt him and he wasn't shaking and seemed fine with me, maybe he thought I had helped him with his ear. 2nyt (or was it last night?) very late I heard a gnawing sound, quite loud.

Sunday 16th March 2003
2nyt start 5:33 pm 45 x 4

2day 12 – 12.30 pm took photos of my garden to show the mess left by Tommys fence erectors.
ASDA WAL/MART AGFA FILM iso 200
1st 4 or 5 of my gardens path mess
Channel 5 finished 5.38 2nyt says modern cars don't survive a 60 – 70 mph crash (head on) nearly as well as a 10 yr old car. Still a long way to go.
Bertie bites off tat on ryt leg.
Heard mouse distress calls about 5.30 pm 2nyt. Petered out about 6.30 pm. Crushed? Or trapped? Cans. Or babies wanting milk? By lounge door to stairs. Heard can/metallic sounds a few times. Is young one trapped with weight of cans above it?

Chapter 17

It just came to me as I was driving past Anfield, the stadium of Liverpool FC. I wasn't even thinking about it, I was thinking of a match I'd been to at that famous stadium what seemed like a hundred years before. And then it just appeared in my head like a magician's reveal.

Urine dries into powder the same colour as the urine. A dead body is lying flat on its back, covered in maggots and beetles. You, a live person, standing up next to the corpse, want to know what state the corpse is in, but you can't tell because of the number of creatures writhing around on it. In an ideal world, if I were in that position, what would I do? I'd pour water on the body and swill them all out of the way. And if there was no water? I'd use any available fluid. And if the only available fluid was numerous bottles of brown urine, then that is what I'd use.

The body had been opened up by rodents and so a deluge of urine would wash into the chest or pleural cavity and some of it would slosh down into the abdomen.

And during the hottest summer on record in the UK, the brown urine would evaporate, leaving a brown powder-like residue and the diners would simply return to the table.

And there you have it ... the two 'strangenesses' of the coroner's report, bottles of urine and the brown powder, the two things I found to be at odds with the dry scientific format of the post-mortem. There they were, interpreted.

Could I prove it? No, I couldn't. Apart from anything else, my brother's remains had been cremated. And according to the post-mortem report, no samples had been kept.

So, the explanation was there *for me*. It satisfied *me*. But of what? That someone, some other person, had been monitoring the corpse of my brother. It seemed ridiculous. Because if that were the case, then someone was doing that for a reason. Who would have such a reason? Only a person who had some kind of, for want of a better phrase, *ownership* of the body.

What kind of person would think that he had *ownership* of the body of my brother? Did someone *kill* Dan? Someone who then *monitored* his body for its state of decomposition. Why?

If some random person killed him, then that person wouldn't monitor his body, they'd just walk away. I would. I'd walk away and never come back.

So, therefore, the person monitoring his body knew him and had a reason to monitor the state of the body. What was the importance of the decomposition?

My logic train hit the buffers. I couldn't work it out. I had to check and double check my thoughts and let whatever was there filter through.

I parked up outside the flat and went back to work.

Chapter 18

I'd been steadily making my way to the first of what I'd mapped out as 'islands'. The cardboard box. It was buried to within eight or so inches of its top and now I'd got there and uncovered it enough to remove it from the embrace of the midden.

The box had been white and had black lettering. It had once contained nine one-litre bottles of vodka. I wondered whether he had bought it as a box of vodka, or whether he'd got it from his booze shop as an empty box to store stuff in.

Sifting the refuse was mind-numbing, yet painstaking. It required concentration. The search had to be meticulous.

It was quite a revelation to me that Dan's midden actually contained photographs, not in packets or envelopes, but just there, mixed up with old newspapers, clothing, and general refuse. It was like he'd been looking at them and then just launched them onto the pile, only for them to get covered up with stuff as the days passed. I imagined him sitting there, looking at a photo, deciding he didn't need it anymore and casually spinning it up into the air, maybe even aiming it at something, like you do with playing cards when you're extremely bored and just happen to have a pack in your hand.

I found a photo of my grandparents standing in their living room, arms across each other's shoulders, posing for the photographer but wearing faces that said they had better things to be doing.

In the fold of a pair of jeans encrusted with something dark brown, was a stained photograph of my parents dressed smartly, sitting in a pub by the looks of it and appearing impossibly young and happy. There was one of my grandad, in his World War One uniform, looking lean and fit, his face all clean lines and sharp angles, handsome, with calm, staring eyes. It was hard to reconcile the photograph in my hand with the place I'd found it. Grandad, calmly staring at the camera, full of the innocence and passion that would take him to the killing fields of France and the photograph, held between the latex-gloved finger and thumb of one of his grandsons, dressed in protective clothing, standing in a midden that his other grandson had both created and died in.

My grandad had survived the so-called Great War, had been gassed, taken prisoner and escaped, had somehow survived decimation of two regiments. He'd married and together with my grandma, brought two children into the world, my Uncle William and my mum, Roberta.

Between the wars he'd moved from Sheffield to Liverpool in search of work, and his daughter had met my father. How proud my grandparents must have been when their daughter and son in law produced their first-born child, my brother Daniel.

And now here we all were. In different forms but all in the same room. What would my grandparents have thought, I wondered? What would they have said if they were stood where I was. Sadly, I didn't care what my parents might have thought or said.

I extracted Cardboard Box Island from its anchorage, put it on the Workmate and opened it up properly.

At one time it had contained nine bottles of Vodka. Now, it contained seven large bottles of urine, all labelled the same as others.

There was a section of the box that was too small to have fitted another of the bottles in but was, instead, stuffed with what looked like a plastic bag. I pulled it out and it turned out to be a lot of little plastic sample bags crammed in together. They had a white strip across one side of them that could be written on.

All of the bags, and there must have been at least a hundred, contained a lock of hair. And every bag had writing in black marker on the white strip.

The locks of hair were all variations of blonde and the notations were in Dan's writing. The first one I picked up had *Front R 110368*. The next one, *Top back L 190571*.

I sat on my toolbox, holding two handfuls of the little bags and let them slip through my fingers, dropping to the floor at my feet. As they landed, some of them landed with notations up and some of them didn't. The slipperiness of the bags dropping from my hands and the soft *plat* as they landed was quite soothing and when my hands were empty, I grabbed another two handfuls, and let it happen again.

I kept picking them up and letting them slide, thinking about Dan and the state he'd got into, using the soothing little bags as a background to thought.

The bags of hair had captured me. In more ways than one, I felt as though I was inside his domain, his castle, holding some of his treasures. What value were these treasures to him? What was their purpose? What did the numbers mean? Did he catalogue them? There had to be a catalogue or inventory. Otherwise, the numbers wouldn't have a purpose, would they? Would they? Numbers are put on things to give meaning. An item number, catalogue number, a fleet number and so on.

As I pondered, I carried on picking up and dropping. *Why did he cut off chunks of his hair and bag them up* I wondered. I spoke out loud to the room, to him, 'What were you doing Dan?' I asked. 'What on earth were you doing?' I heard a little movement and spotted a tiny mouse scooting along the top of Old Dresser Island in the far corner. It stopped when I looked at it, frozen mid-step, head cocked questioningly to one side and seemed to be looking at me. It stood there, probably thinking to itself, '*As soon as I looked at that human it stopped what it was doing, mid-movement and I think it's looking at me.*'

I dropped some more bags, the spell between rodent and human broke and the mouse went about its business.

I watched the last of the bags drop from my hands and wondered if more of them landed writing up or writing down … like dropped toast is supposed to always land buttered side down because it's heavier on the buttered side. I wondered if the side with the writing strip *plus* the weight of the ink, might make the bags mostly land writing side down. Sometimes I hated the way my mind churned on because now that the thought had flitted through, I felt compelled to compare *writing up* against *writing down*. And now that I'd decided to keep score, I felt compelled to keep records, because you couldn't decide anything on just a handful or two of drops.

'ENOUGH!' a booming voice shouted inside my head. Big Joe. 'KNOCK IT OFF!' A quieter voice took over, though it *was* the same person. 'You haven't got time for this stuff, get on with the job and do your thinking later'. It took me a second or two to give an accepting nod to these words because they made sense. I let the bags still in my hands drop to the floor and got a little carrier bag to put them in for the document box.

I stooped to pick them up and the top bag was lying writing up, *Middle back 210576* written on it. I picked a handful up and dropped them in the carrier. 210576, I thought. 210576. A number I'd written dozens, if not hundreds of times in my life, on various forms, was 220576. My wedding day in 1976. 210576 was a date. The date before my wedding. The numbers were dates.

As soon as I thought of the numbers as dates, they started to make sense. No inventory required. Everything you needed to know about the contents of each bag was written on it. I wondered if the dates were significant ones or were just random. I had a quick scan through them. I felt Big Joe giving me a look. 'Just a few handfuls' I said to the room. In a matter of seconds, I picked out some dates that had significance. 010475, was the day I started my firefighter training. 010375, was the day before I became engaged to my first wife, 230973 was my 18th birthday. There were a number of Christmas Eves and Christmas Days, and a number of dates that seemed close to other family birthdays and things. Now, I knew that I'd *have* to go through them all … at a later date of course … and make some sort of inventory.

I wondered why my brother would cut a chunk of his hair off the day before my wedding. Or on my birthday. And what significance did my first day as a trainee firefighter have for him?

I thought of how *fastidious* my brother was, which, given where I sat, seemed a tad incongruous to say the least. When we were young men, he would take ages to shave, actually measuring his sideburns with a little ruler. His eyebrows had to be just right, and he would pluck any stray hairs. His teeth were perfect and white, and he practiced smiling in the mirror, sometimes asking me if I thought his smile was lopsided. He used to measure the distance between the corner of his eyes and the lobes of his ears, he even measured his nostrils. I used to laugh and say he was mad. It would take me no more than a few minutes to shave and combing my hair was usually done with my fingers. I didn't care what my eyebrows did, though, I did get slightly concerned when they decided to meet in the middle, making me look like a Sesame Street character, and my nostril size was beyond my control so didn't concern me in the slightest. I could never understand the attention to detail he gave to everything about his appearance and looking around his flat I thought, *What was the point Dan? What was it all about?*

I got on with the work, but something jarred with me. There was an anomaly that I couldn't pin down. I knew it would come to me in time and got on with the sorting and clearing, next stop Hamster Cage Island.

Chapter 19

Tuesday 15th July 2003

2nyt start 6.14pm 45 x 6 + 112.50

This morning B4 8am took Bertie out. Got to Pat and Wills and there was a fast knocking on a window. I slyly looked but cud not see anyone. My first thought was that it was Will, either cos Bertie had been pissing on his garden and also not far from his front window, or to show me his bird book, or both. I cudn't see his car, and there wasn't any windows opened in his house. Bertie also heard the banging (but I don't think he looked at Wills window) and barked and took off past Brenda's. I end up going around the block. Bertie pulling to go across the road by the bus stop and I end up lifting him from the ground on his lead and walking thru the opening into Cardiff Drive past a schoolboy and gently lowering him back to the ground. Coming back into my close Gary was going to his car, so I stopped. A schoolgirl early teens was coming down the pavement, so I went to walk back home and Bertie pulled against me, so I pushed him violently along the ground on his lead, and went past Garys car. I think Gary was coming back out, or something like that, so I walked, I think, to go back out of the close, towards Garys car, and I can't remember, but I may have pushed/thrown Bertie along the ground again on his lead, and the schoolgirl walked thru the close towards Garys car and she turned her head and stared at me for pushing Bertie. I finally got back home and Bertie didn't seem particularly bothered by the whole episode. He didn't seem frightened, but he must have some thorts. I am feeling really really bad about this. All this is down to u no what. I had dirty jeans and a dirty blue padded jacket on, I must have looked a sight. I didn't really want people to see me like that, and as well as u no wot, this also contributed to me acting the way I did. Shear frustration. If the knocking on the window hadn't happened, I wouldn't have left the passageway, and all of this wouldn't have happened.

Friday 08th August 2003

2nyt start 10.00pm 45 x 5

2nyt I shouted loud at Bertie because he was annoying me by sitting down by my feet again. I can't remember properly, but I think I pushed him, and he turned round and looked at me because he was surprised by my outburst. He then comes back and I shout my head off telling him to come up here! (onto the armchair) He comes up here, but stays facing the back of the armchair, annoying me even more! So I shout my head off again, and hit him on his back (top) leg hardish but controlled – don't know whether it was a full fist, a "palm fist" or a open hand slap. He moved and turned around and sat by me, licking his lips continuously. He was obviously alarmed but not that frightened. So I hadn't really had that much effect on him, which I'm glad about. I stroked him and said I'm sorry. He was ok with me, and still is as the night wears on. It is very hot and humid, his coat needs clipping, he must be suffering, but I don't know how much. I am too hot and I haven't got his fur, or even his shorn fur!

Wednesday 13th August 2003

2nyt start 7.47pm 45 x 6 + 1.5 x 112.50

Bertie 2nyt claws – push – accidentally hit face – hesitant to get on my knees – but he did with gentle coax.

Chapter 20

I had finally uncovered Hamster Cage Island completely. I had to admit, it *was* a clever place to store something you didn't want the mice to get at.

The cage was packed with boxes, mostly shoeboxes. I've always liked shoeboxes. I think it was because as a little kid, I rarely got new shoes bought for me on account of hand-me-downs, so it was a big treat to get proper new shoes. And shoeboxes in a non-shoe shop setting often meant 'treasure chest', as in photographs and the like.

As big as the cage door was, none of the boxes were going to come out of it. I half remembered, from Dan's white-mouse breeding project, aged ten, me being his assistant, aged six, that the wire part was joined to the tray by clasps. I shoved the last bits of refuse away from around the cage bottom with my foot.

The tray was the same colour as our mouse cage from yesteryear, sky blue, and the sight of it brought forward a memory from way back, a picture of my brother, holding a white mouse up by its tail in my grandma's back kitchen.

Early 1960's, North Liverpool

It was about 1960, maybe '61. Dan was ten and I was six. We each had a white mouse. Mine was called Dixie and Dan's was Pixie, after the TV cartoon characters.

We both had a little cage, about the size of a shoebox. The tray was sky blue tin and the cage was strong wire folded into the box shape. The door was a wire gangplank but getting your mouse to walk up it at bedtime was nigh impossible. Pick the mouse up, put hand in cage, let go of mouse, extract hand, close door. Easy. Not. They were like whippets. For me, the whole thing of having pets was just a chore. I really wasn't a pet kind of kid. I loved watching Dan with them, how cool and calm he was, how easily he got his mouse to 'go to bed', and part of me wanted to be like him, but I wasn't. All I really wanted was to be playing with my bow and arrow, my tommy gun or my soldiers and cars. Or galloping up and down the street on my horse, reins in my left hand and right hand smacking my own buttock, urging my horse to run faster, which worked amazingly well. I would've tried the buttock slapping to improve my time on the Ford's 10k run twenty years later but it wouldn't have been a good look.

Our mice must have been different sexes because one day, we had a load of babies. Grandma told grandad to take them down the yard. I was having enough trouble getting one mouse back in the cage after play time so I had no idea how I was going to cope with another six but I thought flushing them down the toilet was a bit harsh. I had an idea.

'Can I shoot them grandad? With my bow and arrow?' I asked.

Dan backhanded me in the chest, making me cough and said that I couldn't, telling me that if I tried, he'd wrap the bow and arrow around my neck. I told him to shove off. I didn't know what it meant but I'd heard someone at school say it. He backhanded me again and grandma told him to 'knock it off.'

Dan used his pocket money to buy a bigger cage and we started breeding mice. When they were the right age, we took them to a shop in the city centre called County Pets, run by a man called Mr Jones, and sold them to him. We did that every two months or so and, because I helped Dan with the cleaning of the cages, he'd give me half a crown.

Taking them to the shop was an adventure for me because my grandma would take us on the bus and when we got to town, she'd go to the market and let me and Dan go to County Pets on our own, but NOWHERE else or we'd get a thick ear.

It was dead exciting; we'd get on the bus and me and Dan would go upstairs. Grandma would stay downstairs because she had a bone in her leg. We'd each have a shoebox with the mice in, the lids fastened on with special elastic bands made by grandma. She used the same elastic that she used for making the garters for our long school socks and so there was no way the mice were getting the lid off. One time mine started to chew and scratch the box and Dan told me to shake it, which I did, but it didn't stop them chewing. A woman in the seat across the aisle could hear the chewing and kept staring at me. I could feel the sweat running down my face. I thought she was going to tell the conductor and we'd get chucked off the bus but she didn't.

When we got to County Pets, Mr Jones would always be happy to see us and would call us Daniel and Joseph. 'Aaah Daniel and Joseph,' he'd say, 'and what have you brought me today?'

He'd open the boxes very carefully and count the mice, then open the till and give Dan the money. On the way home, once we got off the bus, Dan would buy us a Caramac bar, which we'd eat as we walked to the house. When we were eating our Caramac, we'd stop on top of the footbridge at Glendower Street and wait for a steam train to come along so that we could get 'lost in the sky' as the cloud of steam enveloped us.

One time on this return journey, which turned out to be the last time, we stood on the bridge, empty shoeboxes under our arms and waited for a train to come. Grandma had gone on ahead because she wanted a cup of tea. The train came and we were suddenly lost in our own worlds, just two little boys standing on a footbridge over the Liverpool to Southport railway line, daydreaming in a cloud of steam. When the cloud dissipated, we made our way down the steps into Glendower Street and our father was standing talking to a man outside the Glendower pub on the corner. Our father spent a lot of time in the Glendower. 'I'm goin' the Glen.' he would say. Sometimes he'd say to my grandad 'Coming down the Glen for one Albert?' Other times he'd use the full name of the pub, 'I'm goin' the Glendower.' And somehow, I always knew that when the full name was used, there would be trouble.

If grandad went off to the Glen with dad, grandma would moan to mum about it, saying that grandad never lifted a finger around the house. I used to wonder where all the fingers were because I'd have liked to find at least one and keep it in a matchbox so I could be popular at school.

As we walked past our father outside the Glendower, there was no acknowledgement, he just carried on talking to the man but he watched us walk past on the other side of the street. There was something about the way he was looking at us that frightened me but when he came in, smelling of cold and blackcurrants, he never said anything and he didn't hit us or shout at our mum so, maybe, I thought, maybe it was the man he was talking to who was in trouble and not us.

A few days later, when we got in from school, grandma had been crying. Dan must have somehow known what had happened because, straight away, he looked at where our mouse cages should be and they were gone. Our shoeboxes were gone as well. Dan went into the yard. He picked something up off the floor and put it in his pocket. The cages were on the floor, squashed flat and the mice were nowhere to be seen. Grandma told us they'd escaped. Grandad didn't say anything, but I could tell he wasn't happy.

Dan never said anything to our mum or father and they never said anything to us about the cages, or the mice that had lived inside them. Part of me was glad that the chore of keeping pets was over but a bigger part of me was upset at the loss of our adventure on the bus and the Caramac. We would make other trips together, just me and my big brother, but not that one.

'At least,' I'd always thought, 'we didn't get the belt.'

*

I picked hamster cage island up and put it on my Workmate, flipped the clasps and took the wire off the tray. The first shoebox, the one at the top of the pile, had an elasticated band around it, very like the one that grandma made for our mouse boxes all those years ago.

Almost involuntarily, I gave the box a little shake, hearing Dan's voice on the bus to County Pets. I slid the elastic off the box and put it in my pocket and in the act of doing so, saw, in my mind's eye, Dan picking something up from our wrecked mouse cages all those years before. I took it out of my pocket and examined it. It was old and I just *knew* that it was the one that grandma had made for us. A band of knicker elastic stitched into the perfect size for holding a shoebox lid on.

I was overcome with the nostalgia surrounding the simple item in my hand. I could see my grandma sitting on her sofa, stitching the elastic together, listening to the Billy Cotton Band Show, the Sunday roast well under way, filling the place with steam. I could hear the opening of the radio programme, 'Wakey Waaaaake … hey!!!', could smell the pork and potatoes cooking. My mouth watered at the thought of one of my grandma's Sunday dinners, huge Yorkshire puddings, crispy roast potatoes and pork crackling, the gravy, the apple sauce, and the salty dripping me and Dan would scoff on our after-school butties for the next few days.

I suddenly felt that my grandma was behind me, smiling, needle and cotton in hand. I turned, stupidly expecting her to be there. But she wasn't. There was just Dan's midden, becoming less as the days passed, but still there.

I put the elastic back in my pocket and vowed to keep it safe but knew that I wouldn't. I opened Dan's shoebox.

The first thing I picked out was a large brown envelope. Inside, were two colourful pieces of card, our RSPCA certificates, ripped to pieces by our father over sixty years ago. They'd been sellotaped back together. When did he do this? I thought. Where were they hidden in the bedroom we shared for all those years? Why hadn't he mentioned them to me? Maybe he'd thought I wouldn't have been interested in them. He was probably right. I would have written them off, I *did* write them off and Dan knew it. I was so practical about all the stuff that happened in life and Dan was, just … different. I wondered what I would have done with the certificate, had Dan given it to me? I'd have probably kept it for a while, but then, after a time, would have thrown it in the bin. Seeing it revived the memories from that time, the beautiful sunny morning, the crisp box and the drawing pin that hit the potty, but I was glad that Dan had acted so defiantly back then. He'd demonstrated that people like our father, no matter how tough, uncompromising, and devious they are, can never extinguish human spirit. They can seriously damage that spirit but if even a tiny flicker of it burns on, it is they who have lost. Looking about the place, it was apparent that Dan's defiance had turned into self-destruction but in this brown envelope and in this troubled head of mine, the spirit lived on. Of that, I was sure.

Also inside the envelope was a folded page from a fishing newspaper. It was an article about Dan. He'd caught a huge carp somewhere in Bolton, had his mate take a picture and sent it in. I remembered him being excited about the article and rushing out to buy the newspaper. We must have read it a hundred times on the first day. Our father had come into our bedroom while we were out, taken the paper, and used it to line the bottom of the budgie cage and obviously Dan had re-bought the newspaper and secretly kept it. Again, I loved that defiance and wished I'd known he'd done it.

Not for the first time I wished we'd had the chance to talk these things through. I wished he'd answered my letters and taken me up on the offers to sit and talk about our experiences, our lives. But he never did.

It was a truly strange thing about our upbringing. All five of us Croft kids never told each other what had happened on any particular day. I'd pondered that fact over the years and come to the conclusion that the events that shaped us as people, just happened. They were no more than everyday normal things, so why tell anyone about them?

As well as the page from the fishing newspaper was a page from a Beezer comic. I always felt grown up when I read The Beezer because it was like a broadsheet newspaper, but for kids, though I *had* caught my grandad reading it once or twice. I'd seen him reading The Beano and The Dandy too. I unfolded the page. It was Colonel Blink the short-sighted gink, my favourite Beezer character. Every time I thought of Colonel Blink, and I did from time to time, as I was now that short-sighted gink, I couldn't help but recall the trouble I got into with my mum because of him.

Colonel Blink, on account of his short-sightedness, made a number of daft mistakes and when he did, he often exclaimed 'Arf!' He also went 'Arf! Arf!' when he got exasperated and I always found his 'Arfing' to be quite funny.

One day, I'd be about eight or nine, my mum was telling me I couldn't go out to play because it was raining. I tried to persuade her that I'd be ok out in the rain because it would make me grow. She told me it wouldn't and not to be stupid and I said that she'd said that watering her plants made *them* grow so it must do the same for me. She got angry and said that if I didn't stop mithering, she'd give me a smack, so I emulated my Beezer hero and exclaimed 'Arf!'

Early 1960's, Halewood, Liverpool

She went mad. 'What did you say? What did you say to me?' she shouted, 'I'll teach you to use language like that with me!' She grabbed me by the arms and shook me about and said that she was going to scrub my mouth out with soap and water. She finished off with the ultimate threat of telling my father if I did it again.

Colonel Blink had a lot to answer for, to me, when I was eight. A lot to answer for.

The next day, I was sitting on the settee, reading a book. It was about King Arthur and the Round Table. My father was in early from work. Dan was out and mum had gone shopping and taken Carla with her. I was trying to not be noticed by my father and failed.

I was suddenly aware that I was being stared at. That primeval awareness that alerts you to being watched or stalked. There is often an instinct that sits with this awareness, the fight or flight instinct, that rises like boiling milk, fast and barely controllable. I knew my father was staring at me. Stalking me. To run was to invite trouble that might not exist. To run for it if the alarm was genuine would only serve to make the outcome more horrific.

I was pondering any action on my part whilst pretending to be absorbed in my book, though paradoxically, I was absorbed in my book. I had to read every word, trying to memorize them in case he quizzed me, because, if *he quizzed me, because he suspected I was only* pretending *to read, and it turned out that I couldn't tell him what was on that page, then I would be in* serious *trouble. So, to guard against* serious *trouble, you pretended to be* absorbed, *whilst taking in what you were reading, whilst formulating any possible action. Such mental gyrations split your resources and sometimes proved to be too complex a task for a kid to accomplish. The feeling in the pit of your stomach, the tingling, churning sensation deep inside you, as adrenaline pumps into your system ... that feeling ... where you know you're in danger and, rather than running away from it, you're working out how to fight it, how to overcome it or how to just run with it and surf that wave of fright until it subsides, that feeling ... is addictive.*

When I was a firefighter, I shunned promotion for over thirty years because I needed *to be in the thick of things. I* needed *to be in danger as often as I could. On quiet days, or when I had to go on leave, I became anxious and fidgety the longer I was away from the station. I thrived on the adrenaline of my job. I was* addicted *to it. An addiction that I became hooked into as a little kid being stalked by my father.*

I waited for the predator to strike, carried on reading my book and then heard his breathing grow noisy, a slight whistle coming from his nose when he exhaled.

He spoke, and I nearly jumped but caught myself in time. If I'd jumped, he would have asked me if he'd frightened me and if I said yes then he would proceed to give me something to be frightened for. And if I said no then he would call me a liar and quiz me. And then *give me something to be frightened for.*

'Joe.' He said in a strained voice, like he was trying to speak while someone had a grip of his throat. I looked up and he twitched his head to the ceiling which meant I should go up to my room.

I sat on my bed and considered carrying on reading my book but knew that doing so would be a mistake. Even though I hadn't heard him come up the stairs, my door opened, and he came in, closing it behind him.

He motioned with his head and eyes again and I knew that I had to take my pants off and lie face down on the bed. I hadn't seen him take his belt off, so was slightly confused and was thinking that maybe my mum had told him about the 'Arf!' incident and this was going to be no more than a scare for me and that he would tell me to get dressed, point his finger at me and warn me to never use 'that language' to my mum again. But that was just wishful thinking.

I hadn't even heard him move but from out of the blue he slapped my arse with his hand. Quite hard. It shocked me because I always got beaten with a leather belt and this skin on skin, was ... different, shocking in a very distasteful way.

He continued to slap me quite hard, his hand lingering at times, his fingers reaching underneath me, touching me in places that I didn't want to be touched. By anyone. Ever.

He slapped me about ten times or so, and when he told me to get up and get dressed, he stood and watched me, something he'd not done before, and I found the watching to be as unnerving as the beating.

When he went out and closed the door, I sat on my bed and looked at the wall. Inside my mind was blank. I heard cars going past outside, people walking past, some talking. Some birds fluttered past my window and squabbled about something down on the grass. And then I heard the front gate open and close and my mum came in with Carla.

Hearing my mum's voice downstairs brought me tumbling back into my bedroom from wherever I'd been. I landed in a sitting position on my bed, in the house where I lived. Back into my world.

My mind started to do what it has always done. Started to get things into perspective, started to align things, get ready to move on. If my mum hadn't gone out, if she'd got back sooner, if she'd left Carla here as well, if he hadn't been home early from work, if Dan hadn't gone out, if I had been out, if a mate had called for me to play footy. On and on. I was convinced that my mum had told him about the 'Arf!' incident and that I had just been punished for it. I decided that I couldn't or wouldn't ever trust my mother again.

*

Once I got to an age where I knew swear words, I found it quite funny that my mother must have thought, when I exclaimed 'Arf!', that I was about to say 'AAAH fuck off!' but managed to stop myself in time. It has both tickled and perturbed me at the same time, perturbed me because I now believe that there was a more sinister reason for me being isolated that day with the predator that was my father. Similar things happened after the 'Arf!' incident that made me realise they weren't coincidence. Once the principle of Occam's razor, where the occurrence of least speculation was the most probable one, was applied, it was obvious or at least apparent, to me, that she had been coerced by or colluded with the predator.

I wondered why Dan had the Beezer page in his shoebox. Maybe the Colonel was one of his favourite characters too. Maybe he knew about the 'Arf!' incident and kept the page as a reminder of an amusing anecdote. I could speculate all day and still wouldn't know so I moved onto the next item, which was fitted diagonally across the box. It was wrapped in an old Llanberis tea-towel and as I picked it up, the feel of it was strangely familiar. Before I'd got it half unwrapped, I recognised it. It was silver, and encrusted with red, blue, and green gems. It was the plastic scabbard of my wonderful spring-loaded dagger.

Christmas Eve 1964, Halewood, Liverpool

Just like every other kid, or most kids, I was excited. I believed in Father Christmas. I'd seen him. Sat on his knee and told him I'd been a good boy all year.

I was nine, Dan was thirteen and my sister Carla seven in a matter of hours. At that time of my life, on that Christmas Eve, I loved Christmas but I have hated Christmas ever since. Or to be absolutely precise, my overriding emotion is fear and I hate being afraid. I'm sixty-three but still scared of Christmas. It's irrational. Daft. But there it is. I don't care what people might think or say about my fears. I am who I am and I am what I am.

On Christmas Eve 1964, my Auntie Julie and Uncle Barry were over from Manchester for Christmas and the adults were at a party in the pub over the road. My aunt and uncle were sleeping in Carla's room and what that meant to us three kids, was that the single beds of me and Dan were pushed together to make one big bed and the three of us slept in it, Carla in the middle of me and Dan.

We'd gone to bed before they came in and, in spite of my excitement I'd drifted off into a light sleep. I woke up to hushed adult voices outside the bedroom door. I couldn't make out what was being said but there was some sniggering going on so, nothing to be concerned about.

The door handle moved and I pretended to be asleep. Facing the door. If this was Father Christmas coming in, then I wanted to see him.

The door opened and, against the light from the landing outside, I was able to make out a head peeping around the door. My mum. I could tell by the hair. The head disappeared, the door quietly closed and the whisperings and sniggering resumed. I was disappointed. It hadn't been the big man, just my mum.

I opened my eyes properly and could see Carla looking at me. I couldn't tell if Dan was awake, but then, he was an expert at pretending to be asleep. I was just about to tell Carla to turn and face the other way so that she could see Father Christmas when he came in, if he came in, when I heard the door handle move. I shut my eyes again, such that I could peep through a narrow gap.

My mum's head appeared, stared at us for a few seconds then disappeared. The door opened more fully and there he was! Father Christmas himself, with my mum and Auntie Julie watching from behind him. Father Christmas didn't look as fat as he was the last time I'd seen him but, that was about a year ago, I thought.

He came in and placed heavy sacks at the feet of each of us. One of them farted, I'm guessing it was Father Christmas because my grandma had told me that women didn't trump. And when that happened, they all sniggered. Dan moved in the bed, as though he was being roused from a deep sleep. Told you, he was an expert … and Father Christmas, my mum and Auntie Julie melted away and the door closed quietly. I heard them all go downstairs and I supposed they were letting the big man out.

A quarter of an hour later, the adults went to bed, saying goodnight on the landing. The lights went off and bedroom doors closed.

It was dark but I thought I could see Carla's eyes open. Ordinary things can look terrifying when you can't quite see them properly in the dark and it looked like my sister's eyes had dark rings all around them but the eyeballs were huge and staring right at me. I thought I could make out her mouth moving as well, like she was trying to bite me. She'd bitten me before, drawing blood on one occasion and I was getting a bit worried so I kicked her. She moved and said ow! Dan moved as well.

'He's been!' I whispered.'

'I know.' Whispered Carla, 'I felt him putting something at the bottom of the bed.'

'I did.' I whispered, 'Did you Dan?'

'Yeah.' He whispered. 'Have a look, Joe.'

I quietly moved and reached to the sack at the bottom of the bed, grabbed a handful of it and pulled it up the bed towards me. Every time it rustled, I stopped and waited. When no lights came on, I carried on, moving the sack stealthily up the bed. When it got close enough I felt it, trying to make out shapes and sizes, reporting back to Carla and Dan. Quietly.

'Get something out.' Said Dan and so I reached in and had a stealthy rummage. You can't beat a stealthy rummage. Even now at sixty-three, I enjoy the odd stealthy rummage. I eventually found what I knew to be a selection box and reported the facts.

'Have some chocolate.' Whispered Dan and so I did. I opened a chocolate bar and took a bite.

We'd been whispering the whole time. I'd moved everything so quietly. No-one could have heard the rustle of paper. No-one had hearing that good. No-one. No lights had been switched on. No door handles had moved. No doors had opened. No floorboards had creaked. No clothing had rustled. No sound had been made. Which only served to making the bedroom door crashing open and the sudden flood of light as the switch was thrown, all the more shocking. My mouth was full of chocolate and I didn't have time to swallow it before the man wearing white underwear and Father Christmas's hat, rushed at me, picked me up and threw me across the room.

I landed on the floor in the corner, trying, knowing that I had to swallow the chocolate before I choked on it. I managed to swallow half of it before the man grabbed the sack containing my presents and slammed it into the floor over and over and over. I could hear things breaking. The sack became more and more limp as the things inside lost their shape and

I, quite bizarrely, chewed up the big lump of chocolate in my mouth and swallowed it, suddenly feeling safe. From choking at least.

The man in the Father Christmas hat was breathing heavily and glaring at me. I was terrified and my eyes took in the tableau that was my Christmas Morning bedroom. Dan was looking at me, his face still and calm, eyes wide and staring. Carla was looking at Father Christmas and was attempting to make herself look smaller. Father Christmas was standing in his underwear and hat, his chest heaving, his eyes burning into me and behind him, silhouetted in the doorway, the landing light having now been turned on, was my mum and behind her was my Auntie Julie in what I now know to be a babydoll nightie. Her face was a mask of horror, her eyes wide and staring and her mouth making a large black letter 'O'.

Time seemed to stand still. We were like a photograph. You could almost hear decisions being made. Father Christmas suddenly moved towards me, picking up the selection box I'd opened and raising it above his head like a club. I thought to myself that I was going to be beaten to death with a selection box and, again, in super bizarre fashion, found it ever so slightly ... amusing, for want of a better word.

As Father Christmas raised his chocolate bludgeon, my Auntie Julie screamed and shouted 'Charlie! NO!'

So, I thought, it wasn't even Father Christmas.

My father, Charlie, stopped dead in his tracks and glared at me. He squashed the selection box in his big hands, turning all the chocolate bars to pulp, and hurled it at me. It hit me in the face but didn't really hurt. Even if it had, I wouldn't have made a sound.

He turned and stormed out. My mum looked at each of us in turn, turned out the light and closed the door. My Auntie Julie moved her head in line with the reducing gap as the door closed, watching me.

The landing light went off and we were back in complete darkness. There were little pieces of chocolate and paper all over me. I ate a piece of chocolate and stayed on the floor in the corner until I thought it was safe to crawl back into bed.

When daylight came, Dan and Carla sat up and started opening their gifts. I crawled to the bottom of the bed and, laying on it, stared down at my ruined Christmas sack, like a boy peering into a pond for sticklebacks. After a while I reached down and had another stealthy rummage. My hands found something that felt like a jewelled dagger, the one I'd wanted, the one that I would use when I played Robin Hood with my mates. I took it out and held it up. It was silver. And much bigger than I'd thought it was going to be. The scabbard was encrusted with jewels, blue, red, and green. I unsheathed the weapon and tried it out, stabbing myself in the belly with the blade, which, being spring-loaded, disappeared up into the handle.

It was the only one of my gifts that survived. I spent the whole of Christmas Day stabbing people with it. I loved it. And y'know what? Chocolate is chocolate is chocolate. It doesn't matter if it's all mashed up, it just tastes the same. I did, though, have trouble sitting because of the bruising to my left buttock from landing on the bedroom floor. Good job I had two.

*

That incident was never mentioned, by anyone. Sometimes it feels like it never happened but I know it did.

As I took the rest of the tea towel from the scabbard, I could feel a hilt but I knew it wasn't my spring-loaded dagger. As soon as I saw the cream-coloured handle I recognised it as my mum's bone-handled carving knife. I slid it from the jewel-encrusted scabbard and examined it.

It was old and well-worn and must have been sharpened a million times. I tested the blade with my thumb and it was sharp. Very sharp.

I turned it over and over in my hand and recalled the time when I decided to kill my father with it.

1970'ish, Halewood, Liverpool

If I went to Borstal, then so be it. Life was dark, grim and, at home anyway, not worth living. The question was, how could I do it?

It had to be done while he was asleep, but not his night-time sleep because he'd hear me coming into the room, recognise the threat, and kill me. It had to be when he fell asleep in front of the TV, in his chair. But this sleep was a dangerous sleep. Usually, he fell asleep in his chair because he was drunk. Sometimes he could be in a drunken good mood, fall asleep and stay that way for hours. But when he woke up, it was like the circuits in his head had been flipped and he could wake up accusing people of things that ended in violence. Or he'd want a meal that he'd already eaten, and if he didn't get it, then things would end in violence. Or the programme he was watching had finished while he slept and that would end in violence. When he fell asleep in his chair, drunk, no matter what his pre-sleep mood had been, your immediate future was dependent purely on how he woke up. So, to kill him during this sleep had to be swift and sure. Failure was not an option.

I'd read a book about the Romans and learned that a typical military-style execution was done with a gladius, the sword of the Roman army. The method was to have the victim kneeling and the executioner, standing behind. The point of the gladius was positioned to the left side of the neck and, when the order was given, thrust down hard and through the heart. Fast and simple. And apparently relatively non-messy.

Of course, I didn't have a gladius. The closest thing was mum's carving knife. It was long enough and sharp enough to do the job. A gladius was two foot long or thereabouts but I measured mum's knife against my own chest from the shoulder and decided it was long enough, especially if, once the blade was thrust down with all my weight, it was 'wiggled about' inside the wound, slicing everything it touched. The knife was razor sharp and I thought it would do the job.

The occasion arrived. My father was fast asleep in his chair and, cool as you like, I got up and went to the kitchen, got mum's knife out of the drawer and felt the blade. As expected, it was razor sharp. I stood in the kitchen and leaned, with my back to the sink, knife in hand, thinking through what I was about to do. Going through the motions in my head, like football training, rehearsing a corner kick, defence onto attack, over and over until it was perfect.

It would have to be fast, giving no time for anyone in the room to react and cause an alarm, waking him up. If that happened, I may as well use the knife on myself because that is what he would do. I had to walk in swiftly and quietly, knife hiding up the length of my right arm, walk behind him, place the point of the knife next to his neck and thrust my whole weight down onto it. As soon as the blade was buried to its full length, I had to move it about as violently as I could to cause the most amount of internal damage as possible. The attack had to be fast and devastating. By the time an alarm was raised, it had to be too late.

What happened afterwards was what happened afterwards. Simple as that. 'Que Sera, Sera, whatever will be, will be', as my parents were fond of singing in duet. I started to move away from the sink and immediately stopped.

What if I made a noise entering the room? What if he was already awake and just about to exit the room? What if he was looking right at me as I walked in? What if someone reacted much faster than I imagined they would? What if my aim was poor? What if he woke up just as I was about to plunge the blade in? What if I didn't kill him and he got up and killed me? Would he then kill all of us? Would my act of protection and defiance prove to be the end for everyone?

I started to shake, deep seated trembles that shook my whole body. My breathing became ragged and sweat ran down my face. I could feel my eyes bulging and my jaw was set so tight it hurt my face. I felt like vomiting and the trembling became uncontrollable. I knew that I couldn't go through with it. I put the knife back in the drawer, went upstairs to my room and lay on my bed.

I shivered and trembled as if I was frozen to the core, staring at the ceiling, looking for my grandad. He wasn't there, it was just a very badly painted white ceiling. I could hear the TV downstairs ... the end credits of Coronation Street. I imagined the music waking him up and seconds later I heard the living room door open. He came upstairs and went to the toilet. When he came out I didn't hear him go down. Nor did I hear any other door opening or closing. I knew he was standing right outside my door. He was listening. For what, I don't know. Maybe he wanted to hear me listening to illicit music. Seconds that felt like hours passed. I had psyched myself up so that I wouldn't jump when my bedroom door crashed open yet still manage to look startled. I calmed my trembling and very quietly got hold of my latest book, opened it above my face and made it look as though I was reading. I made a point of quietly clearing my throat, a sound I thought of as very natural. I also deliberately rubbed one page of my book against another, a quiet sound but one that he would hear and hopefully consider as normal. I also quickly read the page I was turned to because I could be quizzed. Dan's alarm clock ticked away the seconds. I thought I heard a tiny movement outside and held my breath to listen harder but there was nothing. I resumed breathing and sniffed quietly to hide the sound of a deeper breath. And then I heard stealthy movement and he went downstairs and into the living room.

Did he know? How could he have known? Why did he stand outside my room for so long? What was he listening for? I couldn't know the answers to these questions, but my mind wouldn't let them go, until a voice inside my head said, calm as anything, 'Stop. This is your life. Live it. Read your book.' And that's what I did. I decided to kill my father, bottled it, and read my book.

*

Back in 1970, aged about 14, I decided that execution by *gladius* would be the easiest way for me to kill my father. How sad, I thought, sat in Dan's living room, that I have no remorse at making such a terrible decision, just a bewilderment that a father can engender such desolation in the mind of his son that the only way out of his wilderness is to commit murder.

The last item in the shoebox was a tin. A tobacco tin. Green and gold. I picked it up, shook it. There was a muffled sound to the shake. I opened it. There was a tissue and wrapped in it were two teeth, two front teeth. I knew where they'd come from. They'd come from Dan's mouth. They'd come from his mouth on the day our father gave him the punch that maybe defined my brother, that, looking around the flat, had quite possibly killed him. I remember it like it was yesterday.

1967ish, Halewood, Liverpool

Dan was about fifteen, making me about eleven 11. Carla and the twins were in bed.

I don't know how it kicked off, probably over nothing, like it usually did. A big thing for my mum was my father being late in for his tea, usually because he was in the pub. She would have cooked a meal for the family, and we would have had ours at teatime. If my father wasn't in at teatime, she would put a plate over his meal and either put it in the oven on a low light or on a pan of simmering water.

He would be drunk when he came in. I always knew when he was on his way because I could smell him coming. I'd get this sudden overpowering smell of oranges and would become slightly agitated. 'Here's dad.' I'd say.

Someone would dash to the window and peep out and after a few seconds would confirm that he'd just come out of the pub over the road. No one ever asked me how I knew that he was on his way and I always assumed that everyone could smell what I could smell but I was simply the first to mention that he was seconds from arriving.

We would compose ourselves into a normal looking family scene and try to act as though we weren't afraid for our future.

When his key entered the lock there was an extra second or two where everyone surreptitiously checked their demeanour and stole a glance at others to make sure that one didn't stand out for any reason.

He'd come in and close the door. If he slid the bolt home straight away, you knew, beyond doubt, that there was going to be violence. He was thinking ahead and simply putting an obstacle in the way of anyone's attempt to escape. If that bolt slid home, you had to act as though you hadn't heard it. You couldn't show fear. To show fear was an invite for him to single you out. If he hadn't slid the bolt home, that didn't mean that everything was going to be ok. It meant no more than he hadn't slid the bolt home.

He'd close the front door and hang his coat up on the gas-cupboard door. We had a cloakroom, an actual proper cloakroom, pretty fancy for a 1960's council house. We didn't have any kind of heating except a gas fire in the living room, but we had somewhere to hang our cloaks. My father was the only one who could use the gas-cupboard door to hang his coat on. If anyone made the mistake of doing it, their coat would get flung down the front path, sometimes ending up on the pavement.

Having hung his coat up, he'd come into the living room and we had to go through this act of being surprised at our father walking into the room ... like we hadn't heard him come in ... and we all had to sound really happy to see him. 'Feeling' had to be injected or you could become a target. He never replied of course. Ever. He usually wouldn't even look at you. You had to wait for a few heartbeats at least, to see whether or not he decided *he was going to look at you, because if he* did *look at you it meant that he wanted something and you were the one granted the honour of serving. If you weren't looking at him when this honour was bestowed, then he would have to use your name to issue his instructions, and having to use your name was a reason for you to become targeted.*

So, on this particular night, the night he set in motion a string of events that, in my opinion, killed my brother, I'd smelled the oranges, he'd come into the house, left the bolt alone and hung his coat on the gas-cupboard door.

My mum was in the kitchen and I heard them having words. I could tell that my mum's words were hostile. I caught the word 'slaving'. Whenever she used words like that, I'd be saying to myself 'Shut up mum, shut up.' I knew that if she let it go, we might escape but if she carried on then we'd all suffer in some way. My father was a dangerous man, especially when drunk and, to me, the best thing to do was to placate. You could still end up with a beating, or worse, but to actively encourage it seemed foolish to me.

He came into the living room and me and Dan 'Heil Hitlered' him. That's what I likened it to. He ignored us, sat down, and took his work boots off, which was good because that meant if you got kicked it would only be with a slippered or stockinged foot. The smell of my father's feet, sour and rancid, filled the room within seconds but I kept my face composed, knowing that I'd give it twenty minutes or so, to ensure that he didn't think I was offended by his feet, which could prove costly, and disappear to my bedroom to read. Dan was already reading a book, 'Chemistry made Simple', which, to my mind was a mistake, because he now only had 'walking out' as a strategy.

He crossed his legs and started to read the evening paper, starting with the back page. I was watching something on the TV, and he told me to switch to another channel, which I did. He carried on reading the paper. I now extended my twenty minutes to at least double that. If I left the room after the twenty then I would be making silent protest on him changing the channel.

After a few more minutes my mum brought his food in and put it on the chair arm that he normally ate from. She handed him his knife and fork. He said nothing but carried on reading the paper for thirty seconds. My mum sat down and picked up her knitting. My father made ready to eat his food and spoke to me. 'What's this about Joe?' he asked, pointing with his head at the TV. I knew that he was going to do that and had been paying attention. 'Something to do with apartheid.' I said. 'Oh yeah.' he said, 'What about it?'

I was just about to answer, when I saw him start to cut his pork chop. It was tough and dried out. As were the potatoes and the peas. The gravy had a thick skin on it, and I saw his face change. He glanced at the book Dan was reading, not at my brother but at the book he was reading. He picked his plate up with the thumb and forefinger of his left hand and at first, I thought he was going to take it to the kitchen but he transferred it to the palm of his right hand, stood up and launched it, full force, seemingly straight at my mum.

It went over her head and slammed into the wall, making a noise that was too much for what it was, splattering food everywhere. I watched, in slow motion, a glob of gooey gravy sail across the room and land on the head of a brass flower-seller on the mantelpiece, instantly drooping down over the head like a shawl. I almost fatally laughed. Both Dan and my mum jumped. My mum's knitting hands spasmed so that she looked like me knitting. Dan turned towards our father and he looked really angry. He was glaring and because of that my brain went into a kind of shutdown, where you only think of the things you need for survival and your body gets itself ready for flight, adrenaline surging like a wave into your system.

My mum reacted instantly. 'What the bloody hell did you do that for Charlie!' she shouted. Shit! I thought. This was the kind of thing that would get us all killed.

In an instant, he covered the ground between them, grabbed a handful of hair and pulled her to her feet. She started to protest but as soon as she was standing, he punched her in the face, knocking her back down into the chair. A split appeared across the bridge of her nose, not the first time this particular split had been opened, and blood cascaded down her face and onto her clothing. The sound of fist on face was a brutal sound, a sickening blunt thud of something heavy and hard hitting something made of ... us ... of people. It reminded me of the dull, heavy thud of a butcher using his chopping block.

When my mum landed back down in her seat, the whole chair moved backwards and as it did so, I noticed the dinner plate, which was sliding slowly down the wall, stop, as if it was startled and wanted to know what was going on.

It was only a split second after the blow and my mum hadn't got to the stage of reacting to it, assuming she actually could, when he pounced and dragged her back to her feet, both hands grabbing clothing at chest height and bodily picking her up, moving easily into the middle of the room with her. His left hand kept hold of her clothing and his right fist, hard and bony, slammed into her stomach, once, twice, then he let go of her and she crumpled to the floor in front of me, falling so that she landed on my feet. He shot a calm, flat glance at me, his bright blue eyes looking almost black and I acted as though I was totally absorbed in the question of apartheid, my eyes glued to the screen as if nothing untoward was happening. The transition between a kind of half-peace and this brutal beating of a little woman ... my mum was four foot eleven ... was shocking. A word that doesn't begin to describe what was happening but one that describes the effect on me, on my brain, on my instincts ... which were telling me to run while at the same time telling me to stay still, make yourself small, absolutely non-threatening.

My mum was on the floor but was beginning to get up and I mentally pleaded with her to stay down. He was standing over her, as if ready for a dangerous adversary, his arms outboard from his body, hands clenched into fists. His breathing was deep and calm, his eyes fixed on her, like a cat with a mouse.

Dan still had his book open at the page he'd been reading but had turned his whole body to face our father. His expression was one of pure hatred, and I got the impression he was going to intervene. I prayed that he wouldn't. It sounds terrible that I didn't want an intervention, but I didn't.

When terror strikes, you do what some ancient part of your brain tells you to do. You survive. It was this day, this event, that made me, at age nineteen, become a firefighter and willingly risk my life to rescue people from their own version of the terror I felt at that time.

My mum staggered to her feet and headed towards the unbolted front door. He watched as she staggered past him. I could see his jaw muscles working, like he was chewing something, his blue eyes relaxed, almost amused. She passed him and as she did, he put his foot flat on her back and pushed as hard as he could. She went crashing into the living room door, collapsing into a heap in the corner. As she flailed into her collapse, her hand caught the light switch, turning the lights off. The room was now lit only by the black and white TV in the corner, the programme about apartheid still on.

My father followed her, pulled her up to a standing position, switched the light back on and turned her around to face him. He put his left hand tightly around her throat and slammed her backwards into the door, her head banging violently into it. He then he raised his right fist and hit her hard again in the face, smashing her head into the door. She was like a rag doll, no sounds, no response and I thought she was dead.

Suddenly my brother, my big brother, my all-time hero, threw his book on the floor and rushed towards them. He was bellowing at our father to stop.

It was maybe three or four steps that Dan had to take to get to them, but by the time he reached them, his arms raised to grab hold of something, my father turned to face him, still holding my mum up by her throat with his left hand, his eyes fixing Dan with deadly intent, assessing the threat, working out what he needed to do to fight off this attack ... and brought his right fist across his body, slamming it into Dan's face.

The fist hitting Dan's face made a noise that I can't forget. It was the butcher's block with an underlying crackle. Blood spurted, painting me with red freckles, covering my nose and cheeks. Dan flew backwards, running and falling at the same time, crashing into the corner of the room, the opposite corner to my mum, and slid down the wall, right next to the dinner plate that was still making its way to the floor. Dan's nose and mouth were bleeding profusely. He was conscious and stunned and in pain. He spat blood onto his shirt, a feeble, fat-lipped spit, full of hurt. Two teeth spilled out and slid down his shirt on a river of blood, snot, and saliva. I felt something on my lips, realised it was Dan's blood and involuntarily licked at it, like you do in the sugary doughnut game. I wiped the back of my hand over my mouth but didn't look at it in case my father saw me do it.

My father still had hold of my mum's throat and his right fist was still in mid-air, at the spot in the room where it had connected with Dan's face. My mum's hands came up and tried to wrestle my father's hand from her throat, but it was like he was frozen, staring with his flat black blue eyes at my brother.

I watched the anger fade, watched the black of his eyes change to bright blue. He let go of my mum's throat and she slid to the floor, gasping, and rubbing at her neck. My father sat down in his chair, crossed his legs, picked up the Echo, aimed his head at the TV and said, 'Still the same programme Joe?' I nodded.

*

Over the years, in an attempt, to explain the behaviour of my brother, I've often thought about that punch, a punch made doubly hard by the speed with which Dan approached the accelerating fist. Did the trauma of that punch cause my brother's brain to cannon into his skull? What part of the brain is affected when this happens and what functions does that part of the brain control? I didn't know the answers but my belief was that his brain was injured by his father. Dan was a youth and his father was a seasoned fighter with fists like hammers.

Now, in the hell that was Dan's home, it seemed to me that saving rubbish, doing away with your bathroom and access to water and drinking huge quantities of strong alcohol were not the actions of a healthy brain. Did my father kill my brother with that punch? We'll never know but I think he did.

I re-wrapped the teeth and put them back in the tin.

I went out to the car, took my gloves off, poured a coffee from the flask in the boot and sat on the low wall sipping the hot liquid.

Chapter 21

Tuesday 9th September 2003

2nyt start 8.40pm 45 x 5

No bed. Bad pains + diaorea

Wednesday 10th September 2003

2nyt start 7.34pm 45 x 6

pains – diaorea

This morning, 7 – 9am, couldn't keep eyes open, finally went to bed about 9ish am, got few hours sleep, woken up by Bertie barking from downstairs by the front door. Got up, looked at myself in mirror in bathroom, and was surprised to see how different I looked — much better! Was he barking this morning, or Thursday morning?! I can't remember now! I know I had bad dreams in this sleep, stabbing someone, a man. I may have woke up because of these. Tonight, after drinking what I did, about 10 – 11pm, I almost puked by bringing up a load of half-digested liquid, so I went to bed. Left the TV + PS1 + light on, didn't take Bertie out.

Thursday 11th September 2003

2nyt start 10.26pm 45 x 3 + 112.50

This morning woke up about 6 – 7am 8am(?) was Bertie barking downstairs by front door? I felt absolutely awful and looked absolutely awful! Just shows you what I have been doing to myself for years! Still a few (only a few) pains today, although this morning, stools normal.

Saturday 13th September 2003

2nyt start 8.11pm 45 x 5

Got up around 12pm ish Sunday and wasn't hungover but felt tired and in a bad mood.

11pm! Bertie!! The SLAM!!

Sunday 14th September 2003

2nyt start 7.42pm 45 x 5 + 112.50

1.30pm this afternoon in garden, yanks on lead and Bertie! He instantly annoyed me, and I shudn't have reacted the way I did. I yanked him a few more times on Kittys garden. He can instantly annoy me by going around a tree/object and pulling in the opposite way that I want him to go/come back. I think he gave a few little moans. He seemed ok with me a short while later.

Monday 15th September 2003

2nyt start 6.37pm 45 x 8

Tuesday 16th September 2003

2nyt start ~~9.18pm~~ 9.20pm 45 x 7 + 112.50

Wednesday 17th September 2003

2nyt start 5.42pm 45 x 10½, other ½ poured down sink.

2nyt outside on path I shouted at Bertie to shut up and Brenda shouted allright Dan! I think because Patch was barking. Bertie wouldn't shut up and I think Gary saw me yank Bertie hard, and Bertie went flying along the grass of Wills garden. I think Bertie gave a little moan. I think he had lost his footing and he fell/rolled. He immediately got frightened and ran to the wall, and to my front door for safety. I coaxed him round and went up the path again. He looked at me and wagged his tail a few times, as if to show subservience to me. I talked to him and we (he) seemed OK and friends. Is he? or is he friends with me thru fear? Bertie originally started barking when I was trying to talk to Bethany, telling her not to run out looking for her dad.

Chapter 22

My phone rang. It was Pam. 'How's it going love?' she asked. 'How are you?'

I wanted to say *I'm not so good really*. I wanted to say that my mind wouldn't be quiet, that it wouldn't let me out, that everywhere was barred to me except here, where I was, where it wanted me. I wanted to say that my brother kept talking to me and seemed to be laughing at me when I wanted him to laugh with me. I wanted to say that I was angry at him for not trusting me or wanting me in his life, that I was angry at my father for not acting as a father should, that I was angry at my mother for not protecting us, for not protecting me. I wanted to say that I was angry at myself for failing to be the brother I maybe should have been. I wanted to say that I was despairing of how my sisters acted at times and how they could be so ruthless in their pursuit of self. I wanted to say that I was tired of the constant storm in my brain, the insistent, never-ending vigilance, watching shadows, listening too carefully to words, scrutinising too deeply for that *look*. I wanted to say that I was sorry for the intensity from which I lived my life, that I knew it was frequently intimidating to some people. I wanted to say that I needed to live in the world that I sometimes saw in the mirror, the one from where the real me could sometimes be glimpsed behind the blue veils that could snap shut in a blink. I wanted to say that I didn't need my security team any more, that they could take a long holiday. But I knew that I *did* need them. I knew that they would never take leave, never relax their vigilance, never let a stray word or an interpretable glance go without examination and analysis. I knew that they were with me, in charge of my protection, for ever. I wanted to say that I was glad but sad that they were needed and that there was just too much stuff I needed to say that couldn't be said but instead I said, 'I'm fine thanks love. How are you?'

Chapter 23

The next box was also a shoebox and, at one time, had contained hiking boots so was quite big.

There were a number of items inside the box and the first one just jumped out and smacked me straight between the eyes. I put the box down on the floor, stood up and backed away from the toolbox I'd been sitting on, keeping the shoebox in sight. *Could it be the same one?* I thought, *Why would he have it? Why would he keep it — in this box? A box of keepsakes.*

The item was a hairbrush. A light-green plastic hairbrush. It had a reddish-pink soft pad with black, stiff plastic 'bristles' sticking out of it. The 'bristles' had little balls on the end. My mother used it to brush Carla's hair. I remembered my first wife, Lucy, buying one to use on my daughter's hair and I'd stolen it and disposed of it. She'd bought another one when the first one went missing and I'd done the same thing. Lucy gave up buying the brush and bought a different type.

The brush, the one in the shoebox, had been used to beat me about the face by my father.

About 1960, North Liverpool

Chewing gum. Chewy, in Liverpool. We, the Croft kids, weren't allowed chewy. Like a lot of parents, me included, you don't want your young kids to have chewing gum, for various reasons. My reasons, once I became a parent, were hair, as in my daughters', and car seats, as in my car seats. My grandma used to say that it was dangerous to swallow chewy and that if you did, it would stick to your lungs and kill you. Another Liverpool version of this was it sticking to your heart and killing you. Heart, lungs and chewy ... not a good mix.

One night, probably a Saturday night, because my parents were out, probably at the pub and grandma and grandad were minding us. We were in bed and I had chewy. Dan had given me it. Pink, fragrant, probably a Bazooka Joe. My favourite.

I was furiously trying to blow a bubble like my brother, who was great at it. I was shifting the stuff around in my mouth trying to get it so that I could stretch it with my tongue like I'd been shown a hundred times. I just couldn't get it right and the more I tried and failed, the more agitated I became. But I wasn't going to be beaten by a Bazooka Joe. Suddenly it just disappeared from my mouth and I swallowed it. Panic was instantaneous. I was going to die. This Bazooka Joe was going to stick to my lungs, and I was going to die.

I leapt out of bed and dashed downstairs to my grandma, and she was really cool about it. She tut-tutted a few times and took me to the kitchen where she ripped a two-inch piece of crust from a loaf of bread and told me to eat it. When I swallowed it, she gave me some water to drink and when I'd done that, she declared me to have been saved. I dashed off, like a lunatic, like your dog when you let it free after it's had a bath. I sprinted up the stairs, full of vigour because now, I had a future, I had a life to live when just a few minutes ago I'd only had seconds to live.

So, the hairbrush ... it was a warm sunny day and I'd been playing out in the street with my mate from the house on the corner. He didn't live there but visited his grandad once a week and we'd play together. His name was Robin and he had ginger curly hair, pink cheeks, bright blue eyes and ruby lips. He was straight out of an Enid Blyton book.

On this warm sunny day, he had chewy. Smelled like a Bazooka Joe. Every time he spoke to me or laughed, I got a whiff of it and it was lovely. His grandad came out and called him in for his dinner and Robin spat the chewy out onto the pavement. Right by me. It sat there in the sun and I could smell it. I wanted it but knew that I wasn't allowed. I looked about, there was no one around and I did a really daft thing. I picked it up and put it in my mouth. Just as I did that, Dan came out and sat on the pavement next to me. He picked a lolly ice stick up from the gutter and poked at some muck in between the stone setts of the street. An ant scurried away.

It sounds disgusting, me picking the chewy up and putting it in my mouth but, I was probably about four, nearly five at the time and didn't really know any better. It tasted just how it smelled, fruity and pink. Dan noticed me chewing. 'Have you got chewy?' he asked and I nodded, chewing like a rabbit. 'Where did you get it?' he asked and I told him that Robin had spat it out. He shook his head at me and said that I could get germs. I thought he'd said Germans and was puzzling over that, thinking of bombs, tanks and soldiers. Dan went back into the house.

I was thinking about practicing my bubble blowing and was just about to have a go, performing strange face contortions as I manoeuvred the chewy into the right place. Before I could get my tongue into the middle of it, my father appeared at my side, as if by magic and picked me up. He plucked me off the kerbstones and carried me into the house, into the parlour, our living room. He stuck his big fingers in my mouth and pulled out the chewy, then picked up the hairbrush from the chair next to him and grabbing me by the upper arm, swiped me across the face with the brush. Hard. And then he did it again. And again. And again. And he kept on doing it in spite of me screaming in pain. He threw the brush on the floor then picked me up under his arm and went up the stairs, very fast, two steps at a time, threw me onto my bed, knocking the wind out of me, slapped my arse really hard a few times and slammed the door on the way out.

That night I wasn't allowed any food or anything. No one came to see me. My face was burning hot and I could feel little dimples all over my cheeks where the balls on the end of the bristles had dug in. I cried and cried and when it subsided and I could cry no more, I just whimpered and sniffled every now and then.

It got past teatime and I knew that no one was coming to get me, so I got undressed and put my pyjamas on. I got into bed and because it was still light enough to read, I looked at the pictures in one of my Enid Blyton books. Robin was there, going about his adventures with his rosy cheeks *and all I could think of was what he had eaten for dinner when his grandad called him in.*

*

And now, here, in my brother's flat was that hairbrush from sixty years ago.

Questions leapt into my mind. What was he doing with it? How did he know there was significance to it? How long had he known? Who else knew? Did my father broadcast to everyone what had happened? What he'd done? Did my mum know? Grandma or grandad? Why was nothing ever said about it by anyone? And why was my brother saving it in a shoebox full of mementoes? All questions that I would never have answers to.

I picked the brush up and threw it into the current bucket, took it to the skip outside and upended it, waiting until the stuff slid and settled and when it had and I could still see the brush, I climbed into the skip and kicked rubbish over it.

The next thing I picked out of the shoebox was wrapped in a blue handkerchief. I unwrapped it and the item in my hand acted like a magic portal, drawing me back to a place where two images fought with each other, vying for dominance. The first image was a happy one and the other picture … wasn't.

The item was a snow globe. Inside the snow globe, quite bizarrely, was an igloo, a fir tree and, this is what was bizarre, instead of a Father

Christmas or a polar bear completing the scene, Popeye and Bluto were poised, ready to knock each other about.

I loved the snow globe. My Auntie Marie had bought it for me and it had lived on my little bedside table for quite a while until I threw it away because I *needed* to. I'd seen something in the snow globe that I didn't want to see and once seen, it couldn't be unseen and so I'd chucked it out.

And now here it was. Back in my hand.

1965 – Halewood, Liverpool

It was a summer's day but cool and slightly overcast. The council had been clearing some ground at the top of our road, next to The Grange. The Grange was a big sandstone mansion that, at one time, must have been an incredibly imposing residence. But now, it was black, like sandstone goes, with emerald-green 'spillages' of moss down the walls from leaking gutters and dripping gargoyles. The gargoyles were scary when you really looked at them, which was something I did on a regular basis. All bulging eyes and huge canines, and one of them had horns, like the devil.

The result of the council's ground-clearing was a large hill of rubble and compacted earth. It was probably supposed to have been moved away but stayed there for months. And it was heaven for us. We played on it and around it, all day, every day. We even walked up and over it on the way to and from school, it was that tempting. One of our favourite games, if not the favourite game, was King of the Castle. There was a song or a chant that went with this game. It went,

'I'm the King of the Ca-stle,
Get down you dirty ra-scal!'

The idea of the game was that a team 'assaulted' the hill and once at the top you fought for dominance by throwing everyone else down it, usually, if you had the breath, shouting out the chant and trying to time the *'Get down you dirty ra-scal!'* line with the actual throwing of an opponent. It was a great game. We loved it and would play it for hours, ending up filthy and sweaty. You could play it as an individual or as a team. I always preferred the team game. Me and Dan were World Champions. Me and my mate David were a good team as well. But when me, Dan and David were on the same team, well, we were like a Viking horde, a Roman Legion and the Desert Rats all rolled into one. No one could take that hill from us when we were at the top. And if we weren't at the top, we, almost casually, simply took it off you. Just like that. Some teams came up with fancy ideas of outflanking and making swerving runs designed to split your forces. We never did any of that. With us, it was all about the full-blooded frontal assault. Straight up the hill and cast the enemy down.

We three were Kings of the Castle and a pack of five were trying to take it from us when I caught sight of a man walking down the road, towards where we lived. The man didn't look over or show any interest in us but I recognised our father. It was too early for him to be coming home from work but I knew it was him. He had a folded newspaper sticking out of his pocket. He used to do that on a Saturday when he was off work and going over to the bookies and pub, have the paper sticking up out of his pocket, folded to the racing pages. I could tell it was him from his straight-backed almost regal way of walking. Head held level and shoulders square, his gait measured and steady, eating up the ground without looking fast. I told

Dan that he'd just walked past. He hadn't noticed and told me to never mind and get on with defending the hill. I was worried because the folded newspaper and the earliness of him showing up, signified things to me. That work had finished early, he'd been sacked, laid-off or was on strike. It told me that he'd had time to study the horses, maybe even been to the bookies, which meant that he'd had a drink or two. Maybe not but maybe so. Nevertheless, I got on with defending the hill, just like Dan told me to.

A minute later, Carla came running up fast. 'Me dad wants yer.' she shouted.

My hope was that he wanted Dan, not me. 'Who?' I shouted, as I threw an enemy down the hill and wiped sweat from my forehead.

'Both of yer.' she said.

We instantly stopped what we were doing and walked down the hill, not saying a word to each other or anyone else. We didn't even look at each other. We were now locked into our own worlds, intent only on getting through the next minute and when that one was dead, the one after that. As we walked away we heard the howls of mixed delight and indignation as David was picked up and thrown down the hill by the new Kings of the Castle.

On the way home, maybe a 120 yards walk, my instinct told me we were in trouble, but I couldn't think why. I knew our bedroom was clean and tidy because we'd done it that morning. I knew the grass was cut because we'd done it only a day or two before, Dan on the shears, me on the scissors. I still had the remnants of the blister on my thumb. So, I couldn't think of any reason we'd be in trouble. Logic, my friend, and enemy, often in equal measures, therefore told me that we were being summoned to be congratulated for being such heroic Kings of the Castle. Almost as soon as that thought bloomed in my head it was rejected. Our father never congratulated us on anything so it couldn't be that. Before another useless thought bloomed, we were in the house and the door was closed behind us by our mother. Her face was flushed. She told us to go up to our bedroom.

At first, I thought we'd been sent to bed and was relieved, even though it was only mid-afternoon. Getting sent to bed was a punishment in itself and if I was going to be punished, even though I'd done nothing wrong, then getting sent to bed was a sentence I would happily accept. Much better than the alternatives.

Dan went into the bedroom first and as I followed a step or two behind, I saw his body tense up in front of me and knew that our father was already inside.

He told us to take our trousers down and lie face down on the bed, which we did. Then he told us 'Underpants as well'. Which we did. Lying next to my big brother on the bed, bare arses looking up at the ceiling, I felt incredibly vulnerable and exposed. Nothing was happening behind us, which puzzled me. I heard the door quietly open then close and I thought that he'd gone, that it was some kind of joke, which, if it were, I'd have had to laugh at and find hilarious. But I wasn't going to be the one to turn around and check. Dan could do that. That's what big brothers are for.

I noticed that Dan was looking at the snow globe on the little table at the side of my bed, the bed we were lying on. Popeye and Bluto were squared up, about to have a set-to. As I looked at the snow globe, I could see what Dan was looking at. It was something you could either see or you couldn't, where you can either see one thing or the other but not both at the same time. In this case, you could either see Popeye and Bluto or you could see that both my mother and father were standing behind us reflected in the globe. Just standing there.

The belt landed on me first. Hard and sudden. I almost cried out, which would have been a really stupid thing to do. My fists gripped the yellow candlewick bedspread and, with each stripe laid onto my body, twisted the fabric into tight little folds. I noticed that my brother's hands didn't move, his fingers remaining perfectly spread out. Relaxed looking. I copied him, letting go of the bedspread. The lashings stopped and the room was silent. I heard a little click and then the door opened and closed quietly. The little click, I knew, was the noise my mum's ankles made sometimes when she moved or turned, so I knew my mum had left. I checked in the snow globe. My father was still there, just looking at us. What seemed like an age later, he turned and walked out, leaving us lying on the bed.

We got up, got dressed and looked at each other. I picked the snow globe up and gave it a good shake. Popeye and Bluto glared at each other in the snowstorm. My body was burning, and I could feel the ridges, made by the belt, under my shirt. We couldn't sit down so we stood by the window and looked at the world outside. David was sitting on the pavement outside our garden gate, throwing little stones into the road. He must have felt us watching because we made no sound, but he turned and looked up. He motioned with his head for us to come out. I shook my head slightly. Dan just stared out. David raised his chin almost imperceptibly, a knowing acknowledgment that we were 'indisposed'. He stood, put his hands in his pockets and sauntered off up the road.

I could hear sounds coming from another part of the house. Sounds of a voice or voices but muffled. We both silently crept towards our door though we weren't brave enough to open it. We put our ears to it and strained to hear. It was hard to make out anything but in amongst the sounds I heard a word which I thought sounded like 'Charlie'. I looked at Dan and could tell that he'd heard the same. We looked into each other's eyes, his blue eyes looking into my blue eyes, then he moved his head in the direction of the window and we returned to watching the world slide past our house.

We never played King of the Castle again. We never even mentioned it. But we retired as unbeaten champs. David, my mate, never got to be a man. He was killed by a train on the main Liverpool line. The local newspaper reported that he ran along and then jumped off the parapet wall of the bridge.

*

I sat on my toolbox and thought about David for a few minutes. I could see him, his wavy fair hair, smoky blue eyes and slightly protruding teeth. As a person, he was quiet and thoughtful, and was a great mate to have, though I managed to spoil that friendship by being stupid. I hoped that he had died as a result of misjudgement rather than a desire to die.

The boot box was turning out to be a bit of a Pandora's box. There were some old birthday cards for my mum. I opened the first one and it simply said, "Happy Birthday Mam, Dan, xx". I put it in our document box. Underneath the cards, was a travel draughts and chess set and I picked it up. I remembered it well and opened it. I couldn't believe it was the same set from all those years ago, it looked so new. Even the cardboard sleeve that the set was in looked like new.

Mid 1960's, Halewood, Liverpool

Friday was chess night. My father would have his tea, eating with his plate on the arm of the chair, drink his mug of tea and smoke a rollie, then say to me 'Get the chess board out then Joe.'

The chess board was Dan's pocket-sized set. I never beat Dan at draughts and he didn't play chess. I never saw our father play Dan at draughts. He may have done but I never saw it happen. As far as I was concerned, Dan was lucky that our father didn't play a one-on-one game against him because it was horrible. I hated it. It scared me.

My father had learned that I was in the school chess team and decided that Friday was chess night. And once he decided that something would happen, then it would happen.

Chess was something I took to very naturally. Layered thinking is the key. For me anyway. Layered thinking is what I do. I'm not saying I do it well or even successfully, but it's what I do. My father always won. But I was getting better. I was playing a lot of chess, both in school and against other schools and I was improving all the time.

When I learned the game in the chess club, I was taught to shake the hand of my opponent after a match and always say 'well played', whatever the outcome. I was taught to never gloat after winning. Mr Carstairs used to say to us that there was only one thing worse than a bad loser and that was a bad winner. And so, I have carried that simple little maxim through my life, losing and winning with dignity. Always.

My father won the Friday night chess match all the time and every single time he would wink at me and smile, sometimes laugh and say something like, 'Gotta get up earlier if you wanna beat me Joe' or 'you'll have to be a lot smarter than that if you wanna beat me.' Never once did he shake my hand or say, 'well played'. Not even once. But I was getting better.

And so, inevitably, it happened. It was Friday night and the travel set was on the arm of his chair and, as usual, I sat on a little footstool. The game was well under way. He was being his usual cocky self, making his moves fast and then sitting waiting for me to work out what to do. If I took too long, he would make little noises with his mouth. Or take a deep breath and expel it noisily from his nose. Little signs of annoyance that would always worry me. Scare me even.

I saw the possibility of a trap ... but it seemed too obvious. Nevertheless, I set the wheels in motion and started to lay it. The trap started as a snare to get one of his valuable pieces but, as the game moved on, I realised that he hadn't seen it. That he was too intent on his own moves and was being dismissive of mine. Or maybe, I thought, he has sussed out what I'm up to and was setting a better trap of his own. Was I walking into his trap and getting too excited about my own?

I studied the board. Hard. I could see what he was up to and, it was nothing that I hadn't already seen ... there didn't seem to be any cunning plan underlying his obvious intentions. I couldn't believe that he hadn't seen the trap I was setting for him. So, I studied the board even harder. He rolled himself a cigarette and blew the smoke over me, which, to be fair, I didn't mind because I liked the smell of rolling tobacco smoke and had ambitions to become a smoker.

I decided that I was on top of his plan and turned full attention to my attack on his piece. It became apparent that if he continued with his intended target, not only would he clear the way for me to carry out my planned attack but, in so doing, would also make a possible fatal error and open the way for an attack on his king.

I made my next move and, sure enough, he unwittingly blundered on with his plan. I made my following move and now, suddenly, he became aware that he was in trouble.

He had made a fatal move and I could see that a checkmate was just a handful of moves away. And I could tell that he could see it as well. Now, he was taking a long time over his move. For the coup de grâce to not happen, it would need me to have not realised the position of the game and make an error, or to bottle it and shy away from the win because I was scared.

He tried his best to intimidate me to lose. Staring at me. Making noises. Blowing smoke over me and spitting the little pieces of tobacco from his rollies at me.

Eventually, he made his next move, the only move he could make. And I made my move. I didn't wait. I didn't study the board. I just moved. Then he moved and I took one of his pieces. A smooth action. No faltering. Ruthless. I just took his piece off and dropped it in the plastic lid of the travel set. It made a little plasticky click. 'Check' I said. I know now and, I think that deep down I knew then, that dropping his dead chess piece in the lid, rather than placing it, will have really got right up his nose. Such an action would be an affront to his 'masculinity'.

He studied the board hard again. Moved a piece to block the check ... the only move he could make and now I had a serious decision to make.

I could make the killing move, or I could bottle it. I pretended to study the board, but I was just thinking. Debating. My heart was beating so hard that I thought it would jump out of my chest. I knew that he wouldn't take the checkmate well. I couldn't see me making the move. A voice inside me was telling me to checkmate him and to hell with the consequences. Another voice was telling me to not do it ... was telling me that the consequences could be dire, not only for me but maybe for all of us.

I could feel the colour draining from my face. A tremble began, deep inside me. I knew that he would be able to see the tremble and I knew that he would like that. I knew that he would feed off it and as that knowledge dawned on me and the thought itself raced through my mind, my hand moved all on its own and made the killing move. 'Check' I said. I knew it was checkmate. But I said check. I drew the line at saying the word. I was brave ... or stupid ... but I wasn't that brave or stupid.

He sat there and studied the board. For ages. And ages. He didn't move. Didn't make any noises. It was as if he'd stopped breathing. After a long time, in the quietest voice I've ever heard him use, he said 'That's checkmate that Joe'.

I acted surprised. 'Is it?' I asked in an incredulous voice and studied the board. 'Oh yeah, it is.' I said.

He picked the Echo up and started reading the back page. Crossed his legs and turned away from the board. I asked him if he wanted another game and he simply said 'No.' He didn't even look at me. I put the travel set away.

I stood up and stooped to kiss my mum goodnight. 'Night mum.' I said and she responded with a 'Night' that sounded a little bit cut off, a little curt, like she was unhappy with me. I did the same with my dad, but he didn't lift his head from reading the paper, not offering his cheek, making it almost impossible for me to finish the act, but finish it I did. To not finish the act, no matter how difficult it was, would have been an invitation for my father to visit me. And I didn't want him to visit. So, I somehow contorted my body to kiss his cheek. 'Night dad.' I said. He made no reply.

I didn't know what to do. Do I say it again? Which might attract the wrong attention from him, or do I just walk away and go to bed? Which might attract the wrong attention as well. I decided to meet my fate halfway. I walked to the living room door, opened it and, turning to the room, said 'Night then.' No one answered me and I left, closing the door as quietly as I could.

I brushed my teeth and put my pyjamas on. I switched my little lamp on, got into bed and opened my current book, The Haunting of Toby Jugg, by Denis Wheatley. Dan had told me to read it, said it would scare me.

I was engrossed in the story, reading about the giant spider stalking Toby, when my bedroom door crashed open, swinging with such force that the door handle smashed through the plasterboard and one of Dan's paintings fell off the wall.

My father walked into the room and stood over me. His face was contorted and angry and his eyes blazed at me. I was shocked and immediately started to tremble, my book fluttering madly. I couldn't think, couldn't move. I was terrified. He stood glaring at me, breathing heavily, noisily. He lifted his hand and pointed at me. His voice was hard and threatening, 'Don't you ever …' the ever, was shot out, his face twisting into a snarl, 'get that game out with me again.' He moved closer to me, stooped over, the pointing finger pressing on the side of my nose. I daren't try to move away. If he felt me try to move away, he would hit me hard. He glared at me for a minute, maybe two. I could see the battle raging behind his eyes. I could see him arguing with himself, deciding whether to punch me, slap me, or just leave me. His face was full of turmoil. 'Do you understand?' The words were quiet, hard, flat, delivered with menace. I understood perfectly. To mention even the word chess to him would have been tantamount to suicide. And so, I never did.

He glared at me for another minute, his thick finger still at the side of my nose. He suddenly flicked his hand sideways, swiping my nose and head violently to one side, walked to the door and turned to glare at me again. I could feel blood running from my nose and dripping onto my pyjamas. He slammed the door so hard that another of Dan's paintings fell off the wall.

As he went out, I heard voices on the landing and knew that my mum had been standing outside, and all I could think, now that my brain had unfrozen, was that Dan would blame me for his paintings being off the wall.

My mum never asked me how my pyjama top got to be full of blood.

*

I put the travel chess in the skip bucket. There were a few items left. It crossed my mind that I was wasting time looking at this stuff, but it was mine to waste. The shoebox lay between my feet. It was a portal to the past that I could tumble into just by picking up an item. I thought that if I wasn't careful, I could get drawn too deeply into the world of my brother, a world as remote as the Southern Ocean. I looked about the room that I'd already likened to a sea with islands rearing out of it, Hamster Cage Island, my current berth and in the far corner, Old Dresser Island, and understood that Dan had made this sea, had lived on it, had somehow survived without many of the things we take for granted. He'd shipwrecked himself and the things in these boxes, the wreckage of his life, was the driftwood of my life. It had to be gathered up, looked at for one last time and then it had to be destroyed.

The last thing I picked out of the box was a small black cloth bag with a drawstring opening. I turned it over and it had the word Mitchell on it. I had a vague memory of Mitchell being something to do with fishing reels.

I pulled on the drawstring and emptied the contents into the box lid. I stared at what had come from the bag and thought *what the hell!*

The remnants of a smashed Kodak 110 camera lay in the box-lid. My camera. I turned the smashed camera over and over in my hand. It still had that tangy grease lubricating the winding mechanism, the tanginess quite distinct, sort of sharp and sweaty.

1960's, Halewood, Liverpool

It was coming up to my birthday and I asked my mum to get me a little camera, a Kodak 110. It was too expensive she'd said, so I suggested going halves and she agreed. I had a paper round and always saved my money, so I gave her half of the price and on my birthday, I got this camera. I loved it. The film was in a little cassette that you just clicked into place.

That night, I put my camera, which had been in my hand all day virtually, on the mantelpiece, next to a brass candlestick.

Next morning, I came down about quarter to six for my paper round, went into the living room for something, and there, on the corner of the mantelpiece, next to the brass candlestick, was my camera, just where I'd left it, the exact same place … but it was smashed into pieces. It looked like it had been stamped on. I stared at it for a few seconds and a massive wave of anger flooded my head, pushing all other thoughts out, swamping reason. For the briefest of moments, I was actually, physically moving towards the stairs, moving towards the bedroom where my father slept, when someone inside me, some other person, my man, my aide, sometimes my boss, gripped me, drew me into a bear hug that I couldn't escape from and spoke soothingly, told me that to do what my anger demanded, was what the man upstairs wanted and told me that there was more than one way to skin a cat.

I picked up one of his stinking, sweaty work boots, his right one, and turned it over. There was a tiny sliver of silvery-grey plastic stuck in one of the treads.

I went out of the house and did my paper round.

I left my camera on the corner of the mantelpiece, next to the brass candlestick, just the way it was. I didn't say a word to anyone about it, and, typical of the family I was born into, no-one said anything to me about it.

Two days after my birthday, I got a bus into the city centre, and I bought the same camera. I went home, took the film cassette out of the smashed camera, and examined it. Miraculously, it was undamaged. I put the cassette into my new camera, binned the smashed one and put the new camera in the exact same place on the corner of the mantelpiece. I didn't say anything to anyone, nor did anyone say a single word to me about the rebirth of my Kodak 110.

I left it there, on the corner of the mantelpiece, next to the brass candlestick for exactly one week, and then I moved it to my bedroom. I resolved that, if he smashed my new camera, I would just continue to say nothing and continue to replace it ... and if I had to keep doing that for the rest of my life, that was what I would do.

*

And now here it was, fifty or more years later, hidden in the midden. What on earth was my brother doing, why did he retrieve my smashed camera from mum's copper-coloured waste bin by the side of the fireplace? And why did he not speak to me about it? I couldn't fathom it.

I threw it into the bin for the second time, shook my head and decided that tomorrow was another day and that I'd had enough of this one.

Chapter 24

Tuesday 18th November 2003

2nyt start 9:54pm 45 x 6

2nyt late, another Chicken leg on My garden this time! I shouted fucking hell! And didn't hit Bertie, I just "jumped" him up and down a few times, and he let go. (lessons learned?) I eventually put it in Kittys bin.

Wednesday 19th November 2003

2nyt start 5:11pm 45 x 6

Bertie poo 2nyt Cardiff Drive on the corner where Citreon usually parked (but not 2nyt approx 10.20 pm) Another chicken piece on my garden 2nyt! Saw it after walk (above) when Bertie went for poo no. 2 on my garden. Every chicken piece from start have been covered in some kind of coating and are very greasy. They all have a bone inside which you can feel when u press, and they feel rubbery and return to shape when u stop pressing. The bone feels like a leg bone, but the chicken pieces are different shapes, some look like drum sticks, others look like (thighs?)

Tuesday 27th January 2004

2nyt start 7:15pm 45 x 7

2nyt shouted (the worst yet) at Bertie cos he knocked "my ordered chaos" of mags, PS1 games, clutter etc on the floor by jumping down in response to Katy barking. I told him to stay there (if he jumped down he would possibly have caused damage to what was on the floor) and he did. I don't think he was frightened or shaking, but he must have been alarmed and wondering what was going on. It took me about 15 minutes to put them "back" in the nearest "order" I cud.

Tuesday 3rd February 2004

2nyt start 9:22pm 45 x 6 + 112.50

Late morning, went out with Bertie, checked 3 bins, 65 Cardiff not full, 67 Cardiff full + extra box, checked 18 Middleton, and extra bin bag (clearish) put in, + kwiksave x 2ish bags also. Extra bin bag taken out by me and put into 67 Cardiff bin. I slammed hard several times all 3 bins. Met Kitty on her garden she said I gave her a fright. Having trouble with sticking door offered me the key to try. Bertie barking so I cudnt talk. I yanked him up to my head level on his lead and sed shut up! I don't think I dropped him. I think I lowered him. He must have been quiet cos Kitty said "at least he's quiet now", and I spoke to her about door sticking and keys/locks. She had laft. I went in and dun 3 or 4 carrier bags of rubbish + dog shit off no. 10 garden in to Kitty's bin. Bertie has been fine with me from here, so I don't think I dropped him. If I had dropped him Kitty would have sed Arr!

Thursday 5th February 2004

2nyt start 8:52pm 45 x 6

2nyt bin gone, 11am – 12pm out with Bertie by Brenda's, white haired man walking on W. Derby Rd pavement past Middleton Way towards Tuebrook and is looking and staring at me, so I "head bobbed" and looked mad, deranged, and was obviously affected by the alcohol inside me, although I wasn't obviously drunk.

Sunday 25th April 2004

2nyt start 9:39pm 45 x 6 + 112.50

Bertie didn't cry or whimper. 6am. Once again Bertie is frightened of me. Come here! X so many. Wall, "jumping" him up and down caused by him pulling "this and that way" and stopping i.e. he won't go where I want to go. He heads for the wall where he feels safe and immediately heads for the front door and "safety". Of course I am sorry about what I have done. I cannot trust myself when I am under the influence. I have a terrible personality change which I don't like. Being stressed at the same time doesn't help either. 2nyt I cut grass for first time this year. Finished at 9.03pm by sweeping up cuttings. I started at aprox 8.08pm, it was heavy going because of the amount of growth in some places. My grass and Wills grass was long at the time of "jumping". And Wills grass was in full bloom of dandelions masses of them all over.

Wednesday 28th April 2004

2nyt start 9:11pm 45 x 6 + 112.50 x 2

Mind Out!! Bertie Mind out! at top of my voice and cycle bag (complete with heavy lock and chain) raised, then and only then, did he mind out, onto his chair whereas he had just been turning round and round each time I sed "mind out!" I don't think I wud have hit him. But the more I do these type of things, the closer I get to actually doing something and hurting him. I have got to get a grip on myself.

Chapter 25

I'd reached the window, sifted and shovelled what felt like the millionth shovelful into buckets and skipped them. I wondered how long it had been since someone had stood here and looked out. Five years? Ten? Longer?

I looked down at my car, parked in the same place that I'd always parked in when visiting him and suddenly remembered a time when Dan and I had stood down there, next to the car, on a bitterly cold night, having a conversation that had troubled me at the time and that I'd re-visited on a fairly regular basis.

I remembered the conversation like it was yesterday. I'd called at his home, just because I fancied a cup of tea with my brother. As was the norm, he didn't answer the door to my knocks. I knew he was in because when I opened the letter box and looked through, I could hear movement, so I knew he was there. And when I shouted through, 'Dan! It's me! Joe!' everything went quiet and I could picture him frozen in mid whatever he was doing, a look of annoyance on his face. He usually answered once he knew it was me but this time, he didn't. I knocked a few more times, careful to keep the knocks 'friendly' and eventually I walked away and got in the car. I was just about to drive away when he appeared at the side of me. He had his coat on and looked freezing. 'Hello Joe.' He said in his quiet, unreadable way. 'I didn't know it was you, I thought it was someone else.' *Someone else called Joe*, I thought.

As usual, he never made eye contact with me. It's said that the eyes are the windows to the soul and, for me, my brother avoided looking at me because he knew I'd be looking into his eyes and might see him. I understood that avoidance, I got it. I did it myself but, in a different way. I nearly always made direct eye contact with people but also nearly always summoned Big Joe to look out. It was very rarely me that you were looking at when you looked into my eyes.

I got out of the car. It was freezing and I only had my small jacket on, so I asked him if he was going to invite me in for a cuppa but he said *no, that he was just on his way out*. I asked him where he was going and he said, *just out*. So, I asked him if he wanted to sit in the car where I could put the heater on but he said *no* and that he was going to have to get going *in a minute*.

I asked him what was new and he said that *nothing* was, that *work was work and life was life*. After a while I said that I'd let him get to where he was going and did he want dropping off and he said *no, I prefer to walk*. I said that I was going to have to get going because it was too cold to stand in the street and he said *ok*.

As I was getting in the car he said, 'I've been seeing a psychiatrist y'know.' I got out of the car and asked him should we go inside the house but again he said no. So, we stood on the pavement.

He lit a cigarette. 'I've been regressed and was taken back to when we lived in Germany.' He said, blowing smoke into the cold air. My parents and brother lived in Germany before I was born. My father was stationed there with the army. 'I was in the bath and my dad decided to get in with me but I started crying. He got out, grabbed me by the ankles and pulled my feet up into the air and I slid under the water. My arms were too short to reach the rim of the bath and I was drowning.'

His voice was a monotone and he stared at the ground, never once looking up, one hand in a pocket, the other holding his cigarette. I *always* knew what to say but, on this occasion, I was stumped. 'What do you mean regressed?' I asked.

The smoke from his cigarette spiralled up to his face. 'You get hypnotised.' he said, 'Then they take you back to your childhood and it's like you're back there, like watching a movie and it's about you.'

I was intrigued but irked at the same time. I didn't believe in hypnosis. I thought it was a load of bunkum. But then, this was my brother in front of me and he'd always been able to educate me, always been able to open my eyes to new things. I needed him to satisfy me about this, so I did what I do. I asked questions.

'How do they hypnotise you? Hold a watch up and swing it in front of you?' He glanced at me, then looked back at the ground.

'No.' he said and then stayed quiet. I waited, thinking he was going to tell me, but he didn't, he just looked at the ground. I could see his jaw muscles working, like he was chewing something, like our father used to do.

'So how do they do it Dan?' I asked.

'He talks to you.' he said. 'Gets you to relax.'

'Do you go asleep?'

'Not really.' he said. 'You're aware of where you are but …' He paused for what seemed like an age. His jaw muscles were still grinding away at something and he stared at the same place on the ground. I waited, conscious that I shouldn't interrupt. He inhaled deeply and looked into my face though not into my eyes. He was staring at my mouth. He finished his sentence as though he'd only just started it, '… you're somewhere else as well.'

'So do you keep your eyes open?' I asked.

Now he looked into my eyes and I could see inside for five beats. I could see him and I didn't like what I saw, things that I never expected. I saw contempt, loathing, and rancour. I saw my father. For just the tiniest of moments, the hair on the back of my neck stood up as I looked through the windows of my brother's eyes, and into his soul.

'You know you were his blue-eye don't you?' he asked, a sneer in his voice as he dropped his eyes back to the same place on the ground.

I suddenly felt as though I shouldn't be there, that I wanted to get in the car and drive away. I felt as though I was in danger. I knew I should leave but that natural, sometimes stupid combativeness that resides in me made me quash my instinct and respond.

'Whose blue-eye Dan?' I asked, my eyes boring into him.

'Dad's.' he said, once again looking directly into my eyes.

I was my father's favourite? In a flash, I weighed up everything that had happened in my life whilst under the 'protection' of my father. I was bewildered and appalled that Dan could think that. I was appalled that my clever, intelligent brother, the person who had taught me so much in my life, who had shown me so many things that were good and lasting, could actually come to the conclusion that anyone, any child, any *person* on this planet could be a favourite of the man who was our father. No one person was favourite to our father except our father. It dawned on me that my brother was struggling to rationalise his own life and seemed to be attaching a certain amount of blame to me ... because ... apparently, I was our father's blue-eye.

'I'm not sure how you've come to that conclusion Dan,' I said, Big Joe looking out of my eyes, 'because as far as I'm concerned, that fuckin cunt didn't have any favourites except himself.'

He looked away. Back down to the same spot on the ground. He'd dropped his cigarette and both hands were in his pockets. Fidgeting. I got the strong feeling that if he took them out of his pockets, there would be trouble and I mentally prepared myself for an assault.

Unfortunately, in spite of my loathing for my father, I had his genes. There was always part of him skulking about in my mind and I felt as though the meeting with my brother was on the verge of becoming confrontational and *that* part of me wanted to press the point. 'Did your *psychiatrist* tell you that one Dan?' I asked, infusing a large amount of bile into the word psychiatrist. 'Or have you made that one up all on your own?'

He suddenly looked like a balloon with a slow puncture. His body seemed to sag, and I was ashamed of how I'd spoken; of the hard edge I'd managed to get into my words and radiate from my eyes. I hadn't meant to deflate him the way I had, I'd only meant to defend myself and challenge his perception. I decided, for about the millionth time, that I needed to work on my diplomacy skills.

He pulled his right hand up and looked at a wristwatch that wasn't there and said that he had to go. 'I'll see you Joe.' he said, not looking at me, and walked away.

I watched him for a handful of seconds, a stack of mixed feelings whirling about in me … relief that the meeting hadn't erupted into a confrontation, relief that the feeling of danger had left me and a desperate desire to wash away the wretchedness that emanated from Dan. I got in the car and drove off. A few moments later I caught up with Dan. He was walking quite fast, head downcast and shoulders hunched against the cold. As I drove past, he looked straight at me and I thought I could see the whites of his eyes.

Chapter 26

Tuesday 11th May 2004

2nyt start 8:09pm 45 x 7 + 112.50

Bertie and bin bags This morning either 5am or 6am I put 2 bin bags of tree cuttings into Kittys wheelie, I took 3rd one to Margs wheelie but it was full, probably with soil etc from gutter, so brought it back. I only have one bin bag of tree cuttings left to dispose of now. Whilst I have a bin bag in my hand and Bertie + lead in other going to Kittys bin, he annoyingly pulls on lead as if to say I'm not going that way! Or possibly black bin bag may have put him off for some reason? Anyway he pulled several times and I think I pulled him back either fully possibly sharply, but not violently, or part way, and shouted at him but not loudly like Sunday 25th April 2004. I shouted something like "come here!" I think, and I think I also said "you are a naughty boy!" Anyway he quickly went to the wall again, walking quickly and following the wall to my front door. I don't know if he was frightened of me, or of me and the anticipation of being "jumped" on lead, or just the anticipation of being "jumped" on lead, or not frightened at all, but felt uncomfortable and wanted to go home quickly (he obviously feels "safe" inside). I let him in, put lead on stairs, I think I shut door with yale lock, and did my bin bag tree cuttings to Kitty wheelie bin and Marg wheelie. I finished and went in and up and Bertie was ok with me no shaking or other signs of being frightened. I sat down next to him.

Friday 14th May 2004

2nyt start 8:39pm 45 x 7 + 112.50 x 1.5

2nyt went out about 11pm back by 11:15pm and Bertie either frightened by me or unsure about me. He only had a few pisses for some reason, and then went on "wall walk (shallow V in kittys garden, which he has done several times now over the last several days, I can spot this routine) to front door, to get in. He wants to go in, as if he feels uncomfortable for some reason, but I do think he wants more pisses but won't go for them. I didn't shout at him, but I did "almost shout" at him, saying "come on!" I didn't call his name. I may (only may) have been heard by Brenda, Ken (light on) and Tommy (light on). I also said in a nice voice, "come on," and "this one!" He slightly wagged his tail but didn't go to the tree for a shit + a piss, but just did the "wall walk I'm going home"

Wednesday 02nd June 2004

2nyt start 7.48pm 45 x 8 + 112.50

Both cars gone by 6.05 pm one had gone by 5.46 pm but I can't remember which one. Gold one back by 6.08 pm parked tight by No 4, gold out again don't know when, but back by 8.19 pm parked tight against no. 4. This morning coming in from garden I left tools outside and wanted to come in for something and wanted to go out fast, and I was saying "Bertie mind out!" over and over. I raised my hand at him to move him and he quickly ducked and moved. I don't think I have ever raised my hand to him B4. I wudn't have hit him, and he wasn't affected later on in the morning.

Sunday 11th July 2004

2nyt start 5.00pm 45 x 8 + 112.50 x 1.5

looked out at 6.08pm and Goldie at No 4. No cars been here until now today, except at roughly 12.30pm when there was a dark to mid-blue car at No 4 + 6 (halfway between the 2), looked like an escort, reg possibly a W, cudn't see properly. Don't know when it came, don't know when it left, but it wasn't here long after first seeing it. Blinds are not open, and they have been in the same position (including now) since Friday nyt (Vertical gap in front bedroom blind – on left hand side at the end by vertical frame – has remained the same since Friday nyt).

This afternoon with Bertie outside I yanked him from a bumble bee on the path, and he immediately thought of the comments I was making from last nyt, he immediately took his "path" via walls and Kittys garden to the front door. I coaxed him back, and he also showed other signs that I may or may not have written down before, the best one is standing on 2 legs (back ones) with his front legs on my legs and looking at me. Other signs are stopping and not wanting to go, but to go in, and looking at me intently and constantly as if to try to watch that I "don't do anything to him", and to get back inside, where he thinks its safe (I think he thinks that there is less chance of me doing something to him when he is inside). He is a very intelligent little dog, and I love him to bits. He still sleeps next to my head every nyt, and cries when he can't get up on the bed.

Thursday 15th July 2004

2nyt start 8.08pm 45 x 6

Smiths clock reset this morning to BBC News was about 2 minutes now only 2 seconds slow plus fast a few seconds. Early hours this morning 1.45am, I nearly lost it with Bertie outside. I didn't drag him or do anything, but I did several (stifled) "Commmme Onnn!" cos he was doing his highly irritating stopping dead, looking at me and pulling back, to go in. One or two stifled shouts where done on path outside Kittys, I hope Brenda didn't hear me. One or two stifled shouts were done on path by Wills garden hope Brenda or people in Cardiff didn't hear me. In the end I took him back in, once again his misinterpretations have cut short his pissing outings.

Saturday 17th July 2004

2nyt start 8.59pm 45 x 7

2nyt lost it with Bertie outside on path in garden, side path and even outside Brenda's, hope she didn't hear me, I myt even have lost it outside Kens, I can't remember, but he may have possibly heard me from Brenda's. The "lost it" was controlled, I didn't shout full blast, it was stifled but a **loud** stifle. I may even have been heard round the back by Tommy. What set me off was going out with Bertie then a half strong shout — I can't remember what I said (probably fucking Hell!), I was totally pissed off with myself for getting all the way downstairs and out the door only to realise I had forgotten my left-hand work glove.

Chapter 27

I'd finally reached Old Dresser Island. It had been a long and not very enjoyable voyage. The dresser was an old brown thing, drawers up the middle and doors either side. On top of the dresser was a large rectangular fish tank, upside down. Under the tank, safe inside, were a number of boxes. There was a King Edward cigar box and I remembered him going through a phase of smoking King Eddies especially and cigars in general. He had his pipe phase as well. His favourite pipe, for a while anyway, was a meerschaum. He reckoned it made him look like Sherlock Holmes. I thought he just looked like a bit of a blurt but I never told him.

Dan used to get his tobaccos from a fantastic little shop down some steps off Water Street near the river. I loved that shop. I loved the smell of Dan's pipe tobacco, a lot more pleasant than the dried turds grandad used to smoke.

There was also a red OXO tin under the fish tank as well as a shortbread biscuit tin with a picture of a castle on the lid … the Eilean Donan Castle in north-west Scotland, one of my favourite parts of the world. I'd been there myself, to the castle that is, once or twice and even bought some shortbreads there, in a tin very similar to Dan's tin.

Underneath the OXO tin was a Patrick shoebox. I remembered him buying the trainers. Quite expensive and he loved them but they weren't my type. On top of the shortbread tin was a flattish box, quite ornate. It looked like mother-of-pearl type stuff but dark purple in colour, quite attractive.

I made space and readied myself to lift the fish tank. I knew it would be heavy but I didn't realise it would be as heavy as it was. It weighed a ton, and getting it to a sufficient height to clear the boxes was a bit of a struggle but, I did it in the end, though if I hadn't have had rubberised work gloves, I reckon I'd have ended up smashing it into handleable pieces.

I chose the cigar box first. It felt heavy and when I opened it I could see why. I was surprised, delighted and puzzled to find five Dinky cars inside. Puzzled because they were all mine. Some of my favourites. I didn't know what had happened with them once I left our house to set up a home of my own. I'd looked for them in my mum's loft once our father had left but I never found any of them. Maybe because they were here. I'd always, obviously wrongly, assumed my father had given them away.

There was a black taxi, an Austin FX3, my all-time favourite taxi. One of the tyres was missing. I remembered that when I wanted to play with it I had to change one of the tyres from another car to cover for the missing one.

There was also, probably my all-time favourite Dinky car ... a Standard Vanguard sedan, black, the one that curved all the way to the back bumper.

I loved that car. As I handled it, a memory started to resurface. The Vanguard had gone missing, and I became convinced that my mate David had stolen it. We'd fought over it. I'd accused him and he'd denied it and he wanted to fight and so that's what we did. I seemed to recall that David won the wrestling match.

The more I thought about it the more I became convinced that it was Dan who'd told me he'd seen David putting the Vanguard in his pocket one day. The memory was there but every time I tried to properly focus on it, it slid away. My brother had broken up the wrestling match and I remembered he'd been a bit rough with me when he grappled me from David's grip. I remember that because he bent my ear, which, as I'm sure you know, can be very painful.

Me and David were never the same as mates after that scrap. Understandably so. I'd accused him of something he hadn't done and then fought him over it. I'd genuinely thought he'd nicked my car, but it appears that Dan had it all the time. I looked up at my brother's smoke-stained and beer-splashed ceiling and said 'Sorry David'. A sparrow landed on the windowsill and seemed to look through the glass at me for two heart beats then fluttered off.

In amongst the collection were my Rambler Cross Country station wagon, whitewall tyres and twin headlights, a bluey grey Bentley S2 coupé and last but definitely not least, my beautiful Dinky Pullmore Car Transporter. I bought it myself at a jumble sale from a freckly-faced kid who wouldn't budge from his selling price of half a crown. Which meant I couldn't buy the toffee apple I'd been eyeing up. I've never forgotten that. Freckles saw me coming.

I turned my attention to the OXO tin and prised the lid off. There was a sheet of cotton wool across the entire box and underneath was a set of '00' scale WW2 British soldiers. Hand painted. Very badly. The set had been mine. I remembered sitting at my grandma's table with a page of the Echo laid on it, my paints and brushes spread out and thinking that it wouldn't take long because they were little. And I remembered trying to paint the face of a soldier when the paint on his tunic and helmet hadn't yet dried and grandad telling me I had to wait and be patient. I remember thinking that the painting was stealing my life away and how, outside, in the mean streets of Kirkdale, there were adventures of every kind just waiting for their missing ingredient, me. I remember getting panicky because grandad's clock kept ticking and every tick was a sliver of my life disappearing. And so I ignored the pleas of patience and more or less slopped the paint on and went out. I wondered why Dan had them in his OXO tin.

I lifted my badly painted troops on their bed of cotton wool out, and underneath were Dan's brilliantly painted Bedouin fighters. They still looked bright and colourful, like he'd only just finished them. *Very impressive* I thought. I lifted them out on their cotton wool bed and underneath was a matchbox. I slid the box open and it was filled with tiddlywinks. *My* tiddlywinks. My Shoot! football game tiddlywinks. I tipped them out into my hand, the blues, and the whites, and was whisked back to the 1960's.

Sometime in the 1960's, Halewood, Liverpool

As soon as I was old enough, I became a paperboy. I loved delivering papers. I was always well liked by my boss because I ran my round ... I was fast! Because I ran, I'd be back in the shop in no time and often, when one of the other lads hadn't turned up by the allotted time, I'd be asked to deliver that round as well for double pay. There was one occasion when I delivered three rounds, one after the other. I used to imagine various things that would make me run harder and faster. I was never just delivering newspapers. They were secret documents. And someone was chasing me, trying to stop me from delivering them. Or I was running because I had to be at the football ground to play for my team in a cup final, like Roy of the Rovers. And probably my favourite reason to run the round, the sadistic nazi swine that had kidnapped my beautiful girlfriend and would kill her unless I delivered the ransom, which was inside the last paper in my bag.

I used to go to the barber's in Hunts Cross, Frank Tadini's. He was a great barber, my only other experience of a barber being my grandad with his pudding basin and blunt shears. Next door to Tadini's was a newsagents called Lathom's. When I'd had my hair cut I'd go into Lathom's and get a Marathon, now known as a Snicker, and a Kit Kat and eat them on the way home as an appetiser for my dinner. Sometimes I'd get an Aztec bar instead of the Kit Kat. I was standing waiting to get served, scanning the top shelf, the Christmas shelf, when I spotted it. Shoot! It had a picture of a fella who looked like Roy of the Rovers, scoring a goal, blasting it into the net, and I wanted it. I had the woman get it down for me. She wasn't happy because she had to get the ladder and then climb up it and everyone could see her bloomers. When I say everyone, there was only me. But if everyone had been there they'd have seen what I saw ... which wasn't very nice. They were a dull, grey colour and looked a bit bobbly, like an old blanket.

I had a look at the game and decided to get it. I put a deposit on it and then went back every Saturday to pay a little bit off and was able to get it in time for Christmas.

Shoot! was a game of football played with tiddlywinks. It was brilliant. And I became really good at it but never beat my father. Ever. Not, that is, until the day I did.

Over the months I'd managed to scrounge a piece of pegboard from the newsagent's where I worked and an old blanket off my mum, no bobbles, which was perfect thickness for playing tiddlywinks. I covered the pegboard with the blanket then covered that with an old sheet my mum gave me and I drew the football pitch on it. It was probably about five feet long and half as wide, perfect proportions. I played it a lot, against my mates, when they were allowed in the house, which wasn't often, and against my father quite often, but mostly I played it against myself. Everyone used to say that I couldn't play it properly against myself but my theory was this ... as long as I had rules which made it fair for both teams, and as long as I played by those rules, and as long as I played every move to the best of my ability, the outcome of each game was the right outcome. And the bonus was, that in one game I was able to perfect attack and defence in every move I made. It was like playing two games in one. So I started to get quite good at it in a tactical sense.

If I played against my father he would win every game handsomely. But then, the better I got at playing, and the better I got at stifling the way he played, by positioning my players tactically, the closer the scores became until one night, not only did I beat him but, I thrashed him 3-0. He didn't even get close to scoring. I don't think he even had a shot on goal. He wasn't happy. He didn't speak, didn't congratulate me, didn't look at me. He told me to go to bed. As I started to put the game away he told me to leave it.

I expected him to come to my room, like he'd done when I beat him at chess, but, amazingly, he didn't. I hardly slept that night, waiting for the door to crash open. The next day I got up and went down. I was getting my breakfast and my mum was looking at me funny. I thought my hair was sticking up from sleep or something and I said 'What?' She said that my dad had left something for me in the coal hole. The coal hole was a little room off the cloakroom, that, when we had a coal fire, was used to store coal. And the hole of the coal hole came from when we used to live down by the docks and coal was tipped through a hole in the ground in front of the front door, landing on a brick-built slope. That hole was the real the coal 'hole'. And so now, everything to do with a place where coal was stored was called the coal hole, even when no coal had been near the hole that wasn't a hole for a long time.

Something my father had left me? *I thought.* This was unusual. A present! From my father! What could it be? *I put my breakfast down and rushed to the coal hole, slid the bolt, and wrenched the door open. My football pitch had been snapped into three equal pieces, and the goals, plastic, had been mashed up, the sticks that had a diving goalkeeper attached to them and extended through the back of the goal, had been snapped and the tiddlywinks, lots of them in different colours for different teams, were strewn across the coal hole floor. The box with the brilliant picture of the fella scoring the goal was ripped into little pieces and scattered in with the tiddlywinks. It looked like confetti.*

I shut the door and ate my cornflakes. 'He said to tell you to put it all in the bin.' *My mum said. And I simply said,* 'I'm not touching it. If he wants it in the bin he can put it there himself.' *This was something that, if reported back to him, would result in a serious beating or worse. But this was something that, there and then at least, right there and then, as I chewed my cornflakes,* this *was something I was prepared to die for.*

I never did put my Shoot! game in the bin. I never even looked in the coal hole to see if it had been moved. And I practiced and rehearsed what I would say if and when he asked me if the task had been carried out. I would have said 'No.' *and if he'd have asked me why, I'd have said* 'If you want it in the bin, you put it there.'

*

Of course, the question was never asked. And deep down I knew that I would never say what I wanted to say. Nothing was ever said about the Shoot! incident. By anyone.

And now, here I was, sat in Dan's living room, matchbox in one hand and the two teams that had fought out that match in the other. The sky blues, my team and the whites, *his* team. My brother had picked just those two teams up from the floor, had sorted through the reds, the dark blues and greens, the crimsons, and yellows, he'd sorted them out and extracted just those two teams from that famous night in the cauldron of Boddington Road stadium and put them in a matchbox. Why?

My joy at finding these toys and bits from my past was beginning to wane as I pondered why he had them. Why hadn't he said anything to anyone? Why the secret?

I opened the Patrick shoebox. His View-Master 3D viewer was inside, wrapped in a soft yellow cloth. The grey plastic View-Master was in pristine condition and stacked alongside the viewer were maybe about twenty of the envelopes containing the discs, again, all pristine, looking like they'd just been bought. I leafed through the envelopes, remembering most of them but not all and then, towards the back end of the collection one of them stopped me in my tracks — Wonders of the Deep — a picture of a big shark cruising past on the front. I couldn't believe he'd bought it.

1966ish, Halewood, Liverpool

I'd be about ten or eleven, making Dan about fourteen or fifteen. He was allowed to go to town on the bus on his own and I could go with him as long as he kept his eye on me. One day, during our summer holidays, it was raining heavily and Dan decided he was going into town to buy a new View-Master disc and mum said he should take me with him, probably because I kept asking her when it was going to stop raining. We sat upstairs on the bus, at the front, because we loved the view and I could pretend I was driving the bus, though no-one ever knew I was doing this because I did the steering secretly with my forefinger on my thigh, sort of 'drawing' the turning circle as if I was turning the steering wheel. I'd studied the drivers turning the wheel and copied the speed and everything.

We went to the big department store in Liverpool with the naked man above the main doors. At the View-Master counter, Dan was turning the sales carousel around and around as he couldn't make his mind up. He wanted the Wonders of the Deep, *but he also wanted* Animals of the Galapagos.

The woman behind the counter got bored with him and went off to serve someone else. I was also very bored and wanted him to hurry up because he said we'd walk down to the Pier Head to get our bus home, which meant I'd get to see the ships on the Mersey. I loved watching the ships on the river, especially the ferries as they battled against the tides.

Dan asked me if I thought I could steal the Wonders of the Deep *if he* bought the Animals of the Galapagos. As usual, full of bravado I said yes and he dared me to do it. At first, I refused because I could get into trouble but he laughed at me and said I was a chicken and that he knew I was just talking big. In a blink, I picked up the Wonders of the Deep *and pocketed it*. The woman behind the counter didn't notice and Dan bought the Animals of the Galapagos.

We walked to the bus station through the busy streets, the sense of freedom exhilarating. Dan bought us a Topic each at a booth by Central Station and we ate them as we walked. I liked Topics, though they weren't my favourite chocolate bar.

When we got to the bus station we got hot dogs and ate them while we watched the ferries scooting across to the other side of the river. As soon as we got home, mum made us some cheese sandwiches with a bowl of soup. She didn't know we'd had hot dogs and, more to the point, didn't need to know. I'm not sure what kind of soup it was. Soup was soup and I only ate it because I'd get told off if I left it, because the kids in Africa were starving.

My mum asked Dan which disc he'd bought and he got them both from his coat and put them on the kitchen table. 'I thought you only had enough money for one?' she asked him and, to my complete astonishment he told her that I'd stolen the Wonders of the Deep. She went mad, shouted at me, and ragged me round by my shirt collar, stinging my neck where it rubbed me. She slapped my head a few times as well, told Dan to take me back to the shop and told me to put the reel back. She gave Dan the bus fare and told us to come straight home afterwards.

When we were walking over to the bus stop I looked up at him, 'What did you do that for?' I asked, 'What if she tells me dad?'

He looked down at me and there was a strange look on his face. 'You shouldn't have pinched it.' he said, 'Mam' he always called her mam but I called her mum, 'knew I only had enough money for one, she's not daft y'know.'

'But you could've just put it in your box and she wouldn't have known would she?' I said, then asked 'So what are we gonna do now?' He didn't answer and I got an idea. 'Why don't we just put it in the bin and pretend I've put it back?' I said.

He shook his head, looking past me for the bus. 'No.' he said. 'You pinched it and you'll have to put it back.'

I argued that he'd got me to pinch it but he said he was just talking, he wasn't trying to get me to pinch it. I knew he was lying but I couldn't work out why. I've often thought about it since that day and the only reason he would have done what he did was to get me into trouble. But, to me, it didn't make any kind of sense. I would never have done it to him but then, I suppose, I would never have asked him to rob something in the first place.

He took me back to the shop and pretended to be looking at all the discs, spreading them on the counter top, the same as before. I had my hands in my jacket pockets, the Wonders of the Deep *in my right hand. When the woman got bored and turned away to do something by the till, I just made the thing appear and pretended to be reading the back of the envelope, then I put it down with all the others and that was it, he said he couldn't make his mind up, the woman got a shirty look on her face and we left and got the bus home. We didn't walk down to the river this time.*

On the way home I chattered about this and that and tried to convince him that I could eat a house-full of Milky Ways but all he kept saying was shut up. *And after all that, he'd gone back to the shop at some point and bought the* Wonders of the Deep *anyway.*

*

I picked up the shortbread tin and shook it. It sounded like photographs inside. Biscuit tins *are* a traditional place to keep family photographs after all.

Dan was keen on photography and, as was normal for him, he was *very* good at it.

I opened the tin. I expected the photos to be of grandma and grandad, Avery Street, where we lived with them, the debris at the top of the street by the sidings wall, as made by the German bombers attacking the railway sidings and the north docks. Maybe Dan would've taken some pictures of our old mates in the street or our school, St Paul's, or May's, the sweet shop where the one-armed man worked.

Maybe there'd be photos of Whisky, our black and white border collie or Whisky, our black and white cat, both named after a well-known brand of booze. Whisky the cat got run over by the truck delivering booze to the Glendower. How's that for being in the wrong place at the wrong time, with the wrong name?

I fully expected the tin to be full of old family snaps. But they weren't. They were pictures of my wedding. My first wedding. I'd never seen them before. Lots of formal ones, y'know, the ones you take at any wedding, plus lots of candid ones too. I was, yet again, stunned. The thing was this, when my wedding day was looming in 1976, and I'd been fretting about scraping the money together for a photographer, Dan had asked me if I wanted him to take them. Of course, I agreed to this and that is what happened, Dan acted as the official photographer. But didn't, but, apparently had. Sounds confusing.

May 1976, Halewood, Liverpool

Towards the end of the day, still at the reception, though I'd had enough of it all and was looking to get off home, Dan came to me and we had the strangest conversation.

'Joe,' he said, 'I don't know how to tell you this but, I've just found a roll of film in my pocket.' He held it up between forefinger and thumb.

'Have you?' I asked, thinking, so what Dan? You're the photographer.

'Yeah.' He said, looking me straight in the eye.

'Is that a problem Dan?' I asked him.

'Well, yeah.' he said, 'It should be in the camera y'see.'

I wondered if he was pissed but he didn't sound it and I wondered where the hell this conversation was going. 'Ok.' I said, 'So, put it in the camera then?'

'It's too late.' he said.

I looked at my watch and said, 'It's only half six Dan' and thought what difference does the time make to anything?

'Yeah but I can't take the photographs now can I?' he said.

I genuinely couldn't make out what he was talking about and said so. 'I don't know what you're getting at Dan, what's your point?' He held the film up in front of me.

'It should have been put in this morning but I forgot.' he said.

The penny dropped with a massive clang. 'You mean you haven't taken any photos?' I asked.

'Yeah.' he said.

'None?' I asked.

'Yeah.' He said, moving his feet nervously, 'None.'

'Not even one?' I asked.

'No.' he said, looking me straight in the eyes, 'Not even one.'

'How did you forget?' I asked, frowning.

He sighed, his eyes searching mine. 'I don't know.' he said. We looked at each other for a minute or two. His eyes never left mine. He looked like he was ready to run.

'Well,' I said, 'there's nothing we can do about it now mate, so don't worry about it.' and I wrapped my arm around his shoulders and hugged him to me. He was stiff and resistant to my hug, 'We'll get some from somewhere,' I said, 'loads of people have been taking them so we'll just cadge some.' I laughed and said, 'What are we like eh?'

He'd looked crestfallen. Bewildered. I thought, then, that he'd been truly devastated by his mistake and had thought that same thought ever since and laughed about it ever since. Both me and Lucy, my first wife, had laughed about it dozens of times. All those poses, all those smiles, smiling until our faces hurt, and there was no film in the camera. Neither of us were bothered by it, neither of us cared that much. The wedding day was no less memorable because there were no 'official' photos. I know a lot of people wouldn't go with that sentiment but, we genuinely didn't care that much.

Now, looking at the 'official' photos of my wedding day, the ones taken by my brother, my mind was in turmoil. What possible reason did he have to lie? I couldn't think of anything.

In my mind's eye, I could see him standing in front of me on that day, his suit perfect, the white of his rose buttonhole luminescent against the black of his suit jacket. We'd both bought black suits because it was what I wanted. The black went against the grain for some people and I distinctly remember my mother having a lot of a moan about it, but I was the man getting married and my wife-to-be was happy with my choice and my choice was black, so, 'just get on with it mum', I said to her. 'And what if everyone wears what they want?' She spat back at me, at which I simply laughed and said that as far as we, the bride and groom, were concerned, everyone could wear whatever they wanted, that is what we wanted, for people to not be dictated to and to just do what they wanted. Will you at least wear a silver or grey tie? She asked, or begged would be a better word. We both, groom, and best man, wore navy blue ties. Looking at the photographs now, sitting in the gloom, the groom in the gloom, it looked like the brothers Croft were at a funeral. And now, at age sixty-something, looking back over those years and having more of an idea about what my life up to the moment of my marriage had been like, I asked myself a question — if I'd been raised in a healthier environment, with normal family values and the normal hopes and aspirations that come with those values, would I have dressed more traditionally, more in keeping with the occasion — Yes was the answer. Almost certainly yes.

The mind's eye picture from that day, of Dan standing in front of me, was bright and real. It was like a slow-motion camera tracking my brother's movement, his expressions, his demeanour.

He'd stood square on to me, not too close, his hands up in front of him, using them to express and emphasise what he was saying. I'd always thought that he looked as though, he was ready to run but he wasn't. His demeanour was not that of a man getting ready to run. He looked sharp and alert, his eyes flitting across from my face to my hands, my shoulders, my feet. He was assessing me. Dan had not been in flight mode on that day, he'd been in fight mode. He was poised ... he'd wanted to fight me on my *wedding day. He'd engineered a situation that, presumably, he thought would make me want to strike out. He wanted me to attack him and he was ready for me, his feet positioned well, his hands were up and ready to parry and strike. Not only was he ready to fight me on that day, I thought, but, he was ready, to 'put me down'.*

*

A spotlight suddenly bloomed in my mind, illuminating an anomaly that had skulked in a dark corner for forty-two years. My mind's eye camera rewound to the point of him holding up the film. It was in front of me now as I sat there and I studied it.

It didn't have a tail. It didn't have that two-to-three-inch tail of film that gets slipped into the slot of the film take-up spool. The film that Dan held up in front of me on that day had been rewound into the canister. It had been a used film. Exposed. He'd been holding up, for anyone who happened to be watching, the photographs, as yet undeveloped, of the wedding day.

He and I were the only ones party to the conversation about the missing film … yet the photographs actually existed … which meant that, had I attacked him on that day, my reason for doing so would have been a fit of anger caused by his failure to put film in the camera and that he'd *ruined* my wedding day, whereas, he would've been able to scotch that claim, *prove* it to be wrong, by holding up the film from his pocket and claiming that I'd attacked him for some other reason that he already had waiting in the wings. Had Dan tried to lure me into a wedding day fight, with dozens of people as onlookers? It seemed he had. It seemed that he'd been willing to ruin the day for everyone, bridesmaids, parents and guests ... including all my fire brigade mates. That one simple little lie of Dan's, a lie that he could prove beyond doubt he *would not* have told, would have set me up in the eyes of everyone, that I was some kind of irrational, violent bully, someone who could and would explode over nothing and start lashing out. Just like our father.

Why had he tried to do it? What would it have achieved? And why, having failed in his attempts to have me attack him, had he kept the photos. If the roles had been reversed — and the roles would *never, could* never have been reversed, I wouldn't have kept them. They'd never have been developed, but he had kept them in a tin in a glass case, safe and secure. I was at a loss to explain but the smallest biggest question kept buzzing away ... why? Something nagged at me and I tried to focus on it but couldn't.

Finally, I picked up the purple mother-of-pearl type box. It was about eight inches long, five inches wide and maybe an inch and a half deep. I didn't know what the box was made of. It could have been plastic but I didn't think so. Not that it mattered. I opened it. There was a sheaf of papers in it. The top one was an envelope addressed to Dan. It looked like my sister Carla's handwriting. It had been slit open and I took the letter out and unfolded it. I read it and it shocked me but not because of its content, though the content was, or should have been truly shocking. What shocked me was the emotionless delivery of the words. And it shocked me because it sounded like me.

Dear Dan,

Remember I told you that dad had sex with mum in my bedroom that time, well hes done it again now quite a few times. She doesn't want to and tells me to turn away, which I do but I can still hear everything and feel everything.

They have had a big row about it and he punched her in the face again and cut the bridge of her nose. It needed stitches but she wouldnt go the hospital. She just wore a big plaster on it for ages and now shes got a wide scar. I don't think the twins know what goes on in my room.

The other night they were rowing when they came to bed and I could hear her pleading with him not to. They came into my room and she was trying to get away but he punched her and she landed on my bed. He sat on top of her and poured a half bottle of whisky into her mouth. He held her nose so she would swallow it but she spluttered some and it splashed on my face and I could taste it. I thought she was going to drown and was really scared.

She tried to stop him doing it and I think she crossed her legs but he punched her twice in the stomach I think cos I heard it. He raped her. What do you think I should do Dan, love Carla xxx

PS. Answer your phone please Dan

The letter wasn't dated but obviously it was after Dan had left the house to live on his own, but before our parents got divorced in 1982. So, let's say 1980/81. That would put Carla in her early twenties and the twins at about fourteen.

I read the letter a number of times and wondered why I hadn't been told about it. I wondered why, to my shame, I didn't feel much beyond the words. Had this letter been about my daughters or someone I knew outside my birth family; I would've been outraged. But somehow, for some reason, when it came down to my birth family, I wasn't outraged. I simply accepted such stories. They were normal. It was just the way it was. It was our life. How could we, me, have become so desensitized to such suffering? How is it possible for me to simply shrug off my own sexual abuse by my father? How is it possible for me to put it in a box and cover it all with the phrase 'It wasn't my fault; I didn't cause it.' How is it possible for us all to go through what we went through and hardly even talk about it to each other? I had no answers. Nothing. For most of my life up to the time I became a firefighter, life was perfectly normal to me. I hadn't known anything different, so why would I question things?

Most of the time, our school friends were not allowed in our house, and if they were, they were not allowed to go upstairs. If they needed the toilet, which was upstairs, they had to go home. Going into a mate's house was rare for me. I never wanted to come into contact with other parents. On the odd occasions when that happened I was deeply suspicious of everything said to me and found it very hard to engage in chit-chat. And on the extremely rare occasions I came into contact with the fathers of my mates I was always on alert, ready to flee, and usually left straight away. I never engaged once with any male parent of my mates.

I wondered what, if anything, Carla or Dan had done about the subject of the letter. I wondered what I'd have done had I been told. I decided that I would have done nothing more than taken my mum in at my house where she was safe, but after a week or two she would have gone back because she always did. I could have told the police and they would have investigated, my mother would have denied that it happened and Carla's letter would've been called a lie. There would not have been a case to answer, no evidence, but Carla would have then become a target. I could've taken the law into my own hands and 'sorted him out' … which may have got me beaten up by him or arrested for assault. And everyone in the house would have backed him simply because they lived in the same house as him.

The people who lived in that house were conditioned to simply accept *everything* and *anything* that happened in it. If you've never been 'conditioned' in this way, then thankfully, you can't know what I'm talking about. I imagine most people would think that they would 'not allow' themselves to become conditioned in this way, and I would probably agree with that view, had I not been brought up the way I was. But that's not the way this particular world works. This particular world works exactly the way the perpetrator wants it to, at least until something dramatic happens that brings about an end to their tyranny. In the meantime, the victims suffer and sometimes, as in the case of children, don't even know they are suffering. The funny thing is, when you come across someone from another household who has been or is a victim, you often recognise each other. It's almost telepathic. And when you do recognise each other, you tend to talk freely, something that doesn't often happen within the victim family. Conditioning paints pictures that don't exist, yet become your world. And there you have it.

I slid Carla's letter back into its envelope and put it in the upturned lid of the box. There was another letter underneath. It was the original letter from my mum, the one that had been photocopied and put in a clear A4 sleeve by the living room door, the first day I came to work here.

The mystery of those photocopies would never be solved and like so many things to do with my family, it had to be stored away at the back of your mind. It wasn't healthy to pursue it the way I wanted to.

The last item in the box was a brown envelope. Inside was a sheaf of papers. They were all mine, or rather, all to do with me.

There were five 'birthday cards' from my Sunday school at St Paul's, one for each of my first five birthdays. All sickly angelic and brain-washing.

The card for birthday number one had a little boy sitting in a high chair, presumably me, surrounded by three little angels, or, three little dead children, all blonde girls, all fussing about me, one with a bowl of food, looked like porridge, and the other two amusing me with toys. There was a short verse on the other side, basically telling me, not that I could read at age one, that 'I will fold your hands and pray'. I'm not sure who the 'I' was. Jesus maybe?

The second birthday card had me wearing a golden romper suit and posh sandals. There was an open garden gate behind me and I was standing on the edge of the road. A blonde teenage angel was holding me by the shoulders, either teaching me to cross the road or about to push me into it. I was smiling and I had golden hair peeping out from under the hood of my suit.

The third birthday card had me being taught to read by a blonde adult angel. It told me that on the day of my baptism, 13th November 1955, I was made A MEMBER OF CHRIST. Whatever that meant.

The fourth birthday card told me that on the day of my baptism I'd been made THE CHILD OF GOD. Not A child of God, no, THE child of God. So, at age four I was on a par with Jesus.

The fifth birthday card declared me to be AN INHERITOR OF THE KINGDOM OF HEAVEN.

I held all these cards in my hand, a holy running flush, and thought, so where were you, Holy Father, Jesus Christ and all you squeaky-clean blonde angels, when the Croft kids needed you, eh?

I put the holy propaganda in the lid with the letters.

Next up was my Holy Baptism Card, which was astounding given that my mother had told me on a number of occasions that I had not been baptised. She told me that none of us had been baptised. It didn't matter to me in the slightest whether I had or hadn't but why would she do this? I couldn't think of any reason why this would become a secret.

Last but not least was an *'Out of the everywhere into here'* card, a line from the cringingly honeyed poem called *Baby*. It had a picture of a fat naked baby on the front and inside were all my birth details, weight, name, eyes and hair colour but the interesting thing was this, I mean, it's interesting to *me* anyway, I was born at 5:10 pm or, on the 24-hour clock, 17:10. Nineteen years later I became a firefighter and was given the service number 1710. How weird is that?

What was even weirder was the fact that Dan had all these documents. I remembered going to my mum's and asking her if there was anything from my childhood that might be useful for compiling a family tree and she directed me to a box in the loft. When I found the box there was nothing for me in it. Lots of stuff relating to the other kids but nothing to do with me. She was mystified and couldn't explain and then, when she died and we were all there, all five Croft kids, in the house we grew up in, in the same room for the first time in a quarter of a century, someone started sorting out all the 'baby papers' as we called them but there were none for me. None. No school reports, no cards, nothing. It was like I'd never existed.

Yet all that time, those documents *did* exist. They existed in my mum's loft box but Dan had searched for them and taken them away. Why? When? And why was there an upside-down fish tank in his living room that protected all this stuff of mine from the chewing of the rats and mice? Why did he feel the need to deprive me of these documents but then preserve them?

It was almost like he'd put all this stuff in that safe place, deliberately for me to find after his death. It seemed like he wanted to tell me what he'd done, a *'stitch that!'* moment. Maybe he thought it would hurt me and that thought pleased him. All it actually did was to make me look upon him as a rather sad character, whose actions of spite said more about him than about me. Maybe there were other ways of looking at it but, in my tired and emotional state, I couldn't see anything else.

I sat there. My mind was empty or seemed to be empty. Had I been able to use my mind I would have known, would have recognised that often, when my mind seems to be empty, there is a grenade about to go off and go off it did.

The grenade that went off sent me to the document box, where I got the bags of hair out, sat on my toolbox and sorted them chronologically. The grenade focused me on a date, a significant date that I'd spotted earlier, 210576, the day before my wedding. The thought that blossomed with the grenade was that this date, the 21ˢᵗ May 1976, was the last time he'd cut hair off his head. But that's not what he did. The hair in the bags was mine, all mine. He'd been cutting hair off *my* head and the last possible time he'd been able to do this had been the day before I moved out of the family home for good, the day before my wedding, 210576.

Chapter 28

Saturday 28th August 2004

2nyt start 8.54pm 45 x 7 + 112.50

Fell over, lost balance early hours! Write about it! Shouted my head off! Had to rearrange my left-hand build-up of games + letters, found missing memory card for ps1, Logic 3, no. 2, missing for months as a result of an earlier landslide due to Bertie jumping down towards the left, probably as a result of Patch barking, or he has heard some other sound.

Monday 29th November 2004

2nyt start 7:42pm 45 x 6

Last Monday Bertie/lead chair boing shout, frighten him but, no quivering I come close to breaking down mentally?

Saturday 18th December 2004

2nyt start 8:38pm 45 x 5 + 112.50 x 2

2day between 11am – 12pm out with Bertie and Janet was talking to me outside her gate about the garden back door at no. 02, and Bertie wouldn't stop barking, so I shouted (but not too loud, I tried to control it, cos of other people hearing me, and also disturbing no. 6) at him and "bounced him" a few times on his lead.

Sunday 26th December 2004

2nyt start 7.46pm 45 x 8 + 112.50

Went to bed at 6am Monday morning slept till 11am on and off it was good but light sleep. Dreamed about fighting with a man with blood all over me. Xmas nyt (25/12/04) it snowed heavily. Sunday morning around 8-9am (it was light) I took Bertie out and on my garden and Kittys garden he pulled very fast and heavily, away wide to the left onto Kittys trees (I think) and he nearly overbalanced me on the icy top layer. I don't know why he did this, was it cos Kitty had come out with a bin bag? Or was he excited about the snow? Or both? I was immediately enraged, I can't remember if I pulled him back but I immediately said in a loudish controlled but intensely annoyed voice "What are you doing" and a few other things and probably swore and, I think, "come here!!!" barely controlling my voice. I don't know if he was frightened or not, and I can't remember how long he was out for. But he has to realise this business about being on the lead, also, barking at people, whether they talk to me or are just near me. He can be intensely annoying, and when you shout "shut up" or say "shut up" or say "be quiet" or shout "be quiet" and all the time he won't take any notice, it makes you want to shout into the air "fucking bastard hell !!!" "why won't you bleep bleep shut up???" Kitty was wary about putting her bin bag in the bin in case she slipped so I said to her that I would do it, and I did.

Chapter 29

Days that I'd lost count of had disappeared into my brother's rubbish tip. Days that I'd never get back, but the flat now lay bare and empty. All the rubbish, every single piece, had been picked up, looked at, put into the document box or the skip.

The last rubbish skip had now departed and a new skip delivered ready for the strip-out of floors, walls, and other stuff. The stench of the place still hung heavy over the close, somehow clinging to the fabric of the buildings and trees. I knew that the strip-out of floors and walls would add to the saturation and wondered how long it would take to disperse.

Some of the walls were covered, from ground level, up to maybe two or three feet, by drawings, all in pencil or charcoal. Dan had been quite talented at drawing whereas I was the exact opposite.

There was a drawing that recurred, of what appeared to be a dark forest on a dark night. It was almost completely black. The tops of what looked like fir trees packed closely together were silhouetted against a slightly lighter sky. And that was it. On some of them, there were two lighter points in the trees, like holes in a dark fabric through which a glimmer could be seen. They were easy to not see, like the artist needed them to be included but didn't really want them to be seen.

There was a sequence to the drawings. They started in the bedroom, behind where the head of the bed had been and were duplicated all the way around the room, disappearing into the built-in wardrobe then crossing the threshold into the living room. Strangely, in both rooms, they stopped either side of the window.

The fir trees were the same ones in every drawing, which seemed to imply that this scene was a place he *knew*.

The points of light didn't appear until the drawing moved from the bedroom into the living room, appearing for the first time as the drawing crossed the threshold.

As the drawing moved around the room, the points of light changed slightly and it took me a little while to realise that, as they neared the door to the stairs, the centres of them seemed to have a slightly darker centre. Almost like eyes but not quite.

I pondered the significance of the drawings and realised that I could ponder for the rest of my life and get nowhere. Maybe he had a thing about being watched, felt as though he was constantly under scrutiny. Maybe someone *was* actually watching him. Feeling as though he was under constant scrutiny wouldn't be at all surprising growing up in the house he grew up in. I often felt as though I was under scrutiny by the world at large, as though everyone was waiting for me to mess up so they could punish me. Maybe the drawings were my brother's way of telling the world that he knew what they were up to, that he knew they were watching and waiting. The bottom line was I didn't really have the foggiest idea what the drawings meant. Only Dan knew. Maybe.

I'd told my sisters about them and photographed them properly, well lit, well framed. Dan would have been proud of me. *No he wouldn't*, an inner voice said, *he hated you.* The inner critic was probably right. It seemed obvious from the stuff I'd found that he had *a thing* about me. Maybe it was this sibling rivalry stuff gone mad. I'd never looked upon any of my siblings as a rival in any way unless we were playing a game or wrestling. I didn't get the sibling rivalry thing at all. That didn't mean it didn't exist, I got *that*, but it was hard for me to grasp. Maybe he'd suffered from that First Born Syndrome, whatever that was, though I could guess from its name that it wasn't good for me, being the second born. Again, I'd never know and *so*, I thought, *by all means ponder, but don't get drawn in, because you'll lose out in the end.*

There were no drawings in the kitchen. I checked the bathroom, already pretty sure there were none there but I was just turning out of the bathroom when I noticed a darkness under the filth on the floor in front of where the toilet had been, now just empty floor and capped drain.

I dropped a splash of drinking water onto the floor and rubbed at it with the toe of my boot. There was a drawing under the dirt, so I splashed more water and rubbed the grime away. A forest drawing, the same as the others, was on the floor and the artist must have been sat on the toilet to do it. Had you been sat on the toilet, the eyes, now quite distinct, would have been looking up at you between your legs.

There were half a dozen drawings other than the dark forest. They looked like targets and were on the walls of the same rooms. They were in a range of sizes but otherwise identical, all rings of black and in the middle a black bull's-eye. I counted the rings. Nine of them. Every target had nine circles. In every target there was a black dot drawn on one of the rings, a different ring in each drawing. The last, or could have been the first, ring drawing was behind the door leading to the stairs and had its black dot on the seventh circle. The targets meant nothing to me, and I could speculate till I was blue in the face as my grandma would say. They'd been photographed and I had the rest of my life to ponder them.

I was tired. I'd had enough, went out to my car, got out of the paper overalls, threw them into the skip and drove away.

As I drove to the cottage, pondering on people and their worlds, my phone rang, showing up on the nav screen as Pam. I pressed the button on the steering wheel to answer, thinking, for about the billionth time how I would have loved my grandparents to be in the car with me at that moment. A phone. In a car. And a satnav screen with a person talking to you. I reckon my grandad would have loved it but my grandma would have thought it was witchcraft or something.

'Hiya love, how you doing?' I asked.

As always, the sound of her voice, happy and alive, made me feel good. 'Fine thanks darlin, I was just wondering what time you'll be home and shall I make a nice curry for tea?'

Now that was a question I liked. 'Yeaaaah,' I answered, 'Curry it is. And a beer.' I loved curry as long as it wasn't too spicy.

I told her I was en route and about forty minutes away. Before we cut the connection, and knowing how she liked a puzzle, I described the target or ring drawings I'd found. She said there was something about rings that she thought she knew but couldn't quite drag it to the surface. 'I'll have a little browse.' she said before hanging up. Pam was good at that and not for the first time I thought that she had a talent for research. A broad, non-specific knowledge-base and a memory packed with information was a decent start point, and, apart from her beauty and general loveliness, that sort of summed up my wife.

I got back to the cottage and did my normal disrobing before entering, went in, and headed for the shower. 'Hiya love!' I said to Pam, 'I'm starving.' She blew a kiss at me and said, 'Nine circles of hell.' I frowned a question at her and she said, 'Your targets … they could be the nine circles of hell.'

Chapter 30

The nine circles of hell I thought. Wow. My brother was bleak. Had been bleak. Hopefully he was now at peace but, I'm not sure why, I doubted it. I wasn't a believer in the hereafter but if it existed I expected Dan to turn up somewhere and haunt the life out of someone. Probably me.

Back at the cottage, showered, clean clothes, cup of Yorkshire tea next to me, the smell of curry wafting from the kitchen it was time to take daily stock.

The flat was completely clear of rubbish and the refurb job could begin. Clearing the rubbish was one of the worst things I've ever had to do. I had no understanding of what drove a person to hoard refuse, bodily waste, and locks of hair. I couldn't understand what drove 'sibling rivalry' and I was intrigued about his bathroom and lack of it. What he'd done to himself wasn't normal.

What was the train of thought that ended with him getting rid of his bathroom? How do you even function properly without use of a toilet?

Even before the invention of toilets, we used to designate a place for our 'business' as my grandma would call it.

I needed my brother to tell me how he went about his *business. Where* did he do his business? He had to go, so, how? What are the mechanics involved?

I wondered if a latter-stage alcoholic actually *does* business. Or maybe, because they probably mainly take sustenance of a fluid variety, they don't actually excrete solids? I mean, how does it all work? *Your bowels still function*, I thought, and your bowels empty out from, little bit of science here, that little hole at the bottom of your torso, so, even if you are emptying liquid from that little hole, you can't exactly aim it, or I can't anyway. Not that I've tried. So, what do you do? Use a funnel? With its spout in the neck of, say, a Coke or a 7Up bottle? That sounded like really hard work and he already had a perfectly good funnel, leading into a perfectly good spout, called a toilet and drain. I think that whatever he *was* doing to vacate his bowels was just simpler sitting on his toilet and I struggled to understand his logic. I understood that there *must* have been a logic train running in his mind but I don't think it was calling at the right stations.

Judging by the amount of refuse in his bathroom, he'd done without a toilet for a considerable time and that defeated me. In another world I could imagine the storing of rubbish, but in that world a bathroom is still a relevant requirement of your life. So, why even start using the bathroom as a refuse tip? Doesn't something click in your mind and a little voice says *'Whoa! ... hang on a mo! ... I'm gonna need this room aren't I? ... you can do without some things in life but a toilet is not one of them!'* Doesn't that happen? Apparently not. Or if it does, something else in that mind is stronger and more pressing, strong enough to overcome the most logical, the most human thing. How does a person get to the stage in life where storing refuse overcomes the requirement of a toilet?

My family, just a handful of generations before, had lived in the squalor of the infamous Liverpool Courtyards, where one privy and one cold water pump was used by a dozen families or more. It's hard to imagine how you lived a normal life. What we would consider to be a normal life that is. Even us, me, Dan, and Carla, we started our life in a house with no electricity upstairs, going to bed like Wee Willie Winkie, with a candlestick. We had a potty under the bed. There was no bathroom where we lived our early years, just a tin bath hanging on a nail in the back yard. There was just one source of running water, a cold tap in the kitchen, running through lead pipes into a stone sink. Hot water had to be boiled on the stove. Our toilet was 'down the yard', a squat, brick building with two huge slabs of Welsh slate resting on top of the brick wall, canted down to shed the rain. The walls were white-washed inside and the toilet seat was scrubbed planks of wood with a hole cut in them. A small paraffin heater stopped the pipes freezing in the winter. Toilet 'tissue' was squares of newspaper rammed onto a nail sticking out of the wall, but even this was pure luxury at side of what my brother had lived with for ... how long? How long had he been living like this and why? *Dan*, I asked inside my head, *how on earth did you get into this state?*

I wondered if I could have been a better brother and intervened in some way, could possibly have helped him.

I thought back to the time of the fire in his flat and how, when he was inebriated, he'd needed my help but then, as soon as he was sober, he didn't. He would never have accepted help or even admitted that he needed help. It's possible that in his world everything was ok and by the time he realised it wasn't, he was too far gone for him to arrest it.

The flat had produced some startling finds but, for me the most startling one had been a non-find.

There were no keys. Or rather, there *were* keys, a few bunches of them, but none that fitted the locks of his front door. I was a little bit of an expert, though 'expert' is probably stretching the description, on locks and keys. Many years before I'd owned a lock shop and fitting service, plus I could cut any key you wanted, mortise, cylinder, pipe, flat, double-sided, single-sided, you name it. So, when it came to locks and keys, I wasn't exactly an *expert*, but I was knowledgeable.

The remnants of Dan's front door had been on the garden. The police had smashed their way into his flat on the day his body was found. I'd examined the remnants of the door and discovered that the locks on it were the very ones I'd fitted for him a lifetime ago. They'd been quite expensive at the time, probably still would be today. He had a lot of glass in his door and so I'd fitted a Yale twin cylinder night-latch and also a Chubb Castle 5-lever mortise lock. I remember saying to him that as long as he used the locks in the prescribed way, anyone wanting to get into his house would have to smash the door to bits. And I was right because that was exactly what the police had done.

An examination of the door remnants showed that both locks, the last time they'd been used, *had* been used in the prescribed way, both of them deadlocked. They could have been deadlocked by the occupant of the house, or they could have been deadlocked by someone leaving the house.

A night-latch, or cylinder lock, more often than not a Yale lock, can be easily opened by someone breaking the glass in a door, reaching in, and operating the lever. Hence the twin cylinder lock, which has two cylinder locks, one of them being fitted in the lever on the inside of the door. Operating this cylinder deadlocks the lever, making the breaking of glass a waste of time.

The locks on the front door remnants were fully operated and the keys should have been in the home, but they weren't. Which can only mean one of two things, either he locked himself in his home and disposed of the keys outside the home, or someone else locked the door from the outside and walked away with the keys. I couldn't think of anything else that could have happened. The police and the coroner didn't find any keys on him so, where were they?

I was convinced I'd missed something so I tested my logic. The door was properly locked. This needs keys. Either Dan was the last person to lock the door or someone else was. If it was Dan, the keys should still be in the house — but they weren't. If he locked the door and threw them out of the window, then, why? Doesn't make sense. I know a lot of what he did made no sense, but nevertheless, throwing keys out of the window, no, he didn't do that. If he locked the door and gave the keys to someone outside, dropping them from his window, then, who? When? And why? And where is that person now?

Or … someone else took his keys, locked the door from the outside, and walked away with them. Again, who? When? Why? And where are they now?

I found two bunches of keys in the house, but I could tell, as soon as I found them, that the Chubb keys were not present. I could tell a Chubb Mortise lock key with my eyes shut. There was not a single Chubb key in the home. There *were* a couple of Yale type cylinder keys, but none of them fitted the twin cylinder Yale lock.

So, bottom line … Dan is dead inside his flat, his front door is dead-locked and there are no keys inside the flat. Explain.

The only explanation I could reasonably come up with, was that someone other than Dan had locked the door.

What was it Sherlock Holmes said? '*When you have eliminated the impossible, whatever remains, however improbable, must be the truth*' or something like that.

I typed a message into the group conversation in Messenger. '*Hiya Lyds, hiya Em, I know I've asked this before but I need to ask it again. Dan's keys … do we have any knowledge of them?*'

A few minutes went by. When I'd opened up the conversation, Lydia had been there because her green blob was lit. As I watched, her blob went out and Emily's blob came on. She was typing. '*No, I have no knowledge of them. I was hoping you would find them in the flat. I take it you haven't?*'

I replied that the flat was now empty and that there were no keys that fitted the locks. Lydia's blob lit up. *'You've thrown the door on the skip now haven't you?'*

'Yeah' I replied.

Another message from Lydia flashed up. *'And has that skip gone?'* she asked.

'Yeah' I replied, *'Ages ago. Everything off the garden went in the first skip.'*

'So even if we find keys in the stuff we brought away that first day, we now won't be able to try them in the lock will we?'

That question, to me, felt aggressive.

'Yeah' I replied, *'we will.'*

'How xxx' she asked. Three kisses I noted.

'Because I kept the stile.' I replied.

There were two minutes were nothing was said. No typing was going on. Both their blobs were lit. *Were they having a private conversation?* I thought. Or were they just waiting for me to elaborate?

Emily's dots danced up and down. *'What's the stile Joe?'*

I couldn't help myself. I'm a firefighter. Thirty years of answering questions fully and informatively, made me someone you maybe didn't always want to ask a question of. Nor get stuck in the kitchen with at a family party. *'A door is made up of parts,'* I typed, *'basically, stiles, rails, mullions and panels.'*

Lydia flashed a question at me, *'Dan's door didn't have panels, it was glass.'*

'Glass panels.' I typed, *'In a wooden door. The construction is the same. Anyway, the stiles are the long pieces down each side of the door, the hinge stile, where the hinges are fitted and the lock stile, where the locks and latches are fitted.'*

I let that info settle and then I finished off my explanation. *'I dismantled the door and threw it all on the skip ... but I kept the lock stile with the locks in situ.'*

'Why did you do that?' asked Emily.

I thought it was fairly obvious why I'd do that. *'Because I didn't want a smashed glass panel door hanging about but I did need the locks to test any keys I might find in the place.'* I typed. *'It just made sense to me.'*

'Good thinking fat head.' typed Emily. Fat Head was a family nickname for everyone. We were all Fat Heads. Can't remember how it came about because we haven't got fat heads. We haven't got skinny heads either. We've got what you might call bog-standard heads. Fat Head was an endearment. A strange one but, there you go, families.

Lydia's green blob disappeared.

Chapter 31

So, there were no keys, something which seemed to bother my sister Lydia, though I can't think why it would. As well as the keys, I hadn't found a wallet either.

Dan *always* had a wallet. Or rather, *up until him stopping talking to me*, he always had a wallet. I know that he stopped talking to me a long time ago and that in the intervening time, he could have ditched the wallet but, it was his *habit* to use a wallet. Maybe I'm just someone stuck in *my* ways, but I believe that some habits are hard to get rid of and I think that a man using a wallet is one of them. You go out of the house, you need to take your driving licence, your bank card, folding money, appointment cards and so on and so forth. I believe he would have kept to the habit of using a wallet. Dan was a creature of habit. He never threw anything away, not even his rubbish. He'd been a smoker for over fifty years. He was a drinker. All habits. He didn't seem to have dropped any of his other habits so, why drop the very handy habit of carrying a wallet?

But let's assume he *did* ditch the pointless habit of carrying a wallet, where did he keep his bank card, his driving licence? In his pocket? His rucksack? In a box? An envelope? Where?

Not only had I not found a wallet, but I hadn't found any of those things that a wallet is handy for. So, where were his bank card and driving licence? There was nothing in his flat that would formally identify him. Nothing.

Of course, I wasn't entirely certain that he used a bank card but, he probably did. Doesn't everyone? How could you function these days without a bank card? Functioning without a toilet is one thing. A damned big thing admittedly, but nevertheless achievable, as attested to by Dan, but surely, in this day and age, functioning without a bank card is right up there isn't it? He was a driver, had been for decades, so where was his driving licence?

I texted into the group chat. *'Hiya Em, hiya Lydia, did Dan have a bank card or what?'*

I got a reply within a few seconds. Emily. *'Yeah he did. Just got the last three months of transactions on his account this morning but only just opened them ... been at our Nick's minding the baby all day ... he last used his card on 29th July'*

The 29th of July. I got the calendar up on my laptop. It was a Sunday. My youngest daughter's birthday. His body was found by the police on 14th October, also a Sunday. I worked the difference out ... seventy-seven days. Exactly eleven weeks. During the hottest summer recorded in England.

I texted the conversation. *'Thx Em. What did he buy on 29th July ... and where did he buy it?'*

She replied straight away, *'Didn't buy anything just got cash out'*. This was followed by another text, *'200'*.

'Ok thx Em.'

Ten minutes later Em lit up in a private WhatsApp message. *'Something not right with these bank statements Joe, you need to see them.'*

'I'll be there in 60.' I said.

'OK fat head' she replied.

Chapter 32

I parked outside Emily's house about sixty-five minutes later. On the way there I was thinking about my exchange of texts with her just over an hour ago and the previous conversation about the keys.

It took two knocks to get Emily to open the door. She looked terrible. Eyes red, like she'd been crying. Face a bit puffed. Hair bedraggled. We greeted each other. She sounded tired and gave me a little hug.

I closed the door and we walked down to the kitchen, the centre of all family discussions, and I sat at the table.

'Coffee?' she asked, switching the kettle on. 'Yes please.' I said, so she got mugs out and put coffee in them. I looked out of the kitchen window at the back garden. It was looking a bit sad for itself.

She brought the coffees over and sat opposite me.

'I know the garden looks a bit untidy but, to be honest, I can't be arsed.' She lit a cigarette and blew the smoke towards the open kitchen window. I caught a whiff of it and thought, not for the first time, how nice it smelled. I gave up smoking over thirty years ago, on the fifth birthday of my eldest daughter, an 'extra present' I called it, her dad around the place for an extra twenty to thirty years or so. Hopefully. I've never had or craved another cigarette in all that time, but every now and then, I get a whiff of the smoke from a freshly lit one and I like it. I took a sip of coffee.

'So,' I said, all business and bustle 'where are these bank statements?'

Em put a large envelope down in front of me and I took out the papers. There were about a dozen or so.

I flipped through them a couple of times.

'He was loaded Em.'

'I know.' she said.

'How long have you known?' I asked.

'Since an hour or so ago when I opened them and told you.'

I looked at the statements. He had three accounts. His current account, savings account and ISA account were all very healthy. Plus, the mortgage on his property was fully paid up. Plus, he had a good life insurance policy.

I waved the statements at Emily. I was angry at Dan. Again. 'Why was he living the way he was with all this money Em? What the hell was he doing?'

'I don't know.' she said, 'I just don't know.' Tears started to run down her face. 'The poor man.'

'Em,' I said, 'I can see all this upsets you and it upsets me as well.' She nodded at me and it was like my words had given her permission to let the tears fully flow. 'The thing is Em, from my point of view anyway, is that, in the main, Dan did what he wanted to do and ran his life exactly the way he wanted. He may well have acted the way he did because he was damaged mentally, maybe even physically, from his early years. He may well have turned his back on his family because he simply didn't trust any of us. Which you can understand, coming from where we grew up. We victims should have always been able to trust each other, but, as you must know, it's just not the way this thing works. It's like we've been programmed to never expect too much from life, or from other people, no matter what the relationship is. We have no control over what other people do or think. You only ever have control over what *you* think and what *you* do. And that's it. For me ... I *always* expect people to do me wrong. Always. If they don't, it's a pleasant bonus and if they do, well, it's no more than I expected.' I took a swig of my coffee. Emily was looking at the table, tears dripping from the end of her nose. 'For me Em, and I can only ever speak for myself, I always try to say and do the right thing. I'm not saying I always manage to achieve this because I know I don't. But I *try* to. And if I fail, then the only accusation that can ever be levelled at me is that I'm ...' I paused, searching for the right word, 'fallible.' I said, 'Human.'

'That's pretty bleak Joe,' she said, wiping at her face, 'that's not the kind of world I want to live in, never trusting anyone.'

I laughed. 'You're right Em, it does sound bleak, but it doesn't feel like that to me.'

'Really?' she asked.

'Yeah really.' I said, 'What it means, to me, is that I always have a realistic sense of the world around me, it means that, just like everyone, I get caught out, but maybe because I always have at least a half-expectation of getting caught out, it doesn't…erm…' I finished my coffee while I thought, 'hit me as hard as it might have done, and because I expected it anyway, it's easier to get past it.'

Emily stared at me and blinked a few times while she was digesting what I'd said. The tears had stopped and she smoked her cigarette.

I turned my attention to the statements. He'd made his last transaction on 29th July. Two hundred pounds drawn from an ATM. Looking up the list, he'd drawn a lot of cash out over a relatively short space of time. Looking back at the previous November, it appeared that he was buying his booze, or to be more precise, spending with his card in a shop called BoozeMart up until late April, when he appeared to stop doing that and started withdrawing cash instead. I assumed he was still making purchases in BoozeMart, so, for some reason it appears as though he wanted to buy in cash rather than have the transaction 'traceable' so to speak. If that was the case, why would he want to hide his transactions? Who was he hiding it from? Himself?

I didn't get it. 'See this Em?' I ran my finger down a list of consecutive transactions at BoozeMart then pointed at a list of consecutive ATM transactions, 'He's changed his method of buying booze here, y'see?'

Emily moved her chair to sit next to me. 'Hmmm.' she said. 'So what Joe?'

'Well do you reckon he's still buying booze or what?' I asked.

'Yeah of course he is ... he's alcoholic isn't he, he's not gonna stop buying it. He *can't* just stop buying it.'

That phrase hit home. He was so far gone down the alcoholic route that it was probably dangerous for him to just stop. Not having booze close to him wasn't an option. 'I wonder why he changed his method of buying it though ... is he trying to hide it d'you think?'

Emily moved her chair back to the other end of the table. 'Who from?' she asked.

'That's what I'm saying.' I said. I looked back at the statements. 'It looks like he's trying to hide what he's spending his money on but he's only hiding it from himself isn't he? Maybe that's what he's doing, hiding the facts from himself, I don't know — it just seems strange to me, this sudden change in buying habit.' I thought about the word 'habit' after I'd said it. He was a drug addict. Alcohol was his drug, one of his habits, and his method of paying his dealer, BoozeMart, was to go in, use his bank card, get his stuff, and go home. That was another habit. But he changed it, changed his method of paying. I found that strange, I have to say.

Emily went and stood by the open window and lit another cigarette. She inhaled deeply and started talking as she exhaled, 'Dan wasn't exactly, I don't know, living on the same planet as us, if you know what I mean. Just think about the state of his place, so, I don't know whether we can look at a change in his habit as anything too…*important*. I don't think we can apply any *normality* to anything to do with him. D'you see what I'm saying?' As she'd been talking, she was exhaling smoke and I was amazed at just how much smoke came out and for how long. Five exhalations it took for her to stop breathing smoke out. And then, as soon as she did stop exhaling smoke, she took another drag and set the process in motion again.

I did know what she meant. And it was hard to apply our logic to things he did or didn't do. 'I see what you're saying Em.' I said. 'For me, I just try to cover all bases and, I don't know, it's like, when you're playing a chess game for instance, and you're trying to think about what your opponent is going to do next, you don't think about that from *your* perspective, using your logic, you do that thinking from *his* perspective, using the logic that you think *he* applies to his moves.' A slightly fuzzy head told me that I'd had too much coffee today and I went to the sink for a cup of water, speaking as I got it. 'You look at Dan's place and it looks like utter madness, it *is* utter madness, but only from our viewpoint. There *is* a logic to it. Not *our* logic, but nevertheless, it was *worked* out. The mountains of beer cans, the cardboard bed he died in, the bottles of piss with their notations, the bags of hair and suitcase of mum's clothes … all madness to us, but to him, it all meant something, it was all put in place by him for reasons known only to him.' I drained my cup of water and got another. 'There were reasons for everything he did. It all looks as random as it could possibly be, but it wasn't Em.'

I looked at the last transaction he'd ever made. Four days previously, he withdrew £180. Two days prior to that he withdrew £160. I added up his withdrawals for July. They came to £1700. That was alarming. June was

£1200. May, £750, all drawn out between the 23rd up until the end of May, so, what, a week.

On the 19th May, he used his card in BoozeMart to the tune of £45 and after that transaction, he switched to withdrawing cash only. Except for one transaction. One day prior to his last ever transaction, the £200 cash withdrawal on the 29th, he used his card to top up a mobile phone to the tune of £30. I'd cleared the flat and there hadn't been a phone of any kind.

'What happened to his phone Em?' I asked.

'Well the old one,' she said, 'the one he got off mum when she died, remember it? I don't know where that one went. He probably threw it away because it kept breaking down and the battery wasn't charging properly.'

I did remember that phone and said so. 'He bought a new one from Asda just after Carla died.' she said, 'A basic Nokia, almost the same as the one of mum's that wouldn't charge up.'

'Where is it?' I asked.

'It's in the blue box of stuff that Lydia brought here that first day we went there, remember that day when we just went to have a quick look? Before the door got fixed?'

She went out into the garden, 'The blue box is in the shed Joe, it absolutely stinks so I won't have it in the house. Stay there while I get the phone.' She walked off down the garden to the shed and I could see her rummaging around in the blue box. While she was rummaging I had another look at the bank statements. On the 30th April he spent £40 at Asda

Mobile. That was probably the purchase of his new phone. The only other mention in the statements of anything to do with a mobile phone was the Top Up that he bought with his bank card on 24th July. I was pondering that information when Emily returned with a plastic zip-lock freezer bag and gave it to me.

The phone was quite obviously new. A Nokia 105. I tried to turn it on without taking it out of the bag and it wouldn't. Probably no charge.

'Have we got a charger Em?' I asked. She shook her head. 'Didn't you find one in there?'

'No,' I said, 'I didn't find anything to do with any kind of mobile phone.' I turned the bag over in my hand. 'Did you put it in this bag?'

'No.' She said, 'That's how Lydia found it.'

I was surprised and held up the bag. 'In this?' I asked.

'Yes,' she said, 'Edward found it outside in that bag. The firefighters must have thrown it out when they were clearing the way for the police.'

I shook my head, 'Really?' I asked.

'She said that it was right by the front door, as plain as anything.'

I held the bag up again. It was clear, see-through plastic, with a blue plastic zip at the top. It looked quite new to me. I sniffed it. It smelled faintly of his place. I unzipped it and stuck my nose in. The smell of Dan's place charged out. I zipped it back up again and sniffed the bag. Only faint. 'I don't think this bag has ever been in his flat.' I said. 'It's too clean.'

Emily shook her head and shrugged, 'I'm only saying what Lydia told me, I don't actually know.'

I slid the back off the phone without taking it out of the bag. There was no battery in it. I checked inside the battery compartment and there wasn't a SIM card either.

'Did Lydia take the battery and SIM card out?' I asked.

'What do you mean?' said Emily, 'Hasn't it got a battery?'

I slid the bag across the table to her and she picked it up and examined it. 'Dan must have taken them out.' she said. And then a frown creased her forehead, 'Yeah, Lydia wouldn't have taken them out so, Dan *must* have done it.'

'Yeah but why?' I asked, and held up the bank statement. 'The last proper purchase he made with his card was a £30 top up to his phone, *that* phone.' I said, pointing at the bag in Emily's hand.

Emily sat looking at the phone in the bag.

'And the SIM card.' I said, 'Why would you top up a phone then get rid of the battery and SIM card? Why would you do that?'

I was puzzled. So was Emily. She put the bag down and stood up, walked to the sink and looked out of the window at the bedraggled garden.

Chapter 33

Emily and I had chatted on for another half hour or so, going around in circles and then I'd gone back to the cottage. I went to bed that night and before drifting off I mulled over all the anomalies, getting them into some sort of order.

The next morning, when I woke up, I felt fresh and everything seemed very clear.

We know that Dan's bank card is missing. We know that he last used it on 29th July, therefore, between that date and the date of his death, whenever that was, he either lost it, had it stolen, gave it away, or otherwise disposed of it outside the house and without that card, he would be unable to access his cash or make purchases.

We know that he died inside his home. The only door to the outside world was securely locked and the keys required to get through that door were not found. Therefore, he either lost the keys, had them stolen, gave them away, or threw them out of the window. Without the keys he couldn't get out of his home.

We know he had a new mobile phone and that he'd topped it up the day before his last ever bank card transaction. The phone has been found — minus its battery and SIM card. I didn't find a charger for this phone, or any other phone, so, apparently, he rendered his phone useless, yet preserved it in a clear plastic zip-lock freezer bag.

We know that the very last transaction made with his bank card, was to withdraw £200 in cash on the 29th July, and that during that month he withdrew £1700 in cash … and yet I didn't find any cash in the flat, not even a single coin. I found that strange. I know that cash can be spent and given away but, everything you buy doesn't add up to nice round amounts, there is always loose change.

We know he was addicted to alcohol yet there were no 'live' cans of beer, nothing except empty cans and wine bottles. There was absolutely nothing in that flat to drink, not even water. The only fluids present were bottles of urine.

We know that he was addicted to tobacco and rolled his own. Like his father. And we know, from his shopping lists, that he bought rolling tobacco in pouches, papers, filters, and lighters in packs of five. I did not find any usable smoking materials. No tobacco, no papers, no cigarettes, no 'live' lighters. Nothing.

We know that it was his habit of carrying a small rucksack when he went out. And we know that the only thing found in it, by the police, was an old cheque book and a letter from the Inland Revenue, both items now in our possession.

We know that he had a current driving licence but didn't find one.

And we *think,* or rather, *I* think, that he would have had a wallet, based on the facts that a wallet is so useful and that, when I knew my brother, he always used one. But none had been found.

The only conclusions I could draw from this information was that, in the final weeks of Dan's life, he withdrew a large amount of cash and spent every single penny of it, bought a large amount of booze and drank every single drop of it, bought his usual smoking materials and used every shred of tobacco, every cigarette paper, and exhausted every gas lighter, topped up a new mobile phone, presumably so that he could use it but then got rid of the things that make it work, got rid of his bank card and driving licence, locked himself in the house then made his keys disappear, turned his TV on, lay down the wrong way around in his Skara Brae bed, covered himself with five feet of rubbish, then died.

So, just how feasible is that?

Chapter 34

I'd been working in Dan's place for a while now. The smell couldn't be got rid of without removing virtually everything. The whole floor had been covered in enough refuse to fill three eight-tonne skips. Rats and mice had run riot in the place, entering from the drains, when he allowed the toilet to dry out, and wherever else rodents come from. They'd chewed holes in everything, floors, walls, and furniture. It was like a giant theme park for them, free fast-food thrown in.

Mice are omnivorous, and eating through cable insulation is something they do all the time, causing countless fires and, when they get right through the insulation, their own immediate death. Luckily, they hadn't caused any fires in Dan's flat, but it *would* have to be rewired.

When Dan's body had rotted, especially in the upper torso and head area, the fluid this had created had rotted the chipboard flooring in places. In the vicinity of the chest and head, the flooring had become a slimy mush. Quite interesting to see but not good to deal with.

The refuse he'd stored had created its own moisture and as a result, large areas of plasterboard had become damp and turned into porridge encapsulated in soggy paper.

All of the flooring and plasterboard were stripped out and replaced, together with all the skirtings, door-frames and doors. All the kitchen and bathroom fittings, everything, all skipped.

Now, two weeks after starting the refurb, new floors, walls, woodwork, and doors were in place. All the electrics had been replaced. A new bathroom suite with walk-in shower, installed and working, new basic kitchen fitted and the new boiler and radiators were in and commissioned, courtesy of Billy No Mates, one of my mates. The place was looking good and smelling normal. All it needed now was a good hoovering and a decent paint job.

I was absolutely tired out, ordered a pizza for delivery and opened a bottle of beer. Halfway through the bottle my pizza arrived and I ate it. Didn't take too long. I debated having a second bottle of beer, a rarity for me and promptly fell asleep, mid debate, in my super comfortable deck chair.

And I dreamed. Nightmare is probably a better description. An old dream come nightmare that I'd been having on and off since I was a kid.

That kids dream come nightmare was a *real* one. One that, when you wake up, you *believe* has happened and *don't* believe it was a dream, even when you know it was. It stays with you for ages, days sometimes. Sometimes it stays with you your whole life from the first time you had it.

As this particular dream has done with me. It frightens you and has a real impact on your mind and it's very hard, if not impossible to shake at times.

This dream is a double dream, a dream within a dream. You feel as if you've been conned. You wake up and start to decipher your dream only to find you're still dreaming.

My childhood dream is set in the bedroom I shared with Dan. Boddington Road, number nine.

Our front door had a concrete ledge over it, to keep the weather off the doorway. Our bedroom window could be reached from that ledge and, us being the kind of boys we were, had 'conquered' the ledge by accessing our bedroom from it.

My dream nightmare starts with me walking home late at night from my girlfriend's. It was maybe two to three miles along well-lit suburban streets with a couple of busy main roads thrown in. I could have got the bus, but I had a thing about getting on buses at bus stops. I could get on them at a terminus, when they were empty and still, but I struggled to get on one at a bus stop. I didn't know why and it didn't matter. I could do it if I had to but if I didn't, I'd walk.

In the dream, I walked past a bus stop and as I did, a bus pulls up and stops to let a woman off. I looked up at the remaining people on the bus. There were just a handful or so, two women on the raised seats near the back, chatting and nodding their heads at each other, a man standing talking to the driver, and an old white-haired man asleep with his head resting on the window. The bus closed its doors with a hiss of compressed air and started to pull away and as it did, I caught a glimpse of a man sitting in the front seat on the top deck, craning his neck to look backwards as though he was looking at the woman who'd just got off but he wasn't, he was looking at me. His eyes were black, his face all hard bony edges, his hair thinning but long and wispy. As the bus accelerated away, he turned even further to keep me in view and then he stood up and disappeared as he made his way down the stairs. I saw him reappear on the lower deck as the bus approached the next stop along. The brake lights came on and I saw the man get off the bus. The doors hissed closed and the bus pulled away but I didn't see the man leave the bus stop.

The concrete bus stop was one I knew well and didn't like at all. Not that I have a list of bus stops I don't like. But this one was, *sinister.* Why it was sinister I don't know, but it just was. It was the only bus stop of its type that I ever saw. Anywhere. It had a corrugated roof, probably asbestos, but the end of it, facing the oncoming traffic had a slit in it about average adult eye height. Like a letter box but bigger.

The man had definitely not left the bus stop and as I got nearer I got the distinct impression that he was looking out of the slit at me. I couldn't see him but I knew he was there, a foot or two back maybe, staying out of what light was available. I walked past the stop but my senses were heightened. If a mouse had come up behind me, I'd have heard it.

I got about fifty yards past before turning round to check behind me and there was no sign of the man. I breathed a mental sigh of relief because I'd been sure he was going to follow me. After another half a mile I stopped to light a cigarette. The wind wasn't strong but I still had trouble getting my lighter to stay lit. I turned away from the wind and cupped my hands around the flame and as I did so, I caught movement on the other side of the road, about a hundred yards back. I instinctively knew it was the man off the bus.

I stared in that direction but, if it actually *was* a person I'd seen, they were staying perfectly still in front of some tall dark trees bordering a garden. I stood still, watching the area, smoking my cigarette, feeling quite angry that this man was following me. I stood square-on to where I thought he was standing, making myself straight and as tall as I could, challenging him to make himself known. Nothing moved and I was beginning to doubt myself when, quite bizarrely, what looked like a pair of eyes became apparent, set in the darkest part of the gloom of the foliage. I stared at them, trying to work out whether I could actually see them or whether they were just a figment of my imagination. And then … they slowly blinked and there was a slight shift in the shadows, black on black, as if someone moved. There was definitely someone there, waiting in the darkness of the trees and they were watching me. Following me.

I flicked my cigarette butt in the direction of the eyes, a tiny flurry of red sparks bright in the night, turned, all square shoulders and straight back, and strode off in the direction of home.

I resolved to not turn around and look again, to not give him the satisfaction of showing that I was worried, but inside me was a slowly rising compulsion to bolt, to sprint that last mile. Instead, I walked with my hands open and hanging down by my sides, ready for action. I strode out like I was on a route march and generally tried to make myself appear to be someone you didn't want to mess with.

I turned the last corner and there, two hundred yards away, was my home, the living room light on and you could see through the glass at the side of the front door that the kitchen light was on as well. I saw a figure moving between the two rooms, probably my mum. I started to feel safe. I'd reached sanctuary and I turned around to glare in his direction and give him two fingers. And he was right behind me, his face just inches from mine.

And that was when I woke up with a start and, I think, a grunt.

I lay there, on my back, looking at the ceiling. I was breathing heavily and sweating. I could hear my brother breathing in his bed on the other side of the room. I was amazed at how the dream had been so real, at how I could relive every second of it, seeing the women chatting on the bus and the old man asleep. It was so incredibly real. And I re-examined the eyes in the trees and they were real, they were there, I could still see them in my mind's eye.

I was scared to go back to sleep but at the same time I was calling myself stupid and childish. It had been a nightmare I told myself. Just a nightmare, all in your imagination.

But what if he really did follow me home? I thought. What if he's waiting over on the pub car park for me to come out in the morning? What if ... all sorts of things ran through my head, none of them nice.

I laughed at myself and said, *have a look then! Get out of bed and have a look!* Always throwing down a challenge. *See if you can see those scary eyes looking at you! It was a nightmare! Prove it to yourself! Have a look out of the window!*

I laughed at myself, got out from under my covers and knelt up on the bed facing the window. I steeled myself, pulled the curtains apart and he was there, standing on our ledge, just inches away on the other side of the glass, his flat expressionless eyes staring into mine, and a silvery bead of drool running down his chin.

And then I woke up.

And now, reclining on my deckchair, in my brother's flat, sitting just three or four feet away from his place of death, I had that same dream, that I'd had dozens of times before, except this time, the white-haired man who was always asleep, wasn't. This time, he woke up and looked at me, his head turning to keep me in sight as the bus moved away. And the white-haired man looked familiar. It was my grandad, not my mum's dad, my lovely grandad, this was the father of my father, *that* grandad.

I woke up in the dream and challenged myself to look out of the window and the man on the ledge was there, peering in at me, shocking me into waking up again. For a few seconds I didn't know where I was. I thought I heard my father's voice say '*That's our Joe*' but then I became fully awake and realised that I'd had the dream within a dream. I got my stuff together, locked up, got in my car, and drove away.

Chapter 35

Wednesday 19th January 2005

2nyt start 7:33pm 45 x 1 + 45 x 5 + 112.50

No kwiksave 2nyt. Phone box Difficult woman. Early afternoon. Got to go, the other phone is going. Early hours took Bertie out and he was annoying me with his jerky pulling every time I try to guide him away from anything. I almost lost it with him and really pulled him along the path and grass near kittys wall onto wills grass near to no. 67. I have pulled him worse, it wasn't that bad, but not that good. He didn't stumble over/fall over, but it must have frightened him. He looks up at me and must wonder at what is going on. I shouted at him in a low controlled voice – no one would have heard me – and told him he was a naughty, naughty boy. He then takes his usual route walking fast to the front door, thinking that he will be safe inside, and he always is. He associates going outside with me pulling him.

Thursday 20th January 2005

2nyt started 8:23pm - 24pm 45 x 1 + 45 x 1, or 45 x 2 + 112.50 x 2

Again late 2nyt Bertie annoys me by his pulling, and near Kellys I lost it and yanked him up and down a few times. It must have frightened him at least a little bit, and I think we carried on to Garys etc. While yanking him I shouted something to him in a muffled voice, I doubt if anyone would have heard me. Went to kwiksave, got there late, about 7.55 pm was locking up bike and security shouted to me several times Hey mate you don't need to do that I am locking up now (or soon). I was pretending not to hear him but he wasn't giving up so I turned around and I got the impression that he was going to stay by door so I thanked him and didn't lock bike up. I went in and quickly got what I needed and was out by 8.02 – 3 pm, bike was still there, security wasn't, but Mr McGee and other male(s) staff were going in and out. Mr McGee said Tara matey. He always lets on to me now cos he recognises me as a regular customer.

Sunday 30th January 2005
2nyt start 7:41pm 45 x 5
2nyt lost it with Bertie for barking at Jack Russell. I shouted at him to shut up and at the same tym I yanked him up and down on his lead several times. He landed with his back legs splayed, and he stayed there, no whimpering, so I don't know if he was hurt, or just uncomfortable or just making his landing a bit more comfortable. It shut him up tho. He is 11 years old, not young, and I should remember that.

Chapter 36

Painting. A task that was crucial to how all the rest of the job looked. So, it had to be right, had to be good. Luckily, it was something I was reasonable at and managed to do OK at it by switching off and day-dreaming. My favourite day-dream was what I'd do if I won the lottery and whether I'd be doing this painting or paying someone else to do it. Or what it was like being a top footballer. Or an explorer.

And today, as I brushed and rollered my way towards job-end, I'd been musing on the enlightenment that had occurred whilst thinking about all the strange anomalies and details surrounding Dan's death.

I remember a teacher of mine at school. Mr Adams. Mr Adams didn't like me, nor I him. He used to say that his job was to 'enlighten' us, but that it was our job to comprehend. 'What comes after enlightenment Croft?' He would ask, board duster or piece of chalk in hand, and I would answer 'Comprehension sir.' And he would say 'And *do* you comprehend Croft?' And I would say 'Yes sir.' And he would say 'Prove it, what do you understand from today's enlightenment?'

If you demonstrated your comprehension he would move on until he found someone who didn't comprehend and then he would throw the piece of chalk or the board duster at that unfortunate child. I always thought that if he threw it at me, I would catch it and throw it back at him, so I was always ready for that missile coming my way. And one day, it did. I failed to comprehend the *coefficient of linear expansion*. It went in one ear and straight out of the other. The board duster came hurtling my way but almost in slow motion. I was quite athletic at school and in one movement, I stood, caught it in my right hand and threw it straight back at him. He dodged and it battered into the blackboard emitting a huge cloud of chalk dust. He told me to stay behind after class, which I did, and he asked me why I'd thrown the duster at him. I said that if someone threw something at me then I believed I was entitled to throw something back at them. He looked at me without saying anything for maybe ninety seconds, then told me to bugger off.

Mr Adams was right. After my Enlightenment of the past week, came Comprehension. The comprehension was quite natural, quite normal. It just arrived. After enlightenment, you either have comprehension or you don't and I did.

Dan had died in his flat and someone had knowledge of that. Someone walked away from that flat and locked the door.

Dan did not become teetotal overnight but he did change the way he bought his booze. He usually went into the shop himself and had been doing so for years, using his bank card to buy. And then suddenly he wasn't, suddenly he was withdrawing cash instead. Booze was still being bought in the same shop, because *it had* to be, but with cash because *someone else* was buying it, which meant that he was probably incapacitated in some way.

That *someone else* was trusted with his pin number to withdraw cash ... but couldn't have gone into the shop to use that same card because the proprietor knew my brother.

Who would Dan trust with his pin number? A neighbour? Or his sister, Lydia? Anyone other than his sister would possibly, or even probably, have carried on drawing money out of the account until that account was empty.

Someone else covered Dan up with the rubbish. It wasn't possible for him to do it himself because he didn't have arms that were eight feet long and it wasn't feasible for the rubbish to fall on him to the depth and uniformity that it had done. Who was that someone? Lydia.

Dan was either gravely ill and knew he was going to die or he committed suicide. Let's face it, he'd been committing suicide by stealth for most of his life, which is what a lifetime of boozing and smoking is. In my opinion. Either way, he wanted to stay in his flat after death and become a feast for the beasts, something that I truly believe he would have been fascinated with. He took part in his own version of the cycle of life and did it in a pretty unique way.

Dan somehow persuaded his little sister, Lydia, to assist him. Maybe she was especially gullible, or maybe there was some kind of *lure* to get her to act for him in the way I think she did.

Can I prove anything? No, I can't. But at least what I'm *thinking*, coupled with what I know from the enlightenment, is … *plausible*. Yeah, it's definitely plausible.

If Lydia had been persuaded to do what I think she has, then that will be her burden to carry through the rest of her life, and I had no intention of adding to that burden. I'd get the flat finished, we'd put it on the market, sell it and all move on. C'est la vie.

Chapter 37

The painting had gone well and we had one of our favourite little meals. One of the things about getting older, we find, is that you can't eat big meals every day. We don't eat meat every day, maybe having it two or three times a week, and mostly chicken when we do have it. The sheer number of chickens eaten in the world every day amazed me. And then there are the eggs, probably billions of them used every day. The chicken-rearing industry must be amongst the biggest in the world.

The favourite little meal we had was poached eggs on toast with onion rings. My sister Carla put me onto this and I thought it sounded disgusting but it's actually really nice.

We watched some telly, had a mug of hot chocolate and went to bed. Tomorrow it would all end, the painting would be done and we could get ourselves back to France. I went to sleep almost straight away, hardly even finishing one page of my latest book.

And I dreamed. The dream within a dream again, but it was different. Mostly the same but slightly different.

I'm still walking along. I walk past a bus stop and as I do, the same bus pulls up and stops to let the same woman off. She walks past me and as she does, her eyes slide over me and there's a slight wrinkling of her nose. The woman is my sister Carla, but she looks too old, haggard, her cheeks shrunken and her lips grey. Long strands of grey hair hang down the sides of her face like old curtains.

There are just a handful of people left on the bus, two women on the raised seats near the back, still chatting and nodding their heads at each other, the man standing talking with the driver, I hoped about football but somehow, I knew they were talking about me.

The old white-haired man who'd been asleep all my life until the last time I'd had this dream, was no longer asleep. He was now upright and alert looking, staring at me, his face expressionless. It was my father's father, a man I barely remembered, hardly knew. The bus closes its doors and, just the same as always, starts to pull away and as it does, the man sitting in the front seat on the top deck, stands and leans on the back of his seat, staring at me. The two women stopped chatting and looked at me. The one next to the window has black hair, thick rimmed glasses, and a heavy face, jowly with a big nose … hard looking. It's my grandma. My father's mother. Again, I hardly knew her and barely remembered anything about her, but it *is* her. The other woman is leaning forward slightly, to get a view of me. She looks like she could be nice, her face is triangular and pretty, the mouth nicely shaped and bordered with shiny red lipstick, but where her eyes should be are just dark hollows. She's smiling the smile of someone standing behind a bully, knowing that you are about to get what is coming to you, that you are about to get what you deserve. The woman with hollow eyes is my mother.

Chapter 38

It was done. Everything was finished. It's funny but, you know you're approaching the end of the job, you know you just have one or two things to do but, when you've done them, you can't quite believe there is nothing else to do. You think you're being tricked.

I checked. Walked all around the flat, which didn't take long. Checked everything with a critical eye. Turned every light on and off, opened and closed every tap and flushed the toilet. It was done. Finito!

I got the last bottle of Leffe from the kitchen, opened it, sat in the deckchair, and sighed. I wouldn't have wanted to live here but nevertheless, it was bright, smelled new and looked fresh. I loved crisp lines, so corners and skirtings had to be perfect and they were. I was pleased.

I thought of how it had looked just weeks before, of how it had smelled. It was impossible to envisage it now. But life moved on. The work was done and I could go home. It was beyond sad that Dan's life had ended in this room, that he had lived the life he lived in this little flat, locked up, unable to see beyond the shuttered windows of his mind. I wanted life to have been different for him but, it was what it was. Life, his life, had led him, seemingly inexorably, to his death. As mine would lead me to my death, albeit down a different path.

I sat there in my deckchair and remembered him fishing, messing with his cameras, handling little animals, and breeding maggots. I thought of the things in life that made me who I am, things that Dan had introduced me to. And I thought of the strange urges that drives a man to spurn his sibling, contradictions and conflicts that were impossible for me to fathom because I never had them.

I started to mind drift, beer on an empty stomach conspiring to befuddle me a little and I knew I had to close my eyes for a few minutes, have a power nap. I put the bottle on the floor and allowed my eyes to close. As I was drawn down to the void of sleep, I knew I was going to have the dream within a dream again. I could feel it waiting for me and momentarily tried to fend sleep off. But I couldn't. I knew I should stand up and walk about, drink some water, eat something. But I couldn't. I was exhausted. Physically and mentally exhausted. Part of me, that belligerent part of me that refused to be beaten, wanted to get inside the dream and fight. Wanted to dash onto the bus before it left the stop, sprint up the stairs and throw the man with the indifferent eyes down the stairs and chant 'I'm the king of *this* castle, get down there you dirty rascal!' But I knew I wouldn't. I knew that the dream would take its own course, and that whatever happened was meant to happen, that I had no control over it.

I took a deep breath, tried one last time to move and get away from the beckoning dream and then suddenly, seamlessly, I was walking along the road, on the way home from my girlfriend's.

As I approached the bus stop, a bus pulled up and stopped to let a woman off. It was my sister Carla. As she walked past me, her head moved, as if her lifeless eyes were scanning me head to toe and up again, her lower face distorted in what looked like disgust. She stopped momentarily and opened her mouth as if to speak. The smell of dung and rotting meat washed over me and a single word hissed out, filled with malevolence, and drawn out for maximum effect. *'Cunt.'* I had a strong desire to grab her around the throat and throttle her but I couldn't move from my path. I walked past her.

The two women on the bus were now sitting with the white-haired man. They were all looking my way. My mother's expression was the one she wore when she lay dead in the hospital, an expression of pain and regret, her lips pressed tightly together. She cocked her head slightly to one side, as if she was saying *'I told you not to do that, now look what you've done.'*

The doors closed with a hiss of compressed air and the bus pulled away. The man on the top deck, who was stood, leaning on the back of his seat staring at me, moved and made his way down the stairs. The man talking to the driver turned and looked at me. It was my father. His jaw muscles were working as though he was chewing something and his piercing blue eyes seemed to be illuminated. He spoke over his shoulder to the driver, never taking his eyes from me, and even though the doors were shut and the bus was moving away, I could hear him clearly, *'That's our Joe'* he said, and the driver briefly turned to look at me. His eyes were red and flickering as if they were on fire. He smiled at me and I could see his white teeth gleaming.

As the bus approached the next stop along, the brake lights came on and the man from the top deck got off. The bus pulled away but the man who got off didn't leave the bus stop.

As I got nearer to the bus stop, I could make out that someone was standing looking out at me through the letter box slit and I knew it was the man from the top deck. I stared at him as I walked past the concrete structure, daring him to come out and confront me. I wanted to pulverise him, smash his bony face to a pulp, stamp on him, grind him into the ground. But I had no choice, I had to walk past.

Fifty yards past the bus stop I turned to check behind me. It was clear. I walked for another half a mile and stopped to light a cigarette. I had to cup my hands around the flame from my lighter because of the breeze and as I did so, I caught a movement on the other side of the road, about a hundred yards back. It was him; he was standing in front of some tall dark trees but I could see him, lighter dark on dark, his eyes dimly showing.

I stood still, my eyes fixed on his, calmly smoking my cigarette, feeling angry, murderous, feeling violated, like my mind had been scraped raw and had salt poured onto the wound. I was enraged that I was being stalked. I stood square on, standing as tall and straight as I could, willing him to come out and face me but I knew he wouldn't.

His eyes slowly blinked and I heard a low, phlegm-loaded laugh, then they disappeared.

I flicked my cigarette butt, end over end in the direction of the trees, a trail of red sparks living then dying in the night, turned and strode off in the direction of home.

Every other time I'd been trapped in this dream, I'd felt the need to escape, to run for home, to get away from the man that followed me but this time, it was different. This time I knew that the dream was playing out for the last time, that this time, I would either die in my sleep, or the man on the ledge would be crushed and never invade my world again.

I turned the last corner and there, two hundred yards away, was home. The living room light was on and I could see through the glass at the side of the front door that the kitchen light was on as well. I saw a figure moving between the two rooms, probably my mum making a cup of tea or something, except this time she stopped at the frosted glass, as if she was watching me approach across the pub car park.

I stopped and turned around to glare in the direction of my stalker, to give him two fingers. And he was right behind me.

And that was when I woke up.

I lay there, on my back, looking at the ceiling. I was breathing heavily and sweating. I looked across to my brother's bed but he wasn't there. I was amazed at how the dream had been so real, at how all the usual characters had turned into members of my family. I could relive every second of it, seeing the two women becoming my mum and grandmother, how the sleeping man had become my grandfather. I wondered why I would dream about two people I hardly knew and could barely remember. The human mind and the way it works, marvellous and sometimes scary.

The things you could think and the worlds you could envisage, imagine, and invent, all of it, all of them real, as real as anything else in your life. Until, suddenly it wasn't real, suddenly you were back in the *real,* real world and your made-up one was put away, like a toy, until the next time.

I was still dreaming. I knew I was. I thought I was. I must have been because I knew I wasn't in my childhood bedroom; I knew I was in my dead brother's flat. Reclining in the deckchair. I knew that. I knew there was no ledge beneath the window, no curtains to draw back. There was just a window looking out onto the car park.

Inside my head a voice, hard edged, said to me, *prove it! prove it! go on! go and look out of the window!*

I got up and moved towards the window. As I neared the glass, I remembered that there *was* actually a flat roof beneath the window, the little front door porch of the flat beneath Dan's, and a tingle of adrenaline began in the pit of my stomach, quickly spreading through me, my breathing increased and my eyes came alive and alert to a possible danger.

I got to the window and looked out. There was nothing, just my car in its usual place. *Check the ledge!,* the voice said, *check the fucking ledge! make sure!*

I moved right up to the window and put my face on the glass so that I could look down to the ledge. To the flat roof. There was nothing and I smiled to myself and turned back into the room.

The skin on my arms registered a variation in temperature, the hairs standing up and as I realised the front door at the bottom of the stairs must be open, my eyes registered a hooded figure crouched at the top of the stairs, that suddenly rushed across the room at me. The street lights from outside glinted on a huge knife and then I was battered to the floor and there was a weight on top of me. My face was hit hard and I felt a blade slice into my right arm as I tried to defend myself and then there were a flurry of blows around my chest and abdomen and I could hear inside my head a loud grating noise which I knew was a knife sliding across my bones. A harsh voice, hard and soft at the same time kept saying *Blue eye! Blue eye!* over and over at me, keeping time with the grating sound. I could hear and feel an invasive sensation that was red hot and ice cold at the same time and knew that I was being stabbed. I knew that I was dying and that something truly fearful, much more so than the person slashing at me, was approaching me fast from up to my left, rushing like a gigantic train towards me and I tried to wave it away, tried to shout, to tell it to get away! But I couldn't, and I heard a voice, the voice of my father say, '*That's our Joe … he's coming to join us.*'

A loud crackling noise, like firecrackers exploding out through my scalp felt like a million hot needles piercing me and all thought stopped. I could see myself from above, a dark shape on top of me, I could feel and see my body being battered, shoved about, then another dark shape swiftly entered the room and suddenly that was it.

Epilogue

Three years later…North Wales

It was my birthday, 23rd September. I was sixty-six. Sixty-six. Six times ten plus six. Me. How can I be sixty-six? How can I be that old? I'm still me inside my head, it's just me in here, with my helpers. Just me and them. The same me that fought the German hordes down by the docks in North Liverpool, aged five. The same me that was desperate to shoot a baby bird with my bamboo bow and arrow. The same me that sat on my grandad's knee, coveting his penknife. It's just me.

And then there's my brother Dan. He is now getting on for seventy. Dan, my hero for most of my life, but no more. He didn't die in his midden. Someone else did. An unnamed man who had followed him home one day from the phone box by the tobacco factory. A man who attempted to rob him, fought with him, and died at my brother's hand, probably suffocated say the police, who suddenly became interested in the man in the midden. An unnamed body that was buried in my brother's pile of rubbish and cultivated on its journey to mummification, the maggots and beetles periodically washed from their rotting feast with bottles of syrupy brown urine, so that Dan, the maggot-meister, could assess what could be assessed. Almost the perfect murder.

Dan now resides in a high security psychiatric hospital somewhere in the Northwest of England. Probably not that far from where I now live, having moved back from France. He will never get out.

Some people tried to explain the whys and wherefores of what had happened, but I didn't need anyone to explain it. I already knew all I needed.

Dan attacked me, tried to kill me. I suffered horrific injuries, lost a lot of blood, but I survived. One of the nurses who helped me rehabilitate, said that I was 'too busy' to die.

Lydia, my sister, is in prison, I don't know which one and I don't care. I'll never see her again. Not intentionally. Dan persuaded her to help him once he'd killed the stranger. She hid him, fed him, and, thankfully, followed him to the flat the night he came to kill me. It was her that rushed him and saved my life. It was Lydia that already had the ambulance and police en route, even before he entered the property. She saved my life, but I don't care. I wouldn't have *been* in any danger, but for her, so, she did no more than the right thing. Maybe I'll feel different in time but I doubt it.

My sister Emily was traumatised by the events surrounding the man in the midden. She is recovering slowly but the fact that her twin sister could act the way she did, has done damage that she may never recover from. I help in any way I can but, at the end of the day, we all have to manage our own world, the world behind our eyes, in the best way we can. We see each other every few weeks or so.

Pam and I drank our Earl Grey tea and ate our home-made flapjacks, sitting on the wall of the stone structure at the top of Moel Fammau and looked out across the Denbigh countryside. The sun was bright through the thin cloud and the breeze was cool but not too cool. Life couldn't be better.

*

Monday 31st January 2005

2nyt start 7.57pm 45 x 6 + 112.50

9.50am no cars here, 307 gone 306 gone. 11.10am 307 here at no. 20. After 1 or 2 cans I said to Bertie "Do you want to go out or what? (not?)" It was said in a very loud voice, and it frightened him, and he did want to go out, but he was "walling" quite soon to come back in, B4 he had emptied his bladder. I cud be turning into a monster. I hope not. At least I am aware of it. Was my dad aware of him turning into a monster?

Mortal Monsters

The monsters that invade young dreams
sit pale beside the mortal fiends
who'd, casually, on a whim,
break both your spirit and your limb.
The havoc that such demons wreak
destroys young souls, turns bright minds bleak,
who, seeking solace in addiction,
exacerbate their own affliction.
Junkies, alcoholics, hoarders
all are someone's sons and daughters,
to be cherished and protected – NOT,
insane and bitter, left to rot!
Never can it once be right
to ravage lives and thus ignite
that festering fuse that creeps its path
to such a sorry aftermath.

Elynn Lake

Printed in Great Britain
by Amazon